The
Ninety Days
of Genevieve

Lucinda Carrington

6 8 10 9 7

First published in the United Kingdom in 2012 by
Virgin Books, an imprint of Ebury Publishing

A Random House Group Company

Copyright © Lucinda Harrington 1996

www.randomhouse.co.uk

Addresses for companies within The Random House Group Limited can
be found at www.randomhouse.co.uk/offices.htm

The Random House Group Limited Reg. No. 954009

A CIP catalogue record for this book is
available from the British Library

The Random House Group Limited supports The Forest Stewardship
Council (FSC®), the leading international forest certification organisation.
Our books carrying the FSC label are printed on FSC® certified
paper. FSC is the only forest certification scheme endorsed
by the leading environmental organisations, including
Greenpeace. Our paper procurement policy can be found at:
www.randomhouse.co.uk/environment

MIX
Paper from
responsible sources
FSC® C016897
www.fsc.org

Printed and bound by CPI Group (UK) Ltd, Croydon, CR0 4YY

ISBN: 9780753541241

To buy books by your favourite authors and register for offers, visit:
www.randomhouse.co.uk

1

Genevieve Loften turned and opened the Venetian blinds again, flooding the room with light. James Sinclair leaned back in his chair, watching her. His steady gaze made her feel uncomfortable. She had heard he could be difficult and this session proved once again that the rumours were true.

She thought again how unlike a conventional businessman he looked. A dark tan, dark hair, and a body like a sleek athlete under that immaculate tailored suit. She actually found him attractive but she had no intention of letting him know it. She was not going to stroke his ego. He looked far too self-assured as it was.

It was their third meeting. And this time they were alone. She had worked hard to impress him, to convince him that Barringtons had innovative ideas and could provide the advertising he needed to expand his markets abroad. He had just watched a recording of one of their most successful television campaigns. She had already shown him an impressive portfolio of past assignments, with sales figures to match, but nothing she had suggested or offered seemed to interest him. All she had received for her efforts had been that darkly ambiguous look, a slight lifting of one eyebrow, and no feedback whatsoever. With an inner sigh of regret she pushed the portfolio to one side. She did not like failures.

'If there's anything else I can show you, Mr Sinclair?' she offered. She was surprised to see him smile slowly.

'Maybe there is.' He paused, holding her eye as he stretched out his long legs. He relaxed visibly, but he still had the self-possessed air of a man in control. 'Come out from behind your nice protective businesswoman's desk,' he said, 'and stand in front of me.'

The sound of London's traffic, muted by the double glazing, filtered up from the street below. Genevieve stared at Sinclair, wondering for a moment if she had heard him correctly. Until that moment he had never shown the slightest interest in her. If anything she had felt his attitude was hostile. Now there was something in his eyes that disturbed her. Amusement? Triumph? She was not sure. And there was something arrogantly confident about the way he had shifted his position from formal to relaxed. It changed the relationship between them. They were no longer two business people looking for a point of contact. They were a man and a woman, aware that something was about to spark between them.

Although she felt unsure of herself, she decided to play along. She smiled and walked round the desk, stopping in front of him. 'Well,' she said, with forced brightness, 'here I am. Now perhaps you'll tell me the purpose of this little charade?'

'Turn round,' he said. 'Slowly.'

'Really, Mr Sinclair,' she began. 'I don't see the point of . . .'

'Just do it,' he said.

Genevieve shrugged, and turned. She was suddenly glad that her elegant suit was loosely rather than suggestively tailored, and that her skirt ended discreetly just below the knee. You can look as much as you like, Mr Sinclair, she thought, you won't see much.

But when she turned to face him again her opinion changed. His dark gaze travelled lazily over her body, touching her breasts, moving down her thighs, outlined by the neat seams of the pencil-slim skirt. He admired her legs, glossy in pale-grey stockings, and her narrow ankles neat above her black, medium-heeled shoes. Far from protecting her, she felt that her expensive clothes were being seductively stripped away, and that she was being explored by an invisible hand. It was like being assessed in a slave market. By the time he shifted his eyes back to her face, her cheeks were flushed pink.

He stared at her for a moment, then grinned slowly. 'I have a proposition for you,' he said. 'But it might not be quite the kind of business deal you were expecting.'

'I'm sure Barringtons will be able to meet any of your requirements,' she said.

'Barringtons might,' he agreed. 'But will you?'

'It amounts to the same thing, doesn't it?' she parried.

'Don't play innocent, Miss Loften,' he drawled. 'You're an adult woman, not a teenage virgin. I think you know what I'm suggesting.'

Genevieve had been propositioned before, although never as unexpectedly and blatantly as this. For a moment she was angry. Did he think she was some kind of commodity up for sale? Then the little voice of ambition reminded her of exactly what this arrogant man could be offering: Sinclair Associates were high profile and expanding. The agency selected to handle their advertising would become an international name.

Barringtons *needs* this account, she told herself, and they'll be very grateful to whoever gets it for them. If James Sinclair wants sex in exchange for his signature, then I'll give it to him. It's not as if he's old and fat, after all. 'Of course I know what you're suggesting,' she said briskly. 'I give you sex, and you give Barringtons your account.'

He laughed. 'You make it sound too simple, Miss Loften. I'm not about to exchange an important signature for a few quick thrills.' His voice altered, there was a harder edge to it now. 'I can get that cheaper elsewhere. I want more. Much more. You and I will have to meet and discuss the details.'

She shivered suddenly. This was not quite what she expected. What kind of details were there to discuss? She'd perform in bed for him and try to make it good. She would probably enjoy it. Maybe he would want something a little unusual? Well, if she had to, she would oblige. Anything to close that deal.

She did wonder briefly: why? Sinclair Associates did not really need Barringtons. It was really the other way around. Another thought nagged her: why *me*? She knew James Sinclair was rich, well connected and powerful. He had the kind of dangerous good looks that most women would have found highly desirable. He could have had any of the money or publicity-hungry beauties who frequented the smarter London clubs. Women more obviously glamorous than she was. Women who would have been delighted to be seen with him, and to go home and perform for him, probably far more expertly than she could.

She was not a virgin, but she did not consider herself particularly sexually experienced. Her first affair had been a fumbling, youthful disaster, followed by a couple of brief flings and one longer relationship that had ended because she was always cancelling dates due to pressure of work.

Sinclair stood up. He was a head taller than she was, and she was taller than average. With his glossy black hair, beautifully cut but worn slightly longer than convention dictated, and his natural tan, he had an exotic look. She could imagine him as a pirate, and a ruthless one at that. She remembered the stories she had heard about his business tactics. Perhaps pirate really was an accurate description. She had a brief vision of him dressed in tight trousers, knee-high boots, and a white shirt slashed to the waist, but immediately banished the picture from her mind, determined not to romanticise him. She was quite sure he had no romantic intentions towards *her*.

He was used to power, used to getting his own way, used to being in control. Well, she thought, so am I. You want to play games, Mr Sinclair? I'll play them with you. I might even enjoy them. But it's going to be strictly business. You can have your night of fun. Or several nights, if you insist. And I'll have your signature on a contract. And that will be that.

'Look,' she said, in her best no-nonsense voice, 'I've said I agree. There's nothing to discuss.'

He was still staring at her like a slave master at an auction. She backed towards her desk. Suddenly, knowing it was a pointless gesture, she touched the buttons of her jacket. The way he was looking at her made her feel as if they were undone. She saw his mouth twist into a smile and realised that he knew the effect he was having on her.

'I've said I accept your offer,' she said, hoping to distract him. 'There's nothing to discuss except when you want to meet me. And as this is rather – unorthodox, I hope I can rely on your discretion.'

'Don't worry,' he said. 'I don't boast about my conquests.'

'This will be a business deal,' she said, icily. 'Not a conquest.'

He looked at her for a long moment, then grinned lazily. 'Of course,' he agreed. 'Strictly business.' He paused. His tone changed. 'Undo your jacket.'

Once again she was not sure that she had heard him correctly. 'My jacket?' she repeated. 'What for?'

'Before I arrange our private discussion I'd like a quick look at what I might be getting.' His voice was soft but there was steel behind it. 'I want the jacket unbuttoned. Now.'

She was tempted to refuse. But a glance at his face told her that this might not be wise. Hurriedly, hoping this would satisfy him, she obeyed him. Under the short jacket she was wearing a plain, white silk blouse with a mandarin collar. She knew that he could not see much through the opaque cloth. Maybe a hint of her bra – a rather nice white lace one, she remembered.

'And your blouse,' he said.

This time her fingers froze. 'My blouse?' Her voice was unsteady. 'Certainly not!'

Sinclair's smile turned into a crooked grin. 'Don't play the affronted virgin with me, Miss Loften. Unbutton the blouse, or I'll do it for you.'

Her fingers touched the silk covered buttons. 'Someone might come in,' she protested.

'They might,' he agreed, unpeturbed. 'So hurry up.'

She pulled at the tiny round buttons. They had never been easy to undo and now her hands were shaking. The blouse fell open. She was tempted to hold the edges together but before she could do so Sinclair moved forward and caught her wrists, forcing her arms apart. His eyes moved from her face, down her neck to her breasts. 'Not bad,' he said.

He moved quickly and confidently, taking her completely by surprise, pushing her back until she felt the edge of her desk dig into her thighs. His hands were inside her blouse and under her arms before she could protest. He found the catch of her bra and unhooked it. In another second the bra was up round her neck and she was pushed back against the desk with her breasts exposed.

Her mind froze with the horror of being found like this. Although she knew any of her colleagues would knock before entering her office, they would not necessarily wait before entering. The knock was a token politeness. Would she even hear their footsteps on the carpeted floor?

His knees pressed against hers but he seemed to be deliberately avoiding any other contact. She did not know if he was aroused or not. She was leaning backwards, both arms braced behind her, taking her weight, knowing that in this position she could not prevent his mouth or his hands from travelling anywhere they liked.

He bent over her and touched her left nipple with his lips, brushing it gently then flicking it with his tongue. Within seconds it had tensed and hardened. Taking it in his mouth he began to suck insistently, each tugging movement making her tremble with a shock of pleasure. He seemed to know just how fast and hard she wanted the action. Then his hand closed over her other nipple and he teased it lightly, nipping and pinching, massaging her breast with a circular movement of his palm.

She felt a moan of encouragement rising in her throat and stifled it. She could not believe that she was actually enjoying this. The knowledge that they might be discovered at any moment simply made it more exciting. 'Please,' she managed to gasp, unsure of how far she would let him go. Or how far he would take her. 'Someone might come in.'

He looked up. 'Afraid they'll see you behaving like a whore?' He cupped his hands under her breasts, pushing them upwards, his thumbs rubbing faster. 'They might enjoy the view,' he drawled. 'I bet quite a few of your colleagues wouldn't mind giving your nipples a servicing. Perhaps we ought to call them in. Five minutes each.' His fingers still played with her, lazily. 'I have a feeling you just might like that.'

Normally the idea would have repelled her but something about the tone of his voice made it sound strangely exciting. Not with her business associates, though. But with strangers? Young men that she did not know and who did not know her, and with Sinclair watching, enjoying it? What would she feel like then? She shivered slightly and her tongue moistened her lips. He was still leaning over her but not touching her now.

'The thought of that turns you on, doesn't it?' he murmured.

'You really aren't as strait-laced as you look. I didn't think you would be, but I wanted to be sure. Maybe you really would be interested in doing a deal with me.'

'I've already said I would.' She tried to keep her voice steady, determined to try and regain control. 'A business deal.'

'But of course,' he agreed sardonically. His hand caressed her briefly. 'We barter. You give me what I want, and I give you a signature. The oldest kind of deal in the world.'

'You won't regret it,' she said.

Once again his eyes gave her a quick sexually charged assessment. 'I'm sure I won't,' he agreed.

They both heard the footsteps in the corridor. Unhurriedly, Sinclair backed away. Genevieve managed to pull her blouse together and hastily button her jacket. George Fullerton, middle-aged but still elegant and always with a flower in his button hole, looked round the door and smiled. 'I'm going for lunch. Perhaps you'd like to join me?'

Acutely aware of her blouse and bra bunched up under the now smooth lines of her jacket, Genevieve managed to smile coolly at Sinclair. 'We have a very good executive canteen, Mr Sinclair.'

'Thank you,' Sinclair said. 'But I have another appointment.'

George Fullerton glanced very briefly round the office, but Genevieve knew he had already noted the television and the portfolios. 'Has Genevieve shown you anything that excited you?'

She saw a smile touch James Sinclair's tanned face. His hand brushed an imaginary speck from his immaculate jacket and she felt a sudden sexual tremor as she remembered what that hand had been doing to her only moments before.

'As a matter of fact,' he said, 'she has. But I'll need to see more before I make a decision.'

'I'm sure Genevieve will oblige you,' Fullerton smiled.

'I'm sure she will,' Sinclair murmured.

'Still playing funny games with little balls?'

The voice intruded on Genevieve's daydream. She was sitting at a table in the sports centre bar, pleasantly relaxed after a shower, remembering the confident touch of James Sinclair's hands on her body. The idea of sex without strings, and a nice business bonus at the end of it, was beginning to attract her. So was the idea of finding out whether James Sinclair looked as sexy without his clothes on as he did in his elegantly tailored suit. She wished she had reacted less positively to his advances and not allowed him to have his own way so easily. She should have made a few moves of her own. Wasn't she entitled to know what she was getting too?

She looked up and saw David Carshaw standing opposite her, a can of Diet Pepsi in one hand and a bulging sports bag in the other. 'It beats chasing a few plastic feathers round a court,' she said.

'There's a bit more to badminton than that.' David sat down. 'And it's a damn sight quieter than squash. Are you still in the league? I didn't see your name on the lists.'

'I don't play in the league any more,' she said. 'I had to keep cancelling matches at the last minute. It didn't make me very popular.'

'The problems of being a career woman.' David grinned. 'I'm glad I'm just a humble bank employee.'

Far from humble, Genevieve thought. She had not seen David for some time and wondered why he had suddenly decided to talk to her now. She watched him finish his Pepsi, gurgling the last drops through a straw, then drop the empty can in his bag.

'Recycling,' he explained. 'The money goes to charity.'

Without a pause he added, 'I hear you're flirting with James Sinclair.'

The question took Genevieve completely by surprise. She knew gossip travelled fast in the City and David was in the position to hear it, but for a horrified moment she thought Sinclair's sexual suggestions were now public knowledge.

'Or rather, Barringtons are,' David corrected. 'Don't you think your ambitious little agency might be getting out of its depth?'

She shrugged, composed now. 'We can swim,' she said. 'And every bit as fast as Mr Sinclair.'

'I wonder?' David stared at her levelly. 'Sinclair's one of those men who would never be content with his first million. In fact he obviously hasn't been content with it. He always wants more. Frankly I can't understand why he's even bothered with Barringtons. There are plenty of top-line agencies who would kiss his – er – feet for the chance of handling his account.'

'Perhaps he heard how irresistible I am?' Genevieve said sweetly.

David laughed. 'Well, you're gorgeous, of course,' he said diplomatically. 'But actually I'm not sure you're Sinclair's type.'

'Really?' She was interested. 'And what exactly *is* his type?'

'Models,' David guessed. 'Leggy blondes with silicone implants. Or society types. You know the kind of thing.'

'He likes variety, you mean?'

'He likes women as accessories,' David said. 'Status symbols. I can't really see him going for anyone with brains. Too much competition. They might answer back.'

'He didn't strike me as that kind of man,' Genevieve said.

'That's because you don't know him.' David leaned forward. 'I expect he's played the perfect gentleman with you, but I'll tell you for nothing Sinclair's known to be a bit of a bastard with women. There was this daughter of a politician...' He broke off. 'No, I shouldn't spread gossip. It was all hearsay. Probably a load of lies.'

'Oh, stop acting like a schoolgirl, David,' Genevieve said crossly. 'You know you're going to tell me anyway.'

'Well.' David settled into his chair. 'She was very stuck on him until he started asking her to do some very peculiar things.'

'Like what?'

'How should I know? Kinky stuff. Anyway, she refused.'

'Very moral of her,' Genevieve said dryly. 'I don't believe a word of it.'

'She threatened to sell her story to the newspapers.'

'Don't they all? I still don't believe it. What's the punchline?'

'Rumour has it that Sinclair paid her more than the papers.'

'And you believe that?'

David shrugged. 'He's got the money to do it.' He paused, then grinned. 'Personally, I think it's far more likely that he told her to publish and be damned. And since her daddy was a politician she thought better of it. But that isn't to say I didn't believe the stories of what they got up to. Sinclair likes playing power games. With women especially. Just thought I'd warn you.'

'Where business is concerned I'm not a woman, just a negotiator.'

'For your sake,' David said, 'I hope James Sinclair thinks the same way.'

Genevieve thought about David's words for the rest of the week. Was Sinclair courting Barringtons for reasons of his own? And if he was, what were they? The more she thought about it, the harder she found it to come up with any. And what was his real interest in her? If David was correct in his description of Sinclair's sexual preferences she was certainly not his type. She was gaining a reputation for efficiency at her job but she certainly could not be considered a status symbol. And she had no intention of pretending to be stupid either, just to humour him. Furthermore, she realised, she had made no arrangements to meet him. George Fullerton had stayed with her while Sinclair went down in the lift on his own. She doubted if he would contact her at work, but it would be easy for him to find out her mobile number. Would he do it?

But her phone did not ring, and she began to wonder if she really had been a fool to take him seriously. Sex for a signature? It was like something out of a film. Perhaps David had been right. He was just playing power games? Perhaps it was his idea of a joke. If it was, did she care? She had to admit that she did. Not, she told herself quickly, that she was particularly looking forward to obliging him in bed. She could take that or leave it. It was strictly a career move. She *needed* a break. She wanted to prove that she could win clients.

Barringtons currently had an exciting creative division, but they would not keep their inventive young designers and writers if they did not expand. Sinclair's account would be the first step. And if Barringtons succeeded, Genevieve knew she would succeed with them. Sinclair could give her that. She stared at her phone and willed him to call her, to suggest a meeting. Anything.

The phone stayed silent.

Genevieve had just run a bath and the perfumed water was gently warming her. She lifted one leg and stretched it, smoothing the creamy foam that clung to her skin. Why did the gleam of water always make your body look sexy? Was that why so many men liked giving women an oil massage?

The phone rang. She reached for it, unhurriedly, trying to guess who it might be. At this time of night it was probably her brother, Philip. He knew she worked long hours and usually phoned late – at least when he thought about it. He hadn't rung her for ages. She prepared to tell him off.

'Miss Loften?' She recognised the voice immediately, with its combination of authority and attractive depth.

'Mr Sinclair?' She hoped she sounded neutral. She had no intention of letting him know how relieved she was to hear from him at last. 'I thought you'd forgotten our deal.'

'I don't forget anything,' he said. 'I had a few arrangements to make. Now listen. Go to 43 Harmond Street tomorrow and collect a box. You wear what's inside it under an outfit of your own choice when we meet for our discussion. Just the items in the box. Nothing else. Understand?'

So he's into sexy underwear, she thought. But he sounded as if he was giving orders to his secretary and she wasn't sure she liked it. With her free hand she smoothed the creamy foam over her breasts so that her nipples were just visible then submerged herself in the warmth of the perfumed water again. She thought: If you were here now, Mr Sinclair, I'd make you change your tone.

She decided to make some kind of protest against being dictated to, if only to see how he would react. 'Wait a minute,' she said. 'I'm not sure I'll have the time go anywhere tomorrow. I've got two meetings and . . .'

'Make time,' he said abruptly.

'And if I can't?' she returned, coolly.

'The deal's off,' he said.

'Now listen,' she began.

'No,' he interrupted. 'You listen. This isn't the office. This is just the two of us, and I'm the one who calls the shots. If you don't think you're going to like it, back out now.' His voice softened slightly, and she imagined his mouth with that slightly sardonic smile. 'Try it my way,' he cajoled. 'You know you're curious.'

She was. She was curious about the kind of garments he would expect her to wear. Frilly knickers? The perennial male favourite, a suspender belt and seamed stockings? Open crotch panties? A peep-hole bra?

She stifled a sudden giggle. Surely not. He was so elegant and controlled, she couldn't imagine him being turned on by such schoolboy props. But then you never knew. She slithered further into the bath. The foam came up to her chin. She felt relaxed, hugged by the scented water. 'Well, all right,' she agreed, hoping she sounded as if she was granting him a favour. 'As long as I can go in the evening.'

'You can go anytime,' he said. 'And the day after tomorrow you'll meet me at the Garnet at eight.' There was a pause. 'And like I said, lady, you wear what you like on top, but underneath it's my choice.'

She knew the Garnet to be an exclusive and expensive restaurant. If she had to wear black stockings and open crotch panties to please him it would be a fair exchange for what would certainly be a marvellous meal.

After her bath, wrapped in a silky kimono, she checked out her *London A to Z*. The road name he had given her was in a residential suburb, and not a particularly classy one. It made his instructions all the more intriguing. There were plenty of kinky shops in London ranging from the smart to the down-right tacky. What was so special about 43 Harmond Street?

Genevieve was still thinking about Sinclair's instructions while having lunch the following day. In the summer she often took a break from her colleagues and bought herself a couple of rolls in a small pub that most local office workers had not yet discovered. She had no objection to talking shop, but sometimes she just wanted to eat in peace.

She was still trying to decide what she would find at 43 Harmond Street (her favourite choice being a middle-aged housewife sewing naughty knickers for bingo money) when someone thrust an A4 portfolio under her nose and said: 'Take a look at these!'

Almost choking on her roll Genevieve turned round angrily. She recognised the voice and knew exactly who she was going to see: Ricky Croft, his hair straggling over his collar, and his face unshaven. He wore a battered Levi jacket and jeans. She could not remember seeing him in anything else. His enemies (and his friends) reckoned he slept in them.

'Go on.' He sat down opposite her and pushed the portfolio towards her. 'Look.'

'No,' she said.

'You've never seen anything like this before,' he said.

'Ricky –' Genevieve put down her roll, '– there is no job for you at Barringtons.'

'Oh, I know that,' he agreed. 'I'm not pretty enough, am I? I don't fit the image. Tell me, what are well-dressed graphic designers wearing these days?'

'You know we don't give a sod what you wear,' Genevieve said crossly. 'You're simply unreliable. You haven't learned what the word deadline means.'

'I'm an artist,' Ricky said. 'Artists don't work to a timetable.'

'They don't work for Barringtons either,' she said. 'We employ professionals. And I don't want to see any more lovely logos for non-existent firms.'

Ricky was undeterred. 'Just look,' he said, tapping the portfolio. 'These are reductions. The originals are much bigger.'

Despite herself Genevieve reached for the portfolio and opened it. She knew Ricky Croft's work. She had once given him a freelance assignment. He had turned in some brilliant ideas – six weeks too late.

The first clear plastic envelope contained a pencil drawing. Detailed objective drawing was one of Ricky's specialities, but it wasn't the skill of the almost photographic rendering that surprised Genevieve. It was the subject matter.

A soldier in eighteenth-century military uniform tumbled with a young woman on a four poster. The two of them had clearly been romping together; the girl's full breasts were exposed, and her frilly skirts were bunched up round her waist. She wore dark stockings gartered at her thighs. The man was kneeling between her plump but shapely legs, holding her ankles apart. His jacket and undershirt were undone. Although his own erection was visibly bulging through the tight material of his trousers, he was obviously intent on oral sex rather than penetration.

Ricky had drawn the woman's erect nipples and open sex in loving detail. Her expression was one of slight shock coupled with erotic curiosity. It implied that she had never experienced this kind of foreplay before. The man's face showed only anticipation. His half smile, and the tip of his tongue just showing between his lips, gave the impression that he knew exactly what he was going to do, and he would make sure his partner enjoyed it to the full.

Genevieve found the picture curiously arousing, all the more so because it hinted at what was about to happen rather than displaying it. It allowed an observer to use his or her imagination. A man could imagine tasting the woman's swollen pussy, imagine her writhing in delight as he forced her into willing submission. A woman could imagine the sensation of an expert tongue exciting her into a frenzy, withholding the ultimate release as long as possible, until she begged him for it. Genevieve briefly superimposed Sinclair's face on that of the soldier. Then, furious with herself, quickly turned the page.

The next picture showed the same couple, but this time the man's head was deep between the woman's thighs. His hands were under her buttocks, lifting her. The woman's head was thrown back, her expression clearly orgasmic. She was fondling her own nipples.

'Nice, eh?' Ricky was watching her. 'Like I said, the originals are much bigger.'

Genevieve gave him what she hoped was a disdainful glance. She felt that she ought to slam the portfolio shut, and tell Ricky in no uncertain terms that she was not interested in dirty pictures. But it would not have been true. She wanted to see more. She turned another page.

The characters had changed. The man was now definitely an officer and it gave her a slight – and delicious – jolt of pleasure to realise that this time it required very little imagination to believe that this was Sinclair. In fact she could almost have been persuaded to believe that Ricky had used Sinclair – if not as an outright model – at least as a representative type. Tall and slim, with dark hair and Sinclair's angular good looks, the officer wore a uniform that was probably historically inaccurate, but looked enough like a traditional hussar to give him an aura of macho authority: tight trousers, knee-high boots and a short braided jacket, buttoned to a high-stand collar. The woman looked more aristocratic this time, slightly contemptuous in fact, with elaborately styled hair held in place by a band with a sweeping feather pinned to it, and a high-waisted, low-necked dress that emphasised her swelling breasts but covered everything else.

There was nothing erotic happening in the picture, but it was clear that these two people knew things were about to change. The woman stared up at the officer as if daring him to touch her, and the man's stance and expression showed clearly he accepted her challenge and was planning to do exactly that – and more. Once again Genevieve was forced to admire Ricky's skill. Not only had he depicted his characters with photographic accuracy, he had conveyed their thoughts too. Or, it suddenly occurred to her, was she just reading into the drawing what she hoped to see? She noticed the picture had a caption. It said: 'Military Manoeuvres'.

'It's a set,' Ricky said. 'A sort of picture strip for adults. A bit like the *Rake's Progress*. You know?'

'With an accent on the strip?' Genevieve raised her eyebrows.

'You get the idea,' Ricky said. He watched her. 'Well, don't just sit there. The pages won't turn themselves.'

She felt that this was the time to say: I'm simply not interested in this sort of thing. If the man had looked less like Sinclair she probably would have done. But the likeness intrigued her. She almost felt a sense of power. It was as if she was peeping through a keyhole, watching him. She turned the page.

In the second picture the officer had removed the woman's dress, leaving her stripped except for stockings, gartered at her thighs, and shoes with tiny heels and large bows. She also still wore her jewellery: a choker round her neck and earrings. Her hair was pinned up but the headband and feather had disappeared.

The officer – who had removed his jacket but nothing else – was pressing her back against the wall, his mouth exciting one erect nipple and his fingers teasing the other. The woman had her hands on his shoulders, presumably as a gesture of protest, but although her lips were parted she was clearly not calling for help. Judging from her expression, Genevieve thought a moan of pleasure would be more likely. The picture reminded her of her recent experience with Sinclair. She felt her body begin to tingle, and turned the page quickly.

In the next picture the officer had removed his shirt, and the woman was on the four poster – although it was obvious that the two of them were not preparing for a quick session of orthodox love-making. The woman's hands were already tied to the bed posts and the man was in the process of completing her restraint, holding and tying one ankle. He had positioned her so that her thighs were wide apart. Ricky had drawn her swelling clitoris – and all the other parts of her body – in loving detail. It was apparent from the officer's bulging trousers that he was also aroused.

The woman showed no apprehension about being tied, and certainly no inclination to struggle. If anything she looked excited. Genevieve was shocked to realise that because it was associated with sexual playacting the idea of being held captive in this way did not fill her with either anger or disgust. She tried to imagine what it would be like to be spread-eagled on a bed with a man tying your hands and feet. She stared at the picture of the officer, with his bare chest and flat stomach. His expression as he looked at his willing captive again reminded her of Sinclair. He was smiling slightly. In anticipation, Genevieve thought.

By the fourth picture the action had heated up. The officer's head was between the woman's legs, his hands flat against her inner thighs, forcing them to stay apart while he pleasured her with his tongue It looked to Genevieve as if she had already had her first orgasm. Her head was thrown back and her mouth open as if she was screaming. Her arms were stretched against their bonds, her nipples erect. Her whole body seemed to shaking with sensation. The officer was glancing up at her even as he used his tongue on her, obviously pleased with the result of his actions. Looking at the drawing, Genevieve could almost imagine the warm friction of that tongue lightly caressing her, moving faster as her lover felt her body responding. She imagined his fingers digging into her flesh, holding her firmly as her writhing grew more frantic and the sensations became almost too intense to bear. Genevieve's own body began to respond. She glanced up to see Ricky watching her closely. Assuming what she hoped was a disinterested expression, she turned the next page.

Now the officer had shed all of his clothes. He straddled the woman's body. His buttocks were taut and muscular. His cock was half in her willing mouth. His hands were under her head and he lifted her slightly towards him, encouraging her to give him the kind of pleasure he had just given her. Although she was still tied, and obviously could not refuse, her expression clearly showed that she was equally delighted to be doing so.

Genevieve had only performed oral sex on one boyfriend. It had not been a very loving experience. Jeff, she remembered, had seemed irritable at her suggestion and tense while she was performing – with more enthusiasm than expertise, she remembered. After his orgasm he had rolled away from her and refused to talk. It was only later that she found out he considered such activities unnatural and had only agreed in order to please her. Since she had only done it to please him (having read in a magazine article that most men considered it the ultimate compliment), she had been both angry and upset at his reaction. They parted very soon afterwards, following a heated argument during which Jeff had brought up the oral sex incident again and described it 'animal behaviour'. If nothing else it had at least taught Genevieve that not all men were as liberated as she had been led to believe.

What would Jeff have thought of the sixth picture, she

wondered. Now the woman had been turned over and upended and the man was entering her from the rear. The woman's head was turned sideways, and again it was clear that she was quite happy with the treatment she was receiving. The man had his arms around her and was caressing her nipples as he thrust into her. Again Ricky's skill had invested the picture with a sense of movement. You could, Genevieve thought, almost hear the bed creak, the mattress springs protest, the legs rattle against the floor. Almost hear the two participants breathing faster and more raggedly as their climax approached.

Genevieve had to admit that if the drawings were intended to be arousing they had succeeded admirably. She had never been particularly affected by pictures before – but then she hadn't seen many, and certainly none as expertly drawn as Ricky's. She did not buy women's soft porn magazines, but she had seen those bought by friends. The mainstream ones, with their carefully posed models covered by strategically placed towels, she found irritatingly coy, and those exposed but limp penises were distinctly unexciting. She knew it was the result of censorship, but it was, in her view, defeating the object.

'He'd be interested, wouldn't he?' Ricky's voice intruded on her thoughts. She gazed at him blankly. 'James Sinclair,' Ricky said. 'Your new client.'

'My God,' Genevieve said. 'Gossip does travel fast.'

Ricky leaned towards her. 'He'd buy something like this. He'd love these.'

'If you really think so,' Genevieve said, 'take him some samples.'

Ricky laughed. 'Can't you just see me getting into his building, let alone his office? I wouldn't even get past those Gestapo security men he's got on the doors. He's got to come to me, and he won't unless he knows where to come and what I'm offering.'

'Write him a letter,' Genevieve said. 'Put them up on your website.'

Ricky's expression changed. 'You're not going to help me, are you?'

'Of course not,' she said. 'Mr Sinclair is a prospective client. Do you really think I'm going to use a business meeting to try and sell him dirty pictures?'

'They're not dirty pictures,' Ricky objected. 'This is erotica. There's a difference.'

'Call it what you like, the answer's no. And you're an idiot if you ever believed it could have been yes.'

'I'm not asking you to act as a saleswoman,' Ricky said. 'Just bring it up in conversation. Sinclair's known to be a womaniser, and he's kinky too. I heard this story –'

'Not the one about politician's daughter?' Genevieve interrupted. 'I've heard it.'

'Look,' Ricky said, 'Sinclair sounds like the kind of man who'd be interested in my work. Surely you could find an opportunity to tell him you know someone who can supply some unusual pictures? You don't have to say any more than that. He'll understand.'

'Act as an agent for you, you mean?' Genevieve shook her head. 'Ricky Croft, it's about time you grew up.'

'I need the money,' he said.

'Start behaving like a professional; meet your deadlines and you'll make a fortune.'

'And die of boredom?' Ricky stood up. 'No thanks.'

'It's possible to be creative and commercial, you know,' she said.

'I've never noticed it,' he answered. 'And certainly not in advertising.'

He left her to finish her roll in peace. And to start thinking again. James Sinclair certainly seemed to have a varied reputation, and his message to her indicated that he wanted more than a few quick press-ups in bed. But was the reputation true, or just gossip? She had a feeling that her visit to 43 Harmond Street would be the first step in supplying an answer. She got up, and became aware that Ricky's pictures had aroused her more than she had realised. She felt distinctly uncomfortable as she walked back to work.

It looked like a very ordinary house. A neat front garden, flower-patterned net curtains. Genevieve knocked on the dark-red front door. An elderly lady opened it.

'I'm Miss Jones,' said Genevieve, following instructions. 'I've come to collect some – er – things.'

'Go straight in, dear,' the old lady nodded. 'Georgie's in her workroom now.'

Wondering if Georgie would turn out to be another old lady, Genevieve went through the door and found herself in a room that indicated whatever clothes you bought here they would certainly not include anything either lacy or frilled.

There was leather everywhere. The tangy scent of it perfumed the air. Hides were stacked on the floor. Boots with impossible heels stood against the wall. Whips and harnesses hung on hooks. Faceless tailor's dummies were masked and gagged with demonstration items. There were long gloves, heavy belts and bras so studded with metal they looked like armour. A workbench was piled high with work in progress. Genevieve stared round in amazement.

Georgie was a bubbly blonde who looked hardly out of her teens. She wore an eco-friendly T-shirt and combats. 'It's a terrible mess, I'm afraid,' she apologised cheerfully. 'My girlfriend says she can never understand how I find anything. I've got your stuff all boxed up.'

Genevieve inspected the nearest dummy. It was dressed in a close-fitting female bodysuit made of lustrous black leather. The head was completely covered by a tight cap with holes only for the nose and mouth. Chrome zips, all obviously very carefully positioned, circled the thighs, the breasts, the midriff, the arms, and curved up between the buttocks. The legs ended in high-heeled, front-laced boots.

'Nice, isn't it?' Georgie said proudly. 'One of my specials. Imagine standing there in some kind of restraint harness, not knowing which zip's going to be undone, or which bit of you is going to be used or played with next. But what's really good is that it's a dozen outfits in one. If you fancy a different game you can take the whole suit apart and use bits of it. The leggings can be thigh boots, the sleeves are gloves. There's a bra and a corset, whatever. I always thought anyone would look good in just the hood and long boots and maybe a wide belt. Actually I saw a painting a bit like that once in a proper art gallery, this woman standing there in this shiny leather gear, and there were all these serious people looking at it and saying how symbolic it was.' She giggled. 'I just thought it was a turn-on, and I bet that's why the artist painted it, really.'

Genevieve stared at the bodysuit. A turn-on? Yes, she had to admit that it was. The leather made it seem faintly aggressive but the obvious sexual positioning of the zips implied submission. She imagined the chrome teeth opening slowly. She imagined the cool touch of air on the exposed skin. And then the tips of fingers, or the tip of a tongue, exploring.

Yes, definitely a turn-on for a certain type of person. Her type? What would it feel like to be sheathed in that body-hugging leather? She turned round. A dummy behind her was wearing a complex corset, laced down the back and covered with straps, buckles and studs. She thought it looked incredibly uncomfortable. 'Do a lot of people buy these things?' she asked.

'Gosh, yes.' Georgie nodded. 'And a lot more probably would if they could afford them. I don't come cheap, but I use the best leather and none of my straps pull off at the wrong moment, unlike some of the stuff you can buy. When you're laced up in one of my restraints you stay laced up until your master or mistress releases you.'

Genevieve stared at the corset, trying to visualise where various straps would go, how they would feel when they were pulled tight. The more she stared the easier it was to imagine this blatantly sexual garment on a real body, or to be more precise, on her body.

She had never really understood the erotic appeal of leather clothing before, or perhaps it would be more honest to say that she had never thought about it. But she began to think about it now, surrounded by this cornucopia of fetishist designs. She imagined the leather corset encasing her, the straps digging and constraining, and realised that she found the idea exciting. She reached out and touched the leather. It was smooth and sensual.

Georgie watched her. 'Nice, isn't it? Almost as nice as stroking a cat. Yours is the same quality. The best.'

'Mine?' Genevieve was startled back to the present.

'Your corset,' Georgie said. 'The one your fella ordered.'

'You've made me a corset?' Genevieve felt her face flush. Her eyes returned to the model on the dummy. She felt as if James Sinclair had read her mind.

'You bet.' Georgie nodded. 'Rush job and guess the measurements time, but it'll fit. Your fella gave me a rough guide to your size and I made it adjustable. You'll feel great in it. Promise.'

Genevieve felt her cheeks growing hot with embarrass-ment at the thought of it. It was one thing imagining yourself in one of these unambiguously provocative outfits, or maybe even wearing one for a long-time partner you knew and trusted. But Sinclair was virtually a stranger. 'But my – friend expects me to wear it when I go out with him,' she said.

'Well, why not?' Georgie shrugged. 'Where are you going? To a club?'

'To a restaurant.'

'But I bet he'll take you to a club afterwards,' Georgie said. 'He'll probably want to show you off. I would if I'd paid all that for your gear.'

'Show me off?' Genevieve repeated. Good God, was that what he was planning? She was horrified. And yet deep down in her mind a little tremor of excitement began.

Georgie looked at her in amusement. 'You're really new to all this, aren't you?'

'New to what?'

'Bondage. SM. Master and slave.'

'Well, yes,' Genevieve admitted.

'You'll love it,' Georgie enthused. 'My girlfriend takes me to The Cupboard. I have to wear a collar and chain and this really short skirt, and boots of course. The Cupboard's for lesbians so it probably wouldn't be your scene, but I've had more spank-ings there than I've had hot dinners. There's this marvellous dyke, really strong, she bends me over and really goes to town. My girlfriend loves to watch.'

'And you don't mind?' Genevieve asked in amazement.

'Of course I don't mind.' Georgie looked surprised. 'It turns me on. If I minded, my girlfriend wouldn't let anyone do it.'

'I wouldn't let anyone do that to me,' Genevieve said, with conviction. 'In public or anywhere else.'

Georgie looked at her and then laughed. 'You'd be surprised what you'd do', she said, 'with the right partner.'

Knowing what to expect didn't make the sight of the corset any less startling when she unpacked it. Black leather, dull-sheened, with so many straps and buckles she wondered if she would be able to do them all up correctly. The box also contained a pair of seamed black stockings and some ridiculously high-heeled shoes. She searched for panties and could not find any. Obviously an oversight, she thought, and put on a pair of her favourite black silk bikini briefs.

It did not take her as long to lace herself into the corset as she expected. It was beautifully made and the straps seemed to find their correct position automatically. She soon discovered that they were intended to display and emphasis various parts of her anatomy. They plunged between her legs, scooped under her buttocks, and circled her thighs like narrow garters. They drew black lines round her breasts and she realised that if she tightened them they would pull her into a provocative jutting shape. She deliberately did not tighten them too much. It looked sexy but it was also uncomfortable.

One of the straps seemed to be designed to go straight across her breasts and was fitted with two little expanding rings that she could not see any use for. She could not detach them so she left them alone. The stockings polished her legs with a glossy lustre and the shoes fitted perfectly. How had he known her size?

She looked at herself in the mirror and saw a woman with her face and a stranger's body. A leather queen in fetishist gear. She thought about the fetish clubs. She was aware there were women who would let others see them dressed like this, but she wasn't one of them. Or was she?

She posed, at first self-consciously and then with increasing lack of inhibition. Her figure, she decided, was fine: good breasts, long legs, neat waist. She had nothing to be ashamed of and plenty to display. Would she really do it? The idea was suddenly exciting.

She covered the corset with a dark blouse and a loosely tailored suit made of silk, not wanting anything too tight or the buckles and studs would show through. She twisted her straight blonde hair into a loose knot and applied the minimum of make-up. Outwardly she looked almost prim. Only the shoes and stockings had a sexy look.

But when she walked she was constantly aware of Georgie's leather tailoring. The straps pulled and the studs pressed, reminding her all the time of exactly what she would look like if anyone removed her clothes. And James Sinclair was going to remove them at some point in the evening. That was one thing she could be absolutely certain of.

A taxi called for her promptly and took her to the Garnet. He was waiting, elegant in black. He smiled and surprised her by putting his hand behind her back and drawing her close for a chaste kiss on the cheek. She smelled the faint and expensive tang of his aftershave. His hand moved down her spine and she realised that his apparently friendly gesture had an ulterior motive. He was feeling for proof that she had obeyed his orders. 'Good,' he said, his fingers lightly tracing a line of hidden studs. 'You're obedient. But I always thought you would be.'

The muted sounds of the restaurant murmured round them. A middle-aged couple sat discussing the wine list. A waiter hovered discreetly. The subdued lighting gave the interior a sense of peaceful intimacy.

He took her arm and led her to a table. She had a horrible feeling the leather was creaking, that everyone knew exactly what she was wearing under her primly tailored suit. He held her chair for her, the perfect gentleman.

'No problems dressing?' he wondered mildly.

'I overcame them,' she said.

'A good fit?'

'Tight,' she said.

'It's supposed to be tight,' he said pleasantly, smiling. He leaned across and took her hand, pressing her fingers. 'Like this.' He squeezed briefly and let her go. 'It's a restraint corset. A mild one, but you're supposed to know you're wearing it. There are better versions. Much better. Think about that.' He beckoned to the waiter. 'Did you fit the rings?' he asked her.

'Rings?' she repeated blankly. The waiter hesitated near their table.

'The nipple rings,' he said.

She felt her face growing pink. Surely the waiter could hear their conversation? 'I don't understand you,' she faltered.

He ordered for both of them and the waiter moved silently away. He leaned forward. She reflected that they must have looked like a couple of lovers. 'There should have been a strap with rings on them to cross your breasts,' he said. 'The rings were to fit round your nipples, nice and tight.'

'Oh,' she said, blushing. 'I didn't realise that was what they were for.'

He surprised her by laughing. 'You are an innocent, aren't you? I'm going to enjoy teaching you!'

This simple comment made her skin prickle with sudden excitement. She was already beginning to realise that her erotic education had been sadly lacking in variety. She would enjoy learning with him as her tutor but she did not intend to give him the satisfaction of knowing that he had already virtually won her over.

'I haven't agreed to anything yet,' she said sharply.

He gave her a wry look. 'Haven't you?' he asked softly. 'I'm not going to argue. Enjoy the meal.'

She did enjoy it. He discussed plays, films and music, entertaining her with anecdotes, intriguing her with his ideas. She sat stiffly because of the corset and wriggled occasionally as the metal studs on the leather garter bands dug into her thighs. He said nothing but she knew he noticed her movements and she was sure they amused him.

'Now,' he said pleasantly, when they finished their coffee and liqueurs, 'go to the ladies.' He indicated the door on the other side of the room with a tilt of his head.

'But I don't want to,' she said in surprise.

'What you want doesn't matter.' He smiled and reached across the table to hold her hand. 'Get this straight. If we make a deal you do as you're told. Walk over there. Go in. Stay a few minutes and walk back.' His strong fingers held hers. 'Don't hurry. Just walk.'

'I couldn't hurry if I wanted to in these damned shoes,' she said tightly.

He laughed. 'I like them. They make you walk like a tart. And that's what you are, aren't you? You're with me because you expect me to pay you. With a signature and not money, but the principle's the same. I've bought you, and tonight I'm going to get my money's worth. Starting now. So walk.'

She swayed over to the door past the small tables and the respectable dining couples. There was a large gilt-framed mirror in the ladies. She looked at herself. A fashionable woman in a silk suit, her hair neat, her face discreetly made-up. And wearing a leather bondage corset under her conventional outer clothes, the restraining straps digging into her flesh, reminding her of the other image of herself she had watched earlier on, posing. A tart, was she? In a way she had to admit that he was right. They were negotiating a contract, but he was controlling the terms. She walked back to the table aware that his eyes were on her all the time. He stood up.

'Right,' he said. 'I think it's time for me to inspect the goods I paid so much money for.'

Sinclair lived in a tall Georgian house in one of the more exclusive London squares. She found it difficult to manage the high steps to the front door. He did not offer to help her, but watched her as she tottered uncomfortably. Inside her heels clicked on the marble-tiled floor in the hall.

He opened a door and she found herself in a room that was both masculine and elegant. There were oil portraits on the walls, large leather-covered chairs, a polished wooden floor and discreet lighting from red-shaded lamps. He walked over to one of the chairs, turned it so that it faced her and sat down.

'Get your clothes off,' he said.

'I thought we were going to discuss your terms,' she began.

'We are,' he agreed. 'But not with a desk between us. You're not at work now. Just do as you're told. I want to see if Georgie's work is still up to her usual standard.'

Genevieve stripped slowly and was pleased to see him shift position as she peeled off her blouse. Maybe he was getting an erection already? She hoped so. The sooner he was hard the sooner he would take her to bed and she could remove the now increasingly uncomfortable corset.

She left her skirt until last. When she finally let it fall to the floor she saw his expression change from the relaxed look of a man enjoying a performance to obvious annoyance. He stood up, came towards her and hooked a finger in the front of her silk panties. 'Did I tell you to wear these?' he asked coldly.

'You didn't include any,' she began. 'So I thought –'

'Let's get one thing clear right now,' he interrupted. 'If we come to an agreement we do things my way. If I don't give you panties it means you don't wear panties. Understand?'

She nodded, speechless. He went to a drawer and took out a pair of scissors. He pulled the panties away from her body and cut them. Her favourite underwear ended up in pieces on the floor.

'That's better,' he approved, inspecting her. 'You're a natural blonde. I thought you would be. Turn round.' She did so. 'Spread your legs. Bend over slowly, then straighten up.' She heard the leather creak as she moved. 'You've got a nice, sexy ass,' he told her pleasantly. 'But I guessed that too.'

'I don't see how,' she said, still with her back to him.

'I always let you walk in front of me,' he said. 'The perfect gentleman. Didn't you notice? Then I used my imagination to decide how your bottom would look if I stripped you. And how big your nipples were. And how fast it would take to get them erect. Little daydreams like that help keep me awake at boring shareholders' meetings. Don't feel too flattered. I do it quite often with women that I meet.' She prepared to face him again. He said sharply: 'Stay as you are.' She stood still. 'Now,' he said, 'walk over to that door, and take your time.'

When she reached the door she realised that it was drilled with inch-wide holes.

'Turn round,' he said. 'Back up.'

He went to a cupboard and took out some wooden pegs and narrow leather straps. He positioned her exactly how he wanted her, flat against the door, legs apart, arms stretched above her head, her body forming an X. He pushed the pegs into the holes nearest her hands and feet and bound her wrists and ankles with the straps.

'That's fine,' he said. 'Every house should have a door like this. You know, Miss Loften, it was worth buying you dinner just to see your legs nicely apart like a high-class whore waiting for action.' He stood in front of her. 'Although a real whore would have known how to prepare herself.' His hands took her breasts and his thumbs stroked her nipples lightly. She knew he was watching her face for signs of enjoyment. It was difficult not to oblige him, especially as her body was betraying her anyway and she felt her flesh peaking into two hard buds. He took the strap with the rings on it and clipped one ring over her aroused nipple, tightening it until she gave a yelp of protest.

'Next time perhaps you'll do it yourself,' he said.

Her other nipple was treated the same way. He pulled on the strap that connected the rings forcing her breasts together and giving her a deep cleavage. The pressure and the tugging made her realise how arousing it was to be manhandled in this way. The sensations became even more intense when he began to tighten the other straps so that both breasts were pulled upwards, and then he adjusted the front lacing of the corset, nipping her waist in by at least two inches, so that she gasped.

He backed away from her and gave her a slow once-over. Even the passage of his eyes aroused her. He turned, went over to a chair and pushed it until it came to rest a few feet away from her. Sitting down, he put one leg over the arm and lounged back. A quick glance proved to her that he had enjoyed restraining her with the pegs, the straps and the rings as much as she had enjoyed being his victim.

'I don't think we've got much to discuss,' he said. 'I always knew that under that cool and efficient exterior there was a highly sexed woman just waiting to be liberated, and your behaviour so far has proved that I'm right.'

She wasn't going to give in that easily. 'Don't jump to conclusions,' she objected. 'I want that business contract. That's why I'm cooperating. And I'd hardly describe this,' she tugged at her bound wrists, 'as liberating.'

'Wouldn't you?' he said softly. 'Lots of women would. Right now you haven't got to think. You haven't got to make decisions. You're free just to be yourself.'

'*This* isn't being myself,' she protested quickly.

'Isn't it?' He smiled. 'Are you sure? Do you know yourself that well?' He paused. 'Here's the deal: for ninety days you'll obey my orders. When I want you I'll call you, and you'll play the games I choose, no arguments. When you're with me I'll let you know who you're going to be. A lady, a whore, a slave, the choice is mine. I will promise that whatever I arrange for you, I'll protect you from being recognised by anyone who might know you. If you really object to anything I suggest you can back out, you've got that option, but if you do the deal's off. Agreed?'

'Yes,' she said.

'Don't you mean "yes please"?' he asked her softly.

Ninety days? Three months? She had been expecting all this to be over in a couple of weeks. Did the idea of being his sexual slave whenever he decided to exercise his power over her excite her or appal her? She was not sure. 'I'll do whatever you want,' she said quickly. 'But just remember this is strictly a business deal.'

He stood up and walked towards her. She would never have believed that she could find being forced into this kind of erotically humiliating position exciting. Normally she hated being uncomfortable. Now her swelling clitoris was aching for attention. He put one finger on her and stroked gently. The sensation was so intense that she writhed against her restraints and groaned.

'You'll do whatever I want, will you?' His mouth moved over her neck and his tongue found her ear, lazily tracing patterns, probing. 'Let's see if you mean that. I want you to make me come, but not too quickly. Think you can manage that?'

He took the strap that joined her nipples and tugged. The rings that circled her sensitive flesh caused her tremors of erotic pain. Her body quivered and shook. All she wanted now was relief, either manual or from penetration. She moaned and thrust her hips forward.

'Answer me,' he said.

'Yes,' she groaned. 'Yes.'

She almost said please, her need for relief was so great. Swiftly he moved back, unzipped his trousers and lifted out his cock and balls. His erection was impressive but she did not have much time to admire it before he entered her smoothly, his hands behind her now, cupping her bottom, lifting her towards him. Her wrists and ankles pulled against their restraints. Her nipples, aroused from the embrace of the rings, rubbed against his coat, causing her extra delight.

'I've been looking forward to this,' he murmured.

He plunged into her, slowly at first and she matched his rhythm, clenching her internal muscles, squeezing, relaxing, pulling him deeper, but letting him withdraw far back enough to graze her clit with each thrust. She wanted to make it last too, not only to please him but for her own pleasure. But as his hips moved faster a glance at his face showed her that he was no longer in control. And neither was she. All that mattered now was release from the mounting sexual tension that gripped her. He climaxed just before she did, a hoarse groan of pleasure deep in his throat matching her own intense cry of relief.

She relaxed limply against the door and watched as he tidied himself up. Even returning to its unexcited size, his penis was impressive and she noticed that he was circumcised. He removed the pegs and straps that secured her. For a moment she remained standing against the door, then she took an unsteady step forward. She felt his hand on her arm.

'Sit down,' he said.

She collapsed into one of the armchairs. The leather felt warm and sensual against her skin. He poured her a glass of wine and one for himself, clinked his glass against hers, smiled, and said, 'Here's to the next three months.'

The following day a small parcel arrived by special courier. It contained three pairs of silk bikini briefs, lace-trimmed, beautifully handmade. A simple message card read: BUT NEXT TIME, OBEY ORDERS.

2

'How's your little flirtation with Mr Sinclair coming along?' George Fullerton stood in front of Genevieve's desk.

'Flirtation? What flirtation?' Genevieve had been engrossed in her work and her reply sounded sharper than she intended.

'Well, perhaps that's the wrong word.' Fullerton perched on the side of the desk. He was wearing a fresh red carnation. 'It's just that you seemed to be getting on pretty well with him at that last meeting. I wondered why we hadn't heard from him again?'

Genevieve looked up at Fullerton and linked her fingers together under her chin. 'What exactly is "getting on well with him" supposed to mean, George?' she asked sweetly.

Fullerton had the grace to look uncomfortable. 'I thought maybe things were getting a little personal between you,' he replied.

Genevieve revised her opinion of George Fullerton. He was obviously more observant than she realised. Just how flushed and uncomfortable *had* she looked when he interrupted James Sinclair's unorthodox inspection of her body? 'Mr Sinclair is a rather attractive man,' she said. 'We exchanged a few compliments. It's good for business. But that's all.'

'Fine,' Fullerton said. He paused. 'Do you want my advice?'

Genevieve smiled. 'I rather think I'm going to get it anyway.'

'You've probably heard about Sinclair's business reputation.

He hasn't made himself a millionaire by being Mr Nice Guy. I don't hold that against him, but he's got another reputation too.'

'With the ladies?' Genevieve nodded. 'I heard.'

'And as a manipulator of people,' Fullerton said. 'He uses them. Like chess pieces. I think he enjoys playing power games.'

'Does that concern us?' she asked. 'With luck we could be handling his advertising. Who cares how he makes his money, as long as he keeps on making it.'

'Have you wondered why he came to us?' Fullerton said.

'He saw the campaigns we did for Electa and Thorwoods,' Genevieve said. 'He liked our style. We've got some very exciting talent in our creative department.' She paused. 'I think he knows we're ambitious. We want to grow. He understands that. He likes it.'

'Maybe. But he's with Randle-Mayne at the moment. They already handle several international accounts. Why does he want to move?'

'He's not happy with them. He told me that much. Creative differences.'

Fullerton shrugged. 'He's hard to please. We've all heard that. And Randle-Mayne haven't been the same since they lost Steve Farmer. It's just that I'd like to know if Sinclair's really serious about moving or whether he's just playing with us for reasons of his own. Maybe using us to get at someone else. It's the sort of thing he'd do, and, frankly, I don't like the idea of Barringtons being used like that. We've got an image to consider. I wonder if he's approached anyone else?'

'He didn't say so,' said Genevieve blankly.

Fullerton stared down at her. 'What about your feminine intuition? Did that give you any hints about his motives?'

'Really, George, what a sexist remark. I'm a businesswoman. I deal in facts.'

'You've just told me you found Sinclair attractive. And you've just admitted you traded a few compliments, so you're obviously not totally immune to his masculine charms. Give me an honest opinion.'

'The honest opinion of a poor, weak, starry-eyed woman?' Genevieve smiled. 'Well, if you must know, George, I thought Mr Sinclair was genuine.'

'Let's hope you're right,' George Fullerton said, but he did not sound convinced. 'You've done good work for us. If you get Sinclair's account we'll be grateful. Very grateful. But first I'd make sure the account really is up for offer. I'd like to be sure Sinclair isn't just using us – and you. All I'm saying is, watch your back.' He paused, next to the door. 'And ours.'

The door closed. That was really it, Genevieve thought. To be picked up and then dropped by a client like Sinclair would not be good for Barringtons' image. And George Fullerton had money invested in the agency. He was protecting his own interests. But what have I got to worry about? she thought. If I play along with Sinclair's games he's promised me his signature.

The trouble was she was now beginning to doubt if she could really trust that promise.

'Maybe men find her big, floppy bottom attractive, but I think it looks positively grotesque. And those tights! If I had a figure like that I'd wear a tent.'

Genevieve could hear Clare's harsh voice through the wooden walls of the sauna. She knew who Clare was talking about, and was comforted to know that at least it wasn't her.

'She's always got some man in tow,' another voice commented. 'Obviously some of them like acres of flesh.'

'You might as well go to bed with a whale,' Clare brayed. 'It would probably have more imagination, too.'

Genevieve bundled her things together and left the spacious changing-room. Why did women have to be so bitchy? The woman Clare was discussing had often smiled and spoken to her, although Genevieve had no idea of her name. She had always seemed pleasant and friendly. She was certainly large, but not unattractive, and Genevieve knew that many men certainly did like a partner with more than ample curves.

She suddenly remembered one of Sinclair's comments. What was it he had said? 'I imagined how your bottom would look if I stripped you'? She felt her face growing warm at the thought. It should have annoyed her. What a cheek, treating her as if she was a piece of meat in the market, assuming that she would be available to him when he snapped his fingers.

Somehow the idea of his self-confidence excited her. Very politically incorrect, she thought, but then we're thinking fantasy here. In real life, I'm still in control. I've got my flat, my career, my choices. I can even terminate this ninety-day agreement if I want to.

And if I did, she wondered, would Sinclair really take his account elsewhere? Was he really going to base his decision entirely on her compliance? It had seemed believable when he suggested it, but, she remembered, she had been in a rather compromising position and her mind had not been wholly on business matters.

Maybe she should not have believed him so easily.

She expected to hear from Sinclair quite quickly, but the days passed and he did not contact her either at her office or at home. She began to get irritable, and then angry. Had George been right? Was he simply using her? Had it amused him to trick her into humiliating herself? Was that all he wanted? A private little victory? The pleasure of knowing that he could tie a woman to a door and make love to her? Get her to dress up in leather bondage gear to please him?

So she had enjoyed it, she remembered crossly, but he didn't know that, and she certainly wasn't going to tell him. As far as he was concerned she had simply been fulfilling her part of their agreement. Did that agreement still stand? She was no longer sure, and her pride would not let her contact him in order to find out.

She tried not to think about him. During her solitary lunch breaks at the pub she read a magazine or a book, and deliberately avoided socialising. When she saw Ricky Croft heading towards her with a large smile on his face she felt her heart sink. He was obviously very pleased with himself.

She suddenly had a horrible feeling that he had visited Sinclair with his drawings and pretended that she had sent him. Ricky would lie and name drop if it suited him, she knew that from the past. Maybe that was why Sinclair had not contacted her again. He had promised to keep their agreement confidential and obviously expected her to do the same.

'Mind if I join you?' Ricky sat down opposite her.

'Do I have a choice?' she asked. At least he did not have his portfolio with him this time, she noticed. She carried on eating her roll.

He grinned at her. 'Guess what?'

'You've sold some of your artwork?' she said.

'All of them. Guess who to?'

To James Sinclair, of course, she thought. But if you've told him I recommended you, I'll strangle you. Right here and now.

'To Jade Chalfont,' Ricky said.

'Who?' Genevieve stared at Ricky blankly.

Ricky's infuriating grin did not waver. 'Not up on the latest hot gossip, are you?'

'I don't have time to gossip,' Genevieve said, rather untruthfully. 'Who's this Jade Chalfont, then? A collector?'

'No, no,' Ricky shook his head. 'A businesswoman, like you. Very tough, very glamorous.' He paused. 'Lucci's latest recruit.'

That *did* interest Genevieve. She sat up straight and stared at Ricky, trying to decide if he was telling the truth. Lucci's were a new agency. Equal in size to Barringtons, they were also equally ambitious. Genevieve knew very well that Lucci's had been trying to tempt a couple of designers from the art department. So far Barringtons staff had remained loyal, but Lucci's poaching tactics had not exactly endeared them to Genevieve's colleagues.

'She bought your pictures professionally?' she asked. 'What's Lucci's latest project? Condoms?'

'She bought them privately,' Ricky said. 'For a friend. A male friend.'

'I hope you got a good price for them.'

'Oh, I did.' Ricky Croft stood up. Genevieve knew instinctively that he had something else to tell her. The real reason why he had started the conversation with her in the first place. 'She told me she wanted them as a gift. For James Sinclair.'

So he knows a woman who works in advertising, Genevieve thought as she toyed with her coffee and tried to watch the morning news. And it just happens to be someone who works for Lucci. It's coincidence. If James Sinclair wanted Lucci to handle his account he wouldn't have come to us, would he?

Would he? Irritably she jabbed the remote at the screen and cancelled the picture. Jade Chalfont? What kind of a woman was she? What kind of a woman bought erotic pictures for a friend? Genevieve knew the answer to that. An ambitious woman. A woman who knew Sinclair's tastes. A woman who was willing to fulfil them.

An ex-girlfriend? A current girlfriend? For some reason the idea made her angry. She knew she was being unreasonable. There was no reason why Sinclair should not see other women. Perhaps he had ninety-day agreements with several of them? Perhaps that was why he had not contacted her? He was too busy satisfying his harem of women with fancy names who bought him unusual gifts.

How did he treat them, these shiny career women named after jewels? Did he wine and dine them, build up the sexual tension until they were panting for his touch? Did he take them home and lash their wrists together with silk scarves, or leather straps, or maybe silver chains? And move his hands over their bodies, and then his mouth? Suddenly she felt jealous. Absurdly jealous of these make-believe women she imagined him servicing. Get a hold of yourself, you stupid woman, she thought. He's a business client. Start getting serious and you'll get hurt.

But the daydreams would not go away. She remembered exactly how he had touched her and excited her, the way his fingers had teased her. The way his mouth had felt on her skin. She remembered it, and yet the pictures in her mind were of Sinclair and another woman, a woman with large breasts and flowing hair, and long, slim model's legs. The kind of woman, she realised, that David Carshaw had implied Sinclair would like.

She had never imagined a man she found attractive with another woman before, and the fantasy, though making her jealous, she had to admit also excited her. It was as if she was experiencing his love-making and watching it at the same time. Very stimulating. But she knew that if this mental picture show became a fact, she would not like it at all.

Her phone rang, startling her. She reached out for it, hoping it was Sinclair. The sound of his voice was just what she needed at that moment. It would disperse the fantasies and bring her back to reality.

'Hallo, big sister.'

Genevieve had been so sure it would be Sinclair that, for a moment, she had to reorganise her thoughts.

'Sis?' Her brother Philip sounded anxious. 'Are you there?'

'Of course I am,' she said.

'Thought I'd catch you before you went to work,' Philip said.

'I'm not lending you any more money,' she warned. 'You owe me two hundred and fifty as it is.'

'I don't want money.' He sounded hurt. 'And I'll pay you back. I just want some sisterly advice. I've split with Petra.'

'Well, you've been with her for a month,' Genevieve said unsympathetically. 'That's some kind of record for you, isn't it? Julia only lasted a week. Or was it ten days?'

'That's the point,' Philip said. 'Sis, am I really politically incorrect? Is that why I can't keep a girlfriend for long?'

'Oh, for God's sake,' Genevieve said crossly. 'Whatever gave you that idea?'

'That's what Petra said,' Philip explained. 'I mean, I respect her. She's doing economics. She's clever. I respect that. I don't mind putting up with her friends, although some of them are pretty awful. I didn't even mind her staying overnight with her ex when his girlfriend chucked him and he was really depressed. I reckon I'm a pretty open-minded, modern person. And she calls me politically incorrect!'

'Why?' Genevieve asked.

There was a pause. 'I wanted to tie her up.' Another pause. 'In bed. Not with chains or stuff. I mean, I'm not kinky or anything, just with scarves. It would've been "let's pretend", really. All very civilised. And she could've got free easily enough, if she'd wanted to.'

For some reason hearing this from her younger brother startled Genevieve. She remembered Philip as a cheeky schoolboy, who kept stick insects and gerbils in his bedroom, and once gave her a live spider in a box as a present.

'You're not shocked, are you?' Philip asked anxiously. 'I mean, I wasn't going to whip her or spank her or anything. I just thought it'd be a turn-on to see her lying there sort of helpless, and then make love to her. I thought she might like it too. And it's not as if I tried to force her. I explained what I wanted to do first. I was very clear about my intentions.'

'And she called you politically incorrect?' Genevieve said.

'You bet she did,' Philip agreed. 'And a lot of other things too.'

'Well, I can't tell you how to get her back,' Genevieve said. 'You could try apologising, I suppose.'

'I don't want her back,' Philip said. 'She's with her ex again now, anyway. What I want to know is, am I going to get this reaction from every girl I meet, if I suggest something a little bit – unusual?'

'Of course not,' Genevieve said. 'You just picked the wrong girl, that's all. There's nothing wrong with a bit of play-acting in bed. As long as you both enjoy it.'

'Well, I hope you're right, sis.' Philip did not sound entirely convinced. 'I mean, I know it probably isn't the kind of thing you'd do, but I thought younger women would be a bit more – well – adventurous.'

'Just keep on asking,' Genevieve said. 'I'm sure there are plenty of politically incorrect women out there just longing for a macho man to overpower them.'

'Well, I wish I knew one,' Philip said.

Maybe you do, Genevieve thought wryly, as she put the

phone down. She had to admit her apologetic brother was hardly in the same league as the self-assured and elegant James Sinclair, but surely there were plenty of girls who would find Philip attractive. She wondered suddenly what Philip's girlfriend would have done if he had tried a little erotic force instead of civilised reason.

There was certainly something exciting about being given sexy orders by someone you really fancied, she thought. She began to slip into a daydream again, remembering the authoritative tone of Sinclair's voice, re-living the restaurant meal and her later experiences at his house. A bang on her door startled her back to reality.

The postman handed her a large, well-wrapped box and asked her to sign for it. After removing the heavy-duty tape and outer paper, she found an envelope. The message inside was simple and direct: GET USED TO THESE. ESPECIALLY THE SHOES. WEAR THEM ON SUNDAY AFTERNOON. LEAVE YOUR HAIR LOOSE. WAIT FOR ME AT FOUR.

Inside the box she found a zipped purse containing makeup: eye liner, eye shadow, and bright-red lipstick – a colour she would never normally wear. There was also a pair of black shoes with absurdly high heels and thin ankle straps, a very short black skirt with long zips instead of side seams and a white blouse with three buttons and a plunging neckline trimmed with a flouncy frill. There were similar frills on the elbow-length sleeves.

She stared at the outfit in amazement. Philip's words came to her mind: politically incorrect. Tarty was another description. Get used to these? She held the skirt against her waist and realised that it would barely cover her bottom. And there were no panties in the box. This time she knew better than to consider wearing a pair of her own. She knew that 'Get used to these' meant exactly that. But did he really expect her to go outside in a skirt that looked like an extended belt, and no knickers? She knew that he did. But surely only just to his car? If she ran, she told herself, no one would notice her lack of underwear.

She picked up the shoes. Could she run in these? Could she even walk in them? No wonder he suggested that she get used to them. On impulse she slipped them on. Although they were uncomfortable they also felt extremely sexy. She sat down and stretched out her legs. She had small ankles and the thin straps emphasised this asset. She pushed aside the silky skirt of her loose kimono and looked critically at her legs. Not bad, she thought. Well, quite good really. She found herself wondering what Jade Chalfont's legs were like. What would she look like in these unashamedly erotic and totally impractical shoes? Had Sinclair ever bought her a pair too?

The thoughts spoiled her previously sensual mood. She took the shoes off and glanced at the clock. That destroyed any remaining desire to daydream. It was time for work.

'Fancy a drink?' George Fullerton had breezed into Genevieve's office. She glanced up and shook her head.

'Not now. Too busy. Thanks, though.'

Fullerton did not go away. 'Let's put it another way. I've got to go to Pete Hessler's birthday booze-up and I want company.'

'George, I hate birthday booze-ups,' Genevieve said. 'Especially if it's someone I hardly know. And I really am busy. I don't want to take any work home this weekend.'

Fullerton glanced at his watch. 'I'm not suggesting a drunken orgy lasting for the rest of the afternoon,' he said. 'The taxi will be here in five minutes. Be ready. That's an order.'

During the taxi ride Genevieve checked that her memory was correct. Pete Hessler had worked for Barringtons before

Genevieve had joined the agency and was now freelance. She suspected that George had an ulterior motive in asking her to accompany him but she could not imagine what it was.

The small pub was full of jostling, noisy people. Genevieve could see from the expression on some of the customers' faces that they were regulars who were not happy about this invasion of drinkers.

'See anyone you know?' George Fullerton enquired.

'Yes,' Genevieve said. 'And they're not about to come over and kiss me on the cheek. There's that idiot John Garner. Do you know he once told me that women shouldn't go out to work, they should just have babies.'

'What did you say?' Fullerton asked.

'That unlike men we were capable of doing both,' Genevieve said. 'Or something like that. Shortly afterwards you promoted me. I was very pleased.'

'And you made sure Mr Garner knew about it?'

'Oh, I wouldn't be that petty,' Genevieve said sweetly.

'You knew he'd hear about it on the grapevine anyway,' Fullerton said, smiling. 'Sit here for a moment. I'll get you a drink and then I'll have a quick word with Pete.'

Squashed in the corner and sipping a Barcadi Breezer that she did not really want, Genevieve amused herself by trying to put names to faces. As she watched the packed crowd, she soon noticed that a lot of activity was going on in one particular area. There were sudden blasts of laughter. Drinks were passed over heads. Genevieve observed that most of the men seemed to edge towards this noisy group after having a quick word with the man whose birthday they were supposed to be celebrating. When the crowd parted she saw that it was centred round a woman. As she watched the woman turned. Her gaze was direct and uncompromising.

Genevieve stared coolly back. There was a kind of steely self-confidence about this woman, who looked as if she had just stepped off a catwalk. She was tall and slim with glossy black hair cut like an ancient Egyptian. Her brilliant red mouth was large, perfectly outlined and unusually sensual. She wore a plain dress and some metallic jewellery that winked dully in the pub lights. As the crowd closed round her again Genevieve noticed her shoes. They were black patent leather with high heels, and while they were nowhere near as extreme in either height or design, they reminded Genevieve of the pair that Sinclair had sent to her.

As she watched, the woman leaned towards one of the men and laughed at something he had whispered in her ear. Loving the attention, aren't you? Genevieve thought cattily. I suppose you don't feel dressed unless you've got half a dozen admirers fawning over you, and these men are certainly obliging.

George Fullerton had battled his way back to her table. He glanced at the noisy group and shook his head. 'You'd think it was Miss Chalfont's birthday not Pete's, wouldn't you?'

'Chalfont?' Genevieve repeated. '*That's* Jade Chalfont?'

Fullerton stared down at her innocently. 'Yes. You don't know her, do you?'

'I've heard of her. How could I forget such a phoney-sounding name?'

'Miaow!' Fullerton murmured, grinning.

'She works for Lucci's,' Genevieve added.

'Oh, I know that. A new recruit.'

'What's she doing here?'

'Pete knew her, way back.'

'I imagine half of London probably knew her – way back!'

Fullerton's grin widened. 'You are on form today, aren't you? Actually Pete didn't invite her. I understand she sort of invited herself. She's being picked up by a prospective client, and the parking's easier round here.'

'It has to be a male client,' Genevieve said.

'Come on now,' Fullerton said, 'be fair. You're the one who told me you exchanged compliments with Mr Sinclair because it was good for business.'

'Just why did you really bring me here, George?' Genevieve asked.

'I wanted company,' Fullerton said.

Genevieve heard the brief toot of a horn outside. George Fullerton looked out of the window. Genevieve watched the crowd. It parted to let Jade Chalfont through. She strode forward with the self-confident walk of a professional model. She clearly knew all the men were watching her, and not only enjoyed it but expected it. She swished past Genevieve without giving her a glance, leaving only the faint trace of a very expensive perfume behind her.

Genevieve could not resist standing up and looking out of the window. A Mercedes stood by the kerb, its engine purring. It looked depressingly familiar. As Genevieve watched, Jade Chalfont swung towards the car. James Sinclair climbed out of the driver's seat, walked round and opened the passenger's door for her. She kissed him on the cheek and slid elegantly into the car, making sure she displayed a long length of leg and a brief tantalising glimpse of stocking top as she did so. She obviously knew that she had an appreciative audience watching her from the pub.

'Lucky man,' someone said.

'It's strictly business. You heard what the lady said.'

'I wouldn't mind a bit of that kind of business myself,' another voice added. They all laughed.

'All you need is a few million, a Mercedes and plastic surgery to make you look like James Sinclair,' someone suggested.

'George,' Genevieve accused, 'you knew that woman would be here.'

'I didn't,' Fullerton said. He paused. 'Well, not definitely. I suspected that if Miss Chalfont knew that Pete and I were friends, she might come along to size up the opposition. In fact it's worked out far better than I hoped. Obviously Lucci are courting Sinclair too. That would certainly imply that he's serious about changing agencies.' He paused. 'It also means that you've got Miss Chalfont as a rival.'

A rival? The words haunted Genevieve for the rest of the day and into the weekend. She knew that George Fullerton was talking about business rivalry, but she could not help wondering if Miss Jade Chalfont was also going to be a sexual rival as well. Had Sinclair offered her an agreement too? Was he going to compare performances? Had he sent her a box of clothes too, and a curt note to 'get used to them'? Had she been obliged to dress up to please him, or did he arrange some other kind of fantasy for her?

Genevieve knew she was being ridiculous. She had no proof that Sinclair was interested in Jade Chalfont as anything other than a business contact. The fact that she had kissed him meant nothing. She was obviously a touchy-feely kind of woman. She probably kissed everyone she met.

On Sunday afternoon Genevieve laid the clothes Sinclair had sent her out on the bed. Unfortunately the black high-heeled shoes once again reminded her of Jade Chalfont. She banished the thought. What was more important was to decide whether she really could walk outside dressed in this micro-skirt and plunge-neck top.

It was only a short journey from her apartment door to the street, and then she assumed that she would just have to walk to Sinclair's car. It was also true that most of her neighbours had gone to their country cottages for the weekend, but how would she feel if someone did appear unexpectedly and recognised her?

Her apprehension disappeared after she had applied the make-up. She stared at herself in the mirror. With her eyes darkly outlined and heavy with mascara, and wearing the bright-red lipstick, she had completely altered her appearance. When she loosened her hair and put on the clothes the transformation was complete.

She had not tried them on before because she had not had time. Apart from her first attempt at balancing she had not tried the shoes on either. Now she realised that the skirt was even shorter than she had first believed. It barely skimmed her crotch. And the blouse was too small. It tugged across her breasts with the buttons pulling and her nipples showing clearly through the thin material. She looked like a hooker. No-one would ever recognise her. She could not believe that a change of make-up and these tarty clothes would make such an instant difference.

She put on the shoes and stood up. Despite the fact that the shoes were obviously meant to restrict her to tiny steps, and curtail her freedom, there was something about their overtly sexy design that made her feel strangely powerful. It was as if by trying to control her they actually captured and controlled the men who enjoyed looking at them.

She practised walking and realised that if you altered the way you moved it was not too difficult to strut about. Her main problem was not balancing or walking but preventing the skirt from riding up with each step she took until both the curving underside of her bottom and the golden triangle of her pubic hair were clearly visible.

She hoped she would not have to walk far. Just to the car would do fine. She had no doubt that Sinclair would be picking her up by car and that wherever he was taking her, whatever he had planned for her, it would be indoors. He surely could not expect her to go out on the street dressed like a this?

She heard the powerful sound of an engine and went over to the window. A massive black and chrome motorcycle pulled up to the kerb. The rider was clothed from head to foot in tight, black leathers, a space-style helmet with a dark visor covering his head. He carried a similar helmet under his arm. She tried to persuade herself that this was a stranger waiting for someone else. In a minute he would mount his machine and ride away.

But even in leathers there was something familiar about the tall, slim figure. When he blasted impatiently on the horn she knew she was right. A motorcycle? How could she ride on a motorcycle in this skirt? It was hardly long enough to cover her bottom. If she sat astride the pillion it would probably go up round her waist.

Did he really expect her to show herself in public wearing the kind of clothes that made her look like a total exhibitionist? The kind of woman men instantly thought of as a dirty shag? Her first reaction was anger, but she had to admit that the idea excited her too.

And, she reminded herself, she had not chosen this situation. It had been forced on her. Well, more or less. She knew she could invoke the back-out clause but that would be the end of any chance of a deal with James Sinclair. It would also probably be the end of her chances of early promotion. She went downstairs and into the street.

He stood by the powerful, chrome-tanked machine. His leathers fitted him as if they had been tailored, accentuating his broad shoulders and slim hips. She found her eyes drawn to the bulging trouser zip and quickly looked away. She wasn't going to give him the satisfaction of knowing that she found his sexual equipment exciting.

He hardly moved his head but she knew she was being checked.

'Very nice,' he said. His voice was unexpectedly clear and she realised there was small speaker in the helmet. 'Lift your skirt.'

There was no one else on the street but she still flattened her hands protectively against her thighs. 'I'm not wearing anything under this,' she said.

'You'd better not be,' he said. He handed her the helmet. 'Put this on.'

She took it and held it. 'I can't ride pillion dressed like this.'

'Why not?' He sounded surprised. 'It's a nice warm day.'

'It's obvious why not.' She tried to tug down the ultra-short skirt. 'You've only got to look at this outfit to know why not.'

'You look fine,' he said, and she guessed he was grinning. 'Put the helmet on.' She lowered the helmet over her head. There was a click and his voice sounded in her ear. 'You look like a typical biker's tart. I'm going to take you for a ride, and I guarantee you'll remember it for the rest of your life.' He swung one long leg over the saddle, kick-started the bike and his dark-visored helmet turned towards her. 'Get up behind me.' She hesitated. 'Get astride.' His voice was hard. 'Or I'll pick you up and dump you on and if any passers-by get a good look between your legs that won't bother me at all.'

The street was empty but she wasn't sure if anyone was watching from the windows. She approached the bike cautiously. Suddenly she felt as if she was acting in a play. She was a different person in these clothes and with the added disguise of the helmet no one would ever recognise her. Let him take her for a spin round the block. If anyone saw her they wouldn't have time to realise that she was more undressed than dressed.

She climbed astride the pillion. The saddle felt warm against her naked skin. She managed to tuck the lower edge of her skirt under her bottom. If she sat down hard she thought she could keep it there. Well, she decided, this isn't so bad after all. She slipped her arms round his waist, feeling the smooth, sexy texture of the leather. The bike roared away from the kerb.

It soon became obvious that he did not intend to take her for a short ride, but he did stay on the side roads and, before long, they were passing boarded shop fronts and a rough-looking housing estate. The few pedestrians out walking turned to stare, although whether it was at the powerful, macho lines of the motorbike or at her she wasn't too sure. But she was sure that it was going to be impossible to keep the skirt secure.

He slanted round a corner and she slithered towards his back. The skirt slipped from under her bottom and she was acutely aware that anyone in a car behind them would have a perfect view of the cleft between her buttocks and her white, rounded cheeks spread by her weight against the black padding of the pillion seat.

And there was a car behind them. She glanced over her shoulder. She could see the driver grinning. She tried unsuc-cessfully to tug the skirt down.

'Stop,' she requested through her helmet speaker.

'What for?'

'There's a car following us. The driver's looking at me.'

He laughed. 'Looking at your ass, you mean? And you're enjoying it, aren't you?'

'Certainly not.' It was her best boardroom voice.

He laughed again and reached behind her, clasping one of her buttocks with his leather-gloved hands, pushing her skirt up even more. His strong fingers massaged her flesh, squeezing and pinching, forcing her to wriggle and shift her position, lifting her bottom off the pillion seat. The car driver tooted enthusiastically on his horn.

'Stand up.' His voice was hard now. 'Unzip your skirt. Make his day.'

'No,' she protested.

'Do it!' he said.

He turned the bike into a narrow side street and slowed down. They were between high padlocked wooden gates and disused buildings now. There were no pedestrians. The car stayed behind them. Suddenly she felt a great sense of freedom. She was anonymous in these clothes, with only her over made-up eyes showing behind the helmet visor. Her best friend wouldn't recognise her. To hell with modesty and convention.

She stood up on the footrests, her legs bent, knees pointing outwards. He kept the bike upright and slow. The car braked gently behind them. She found the zip tabs and pulled, opening the skirt at both sides. The zips made a tearing noise. The skirt was reduced to two flaps.

Sinclair reached behind again and lifted the back flap, exposing her fully. She knew that the unknown voyeur now had a perfect view of her naked bottom.

'Loving this, aren't you?' The car crawled behind them showing no inclination to overtake. Sinclair's voice sounded mockingly in her ears. 'I bet our Peeping Tom thinks he's in heaven. It can't be every day you get to see an ass like yours for free.' He slowed down and beckoned to the car. 'Well, he's seen you. Now we'll have a look at him.'

The bike glided to the kerb and she lowered herself back on the saddle. The car slowed until the driver was level with them. His window was open. Genevieve thought he looked like the kind of man who would have two teenaged children and a nearly paid-for house. She found herself wondering what his wife was like. Middle-aged, she guessed. Not the kind of woman who would wear a frilly blouse with the buttons coming undone.

'You've seen her ass.' Sinclair's voice startled her, coming clearly from the helmet speaker. 'Want to have a look at her tits?' She was surprised to find that the unexpected schoolboy crudity of his language excited her. His voice in her helmet ordered, hard-edged: 'Show him.'

She tugged the flouncey frills aside without a second thought and displayed herself. Behaving like this was so out of character that she felt as if she was acting in a film. The driver's smile turned into a gape of surprise. She put her hands under her breasts and lifted them slightly. The man pursed his lips in a silent whistle.

'Delightful, isn't she?' Sinclair observed. 'And she likes being handled.' His voice switched inside her helmet too. 'Lean forward, my darling. Let him touch.'

Again she felt a strange sense of unreality. She turned towards the car window. The man swivelled in his seat and reached for her. He squeezed and cupped her, bouncing her breast appreciatively. His thumb found her semi-erect nipple and rubbed it into full and sensitive hardness. She felt her breath quicken.

'That's enough.'

The motorbike rolled forwards, taking her out of the driver's reach. He grasped the steering wheel again.

'Put her on the back seat,' he suggested. 'I can think of some other bits of her I'd like to rub.'

The visored helmet turned. Sinclair's voice sounded faintly amused. 'Save it for your wife. Go home and give her a treat.'

'I couldn't...' The man faltered in surprise. 'I mean, she wouldn't...'

'How do you know what she'd do? Have you ever suggested

anything unusual? Whatever you're thinking, go home and do it to your wife. Surprise her for once. I bet she'll love you for it.'

He accelerated and roared off down the road. Genevieve had to circle him with her arms to keep her balance. Her exposed breasts pressed against the sensual smoothness of his leather-covered back. Her skirt flapped behind her. For all the protection her clothes were giving her now she might as well have been naked.

'Stop,' she cried.

'Why?'

'I want to make myself decent.'

'I'd rather you didn't bother,' he said. 'Anyway we're nearly there.'

They pulled up outside an anonymous, high gate. He dismounted and pushed it open. The bike cruised into what had probably once been a builder's yard, a small paved area surrounded by ramshackle sheds and garage doors.

He dismounted and watched her slide off the pillion. Then he stood the bike on its stand and closed the gates. She fumbled with the buttons of her blouse and he came over to watch her, standing with his booted, black-clad legs apart, his face hidden behind the dark visor.

'Did it turn you on?' he asked. He sounded interested.

She glanced up. 'Having to behave like a whore on a motorbike? Certainly not!'

He laughed. 'Lady, you're a liar.'

He was right, although she would never have admitted it to him. It was a little difficult to admit it to herself. It *had* turned her on. The freedom of it, knowing that she was unrecognisable. She would never have believed that the hard insistent fingers of a stranger fondling her could have given her a sexual thrill.

She reached for the helmet strap wondering what he was planning now. Did he intend to take her into one of the disused sheds? Stretch her out on the paving stones? Not very imaginative, she thought, but what else could you do in a place like this?

'Leave the helmet on,' he said. 'Get back on the bike.'

Surprised, she went to straddle the pillion.

'Not that way.' He walked towards her. 'Turn round.'

She obeyed, lying with her back against the petrol tank, her legs apart. He took two narrow silk scarves from one of his pockets. Lifting her arms above her head he positioned her exactly how he wanted her and bound her wrists to the handlebars.

After looking at her for a moment he pushed up her skirt and fondled her clit gently. The touch of his leather-covered finger made her gasp. She waited for him to unzip his trousers, straddle the bike, start to give her some lasting relief from her mounting sexual tension, although she hoped he would arouse her for a little longer first.

Instead he stepped back. 'You're about ready,' he said. He turned. 'Gentlemen, she's all yours.'

Four young men came out of one of the sheds. They wore T-shirts and jeans and looked fit and muscular. She could imagine them working out with weights. They stood round the motorbike, two on each side, and she saw their eyes admiring her.

The man in black leathers said, 'Get on with it.'

They each took up a position where they could reach her body easily and began to play with her. Unhurriedly. Expertly. One of them kissed her arms, his lips tracing lines to the crook of her elbow, licking and teasing the delicate inner skin. Another caressed her ankle, undid her shoe, removed it and lifted her foot to his mouth. He sucked her toes one by one, taking his time. The third man kissed her neck under the padded rim of the helmet. One finger stroked the underside of her breasts. He avoided her nipples although they were hard with obvious desire.

Her fourth tormentor ran his tongue round her navel. She willed him to move his mouth down to her clit, but he didn't. He flicked and tickled her skin. His fingers tantalised the top of her thighs but stopped short of her pubic hair. It was an incredible sensation, to have so many men working on her at once, teasing her, finding erogenous zones she did not know existed.

Someone was drawing light patterns on the palm of her hand. Someone else was massaging her shoulders. A gentle slapping made her breasts jiggle. The man stimulating her toes now moved to her kneecap, making it tingle with the same lightly sucking kisses he had used on her foot. The hands working on her breasts teased insistently but avoided the two hard buds that she most wanted them to handle.

She suppressed a groan of sheer frustration. She was wet and throbbing, aching for a male touch between her legs and on her nipples. The tall figure in black leather stood watching her from behind the blank black visor, legs braced apart. She could see his erection bulging against his zip and hoped he felt as sexily uncomfortable as she did.

The fingers and tongues moved over her skin. She strained at the scarves that held her captive. Hands slid under her buttocks and lifted her slightly. Hands pushed her thighs wider apart. She imagined a tongue on her clit giving her relief but instead a mouth merely kissed her inner thighs. She moaned with delicious frustration.

'You want them to fuck you, don't you?' The voice in her helmet startled her. 'Well, they're not going to do it, lady. Their job is to warm you up. When you want it badly enough you can try asking for it, and I might oblige.'

A mouth nuzzled the underside of her breast, a tongue tickled her belly, another licked the sole of her foot.

'You want it good and hard?' He was actually voicing her exact thoughts. 'Then beg for it. I want to hear you beg.'

But a perverse obstinacy gripped her. If she didn't obey what else would he make them do to her? 'I won't beg,' she said defiantly. 'Never!'

He laughed. 'Enjoying yourself too much, are you? Let's see how you like it when it gets a bit rougher.' She heard the outside speaker click on. 'Gentlemen, turn her ladyship over. And then get to work. Warm up her ass for me.'

The scarves were loosened. They lifted her bodily, forced her to straddle the bike face down and retied her wrists to the handlebars. She stood with her legs braced apart. But not for long. They caught her ankles, lifted her feet from the ground, stretching her out. She felt the cool chrome of the petrol tank against her breasts, the smoothness of the saddle between her thighs.

'Let's see how you like this,' James Sinclair's voice said politely in her ears.

The hand that landed on her bottom made her yelp as much in surprise as pain. The slaps that followed were hard and stinging. Watched by the blank-visored man in leathers, they took it in turns to give her a thorough spanking. And they made no secret of the fact that they were enjoying every minute of it, enjoying the way she struggled, the way her body reacted, the way her hips jerked when she tried unsuccessfully to evade the undignified punishment. But whichever way she wriggled and twisted, the descending hands always found their target and left their glowing pink imprint on her flesh.

She guessed they were probably turned on by the noises she was making too, and she knew her gasps, squeals and protests were quite clear to Sinclair although he did not seem in the least bit inclined to heed them.

And did she really want him to? Not just yet, she startled herself by thinking. She had never been spanked before but it was arousing her as intensely as all the previous sexual tricks she had been subjected to. She was wet and her swollen clitoris ached for relief.

She remembered Georgie. Was this how Georgie had felt when her dyke friend up-ended her? No wonder she went back for more. As each hand landed, her pussy clenched and unclenched. Her moans took on a new urgency. finally she gasped: 'Make them stop.'

'I thought you were enjoying it?' He sounded faintly mocking, pretending surprise.

'Just stop,' she groaned. She knew she could not bear this mounting sexual tension for much longer.

'You want fucking, lady?' He might have been asking her if she wanted a drink. His voice was suddenly hard. 'You want it, you ask for it. Properly.'

The young men changed over. New hands gripped her ankles. A new palm left its stinging imprint on her bottom. Her body jerked and quivered.

'I've asked,' she said. 'I've asked already.'

'Wrong words,' he said. 'I want it plain and simple. I want it basic. I want to hear that snooty boardroom voice of yours begging for it.'

'Please,' she said.

'Try again.'

'Fuck me,' she moaned. 'Please.'

'And again,' he ordered. She repeated the request, more urgently this time. 'Not bad,' he said. 'You sound as if you mean it.' He touched the external speaker. 'Playtime's over, gentlemen.' They stopped at once, standing back. 'Now it's my turn.'

He straddled the bike behind her. His leather-gloved hand smacked her behind. 'Straighten up.'

She jumped with surprise and did as she was told. Was he going to untie her? She heard the zip of his trousers opening and the next moment he had leaned over her, his hands slid under her armpits and captured her breasts. His erect cock pressed against her bottom as he fondled her. As she wriggled she felt it growing even harder from the friction she was providing.

She found it intensely stimulating to be bent forward, hands tied, and used like this. The fact that he was fully dressed in his black leathers added to her pleasure. His gloves were tight fitting. The leather gave his fingers a sensual smoothness. Her nipples were already aroused by the spanking. When he rolled them between his finger and thumb the sensations shuddered down to her clit.

He entered her easily. She was so wet she felt she could have taken a cock twice as big and twice as long. Not, she remembered, that there was anything small about his.

Rhythmically he began to thrust. She let her head fall forward and saw the reflection of his hands massaging her in the chrome petrol tank. The image excited her. It made her wonder what she looked like, half-naked, being taken from behind by an anonymous man in leathers.

It was then, as the sensations mounted, that she realised the four men were still watching. Instead of embarrassing her, it added spice to her predicament. And they could not see her face. They had never seen her face. The helmets guarded them both from recognition. She could be as wanton as she liked. The thought encouraged her to try and control her partner's orgasmic thrusting. When she felt him speeding up, felt his body trembling with imminent release, she moved away from him and nearly broke contact.

Angrily he grasped her thighs and pulled her close, pushing into her again, filling her. She teased him with quick vaginal contractions and was delighted to hear him groan with pleasure. Her apparent compliance fooled him into thinking that she was going to let him have his own way. He relaxed his grip and she immediately pushed forward again.

But this time he grabbed her more roughly. She heard his breath rasping in the confines of his helmet, coming clearly through to hers. His superior weight pinned her down on the bike. Her knees bent and her high heels slipped on the ground. His hands held her close. He thrust deeply, pulled back, and thrust again until she began to match him with her internal muscles and the smooth pumping of her own hips.

'That's better,' he said softly in her ear.

His fingers slid round to her clit. He rubbed it lightly and thrust faster. The stimulation was so intense that she felt herself coming and could not control it. She cried out, 'Yes, now! Please!' Her legs kicked and her feet slipped and it was only his hand round her waist that kept her in position as they both climaxed together in a violent spasm of delight.

The men had gone. Sinclair took off his helmet and unlocked one of the garage doors. Inside there were two chairs and a table. She sat down and felt the chair's padded PVC seat cool against her skin. It reminded her of the saddle of the motorbike.

'Not a very glamorous venue, I'm afraid,' he apologised. 'But it doesn't get used very often.'

'You don't bring all your girlfriends here?' she asked, extra polite.

He gave her a quizzical look, then grinned unexpectedly. 'You're the first. I arranged this just for you.'

She wanted to believe him. She was tempted to mention

Jade Chalfont's name but instead she allowed herself to feel both flattered and fulfilled by the knowledge that he had taken all this trouble to provide what had been an exciting, revealing and sexually satisfying experience. She knew that while he had undoubtedly enjoyed every minute of it, he had always intended her to enjoy it too. She guessed instinctively that Sinclair was not the kind of man who got his kicks from forcing a woman to do something against her will.

He went to a cupboard and took out a bottle of white wine, two glasses, a large cardboard box and a mobile phone. He poured her a glass of wine then opened the box. Inside was a full-length fur coat.

'Put this on,' he said. 'I'll call a taxi.' His eyes ranged over her, amused. 'You're in no fit state to ride back with me. You look as if you've been gang-banged.'

'Well, that's more or less how I feel,' she said. She took the coat dubiously. 'I hope this is fake fur. I hate the idea of animals being killed for fashion.'

'So do I,' he said, surprising her. 'Don't worry, it's fake, but it cost almost as much as the real thing and you'd have to be an expert to tell the difference. Keep it. I might want you to wear it again.'

She stood up. She knew she looked tantalising and sexy with her leather skirt split to her waist and her blouse open. He watched her, enjoying the view with undisguised delight. She couldn't remember when a man had last looked at her that way. It made her feel powerful.

She took the coat, standing with her feet apart, and swung it elegantly over her shoulders like a cloak. Twisting, she shifted her body provocatively as she pushed her arms into the silk-lined sleeves. His eyes followed every move she made but he didn't make any attempt to touch her. She sat down, swathed in the soft weight of the fur, stretched her legs out and crossed them. Then she picked up her glass of wine. He sat opposite her.

'Who were those men?' she asked.

'Friends of mine. We share similar interests. We help each other out.'

'And the man in the car? Another friend?'

He laughed, relaxing in his chair. 'No. Just a lucky punter. A bonus for us both.'

'A bonus for me? Being touched up by a stranger?'

'You loved it,' he said, 'and so did he. He'll be telling his mates about it for years, and they won't believe him.'

If I told my friends about it they wouldn't believe me either, she thought.

'If only you could have seen yourself,' he said suddenly, 'tied to the bike and wriggling about, getting more and more frustrated. It was the greatest kick ever, watching you. Do you know, some idiot former colleague of yours told me he thought you'd got a low sex drive. He should have seen you out there on the saddle. He'd have certainly changed his mind.'

'Whoever was that?' she asked.

'Harry Trushaw.'

'I thought he'd be retired by now,' she said. 'He tried for years to get me into bed.'

'Why didn't you oblige him?'

Because I didn't fancy him, she thought. Lecherous old sod, never looks at your face, always stares at where he thinks your nipples are. Aloud she said: 'Mr Trushaw never offered me anything I wanted.'

'Like a good business deal?' Sinclair's dark eyes were serious now. 'That's why you're doing this, isn't it? It's purely mercenary.'

'Dead right,' she agreed. She finished her wine.

He picked up the mobile phone and called her a cab. 'Has this taught you anything?' he asked her. 'Anything about yourself?'

She knew that it had, but she was not going to admit it to Sinclair. 'Only that I'll obviously go further than I thought to get our deal closed,' she said.

'You'll go further yet,' he said. 'You'll learn more. Believe me.'

A week ago she would not have believed him. Now she did.

'You'll be hearing from me,' he said. 'Soon.'

The next day a small parcel was delivered by courier to her London apartment. It contained a model black and chrome motorcycle and a neatly printed card enquiring: MEMORIES ARE MADE OF THIS?

She smiled, and stood the model next to her bed.

3

Genevieve saw Mike Keel, the assistant manager of the sports centre, coming towards her and deliberately walked faster. Mike ran. Knowing that if she ran too it would look unkindly obvious, Genevieve stopped and turned. 'No,' she said.

Mike grinned. 'That's what they all say.'

'I haven't time.'

'You could make time,' he said, teasing now. 'For me. You won't regret it. I can promise you an experience I'm sure you've never had before.'

Well, Genevieve thought, I doubt that. Even though I imagine you're only talking about squash. 'It's not fair on the others in the league,' she said. 'I can't help missing games when I'm busy.'

'Who's talking about the league?' Mike asked innocently. 'Are you trying to tell me you can't spare an hour on one solitary Saturday afternoon? And for charity too?'

'It's not one of those awful sponsored press-ups? I'll give you a donation but I'm not doing a single press-up.'

'Nothing like that.'

'I'm not doing a two-legged race round the grounds either,' Genevieve said, remembering a previous sponsored event which had a variety of people tripping over each other and falling into the flower beds.

'For heaven's sake,' Mike said. 'All I want you to do is demonstrate some squash moves while an audience of admiring men stand and watch.'

Genevieve stared sat him in surprise. 'You're joking?'

'I'm not. Don't you read company-wide emails?'

'Well – sometimes.'

'That means never. I don't know why I bother to send out any information. If you *had* paused to read my missives occasionally you would have seen that we're having an open day in a couple of weeks time. Basically we want people to explain their particular sport so that anyone interested can get some idea of what it's all about, and in some cases maybe try it. The entrance money will go to the local hospice fund.'

'What about the admiring audience? Is that guaranteed?'

'If you'd be willing to wear a bikini, it would be.'

'No way!'

'Well, I'll come and admire you, anyway,' Mike offered, gallantly.

'What exactly do you want me to do?'

'Whatever you like, really,' Mike said. 'Just give the audience the feel of what squash is about. You can do a bit of coaching. Demonstrate some shots. Answer questions. John Oldham said he'd come and help. The whole thing needn't take long. We just want visitors to see as many sports as possible, even though most of them will probably be coming to watch the demonstrations.'

'What have you got?'

'Ladies in sexy lycra doing aerobics. Trampolining. The kids are doing a gymnastic display. And we've got karate, aikido and even kendo. It should be good.'

'I didn't know we did kendo here?'

'We don't,' Mike said. 'But one of our new members does. Apparently she's well up in the sport. She teaches in London, and she's agreed to arrange something for us. If there's some interest she might start classes. I think her name's Chalfont.'

'Not Jade Chalfont?' Genevieve asked.

'Sensei Chalfont,' Mike agreed. 'That's right. Do you know her?'

'No. Well, not really.'

'You know her but you don't like her?' Mike guessed. 'I agree, she is a bit – overpowering.'

'I don't know her personally,' Genevieve said. 'She works in advertising, but not in my agency.'

'A rival?'

'I suppose so.' Genevieve shrugged. 'But then anyone who doesn't work in my agency is a rival. Advertising is a competitive field.'

She agreed to help out on the open day and found herself wondering about Jade Chalfont's demonstration. Kendo was a fairly unusual sport but she thought it suited the self-confident Jade. It was easy to imagine her as a warrior. *Sensei* Chalfont, she thought. I bet she just loves strutting about waving a sword, turning on all the men who like dominant women.

And James Sinclair? Would it turn him on to see a woman fighting like a samurai? Perhaps he had seen it already? Maybe he also practised kendo? She realised that she had no idea what he did in his free time – apart from arranging sexual fantasies and playing them out. Perhaps he listed sex as his hobby? He was certainly good at it.

She tried to visualise him wielding a sword. It wasn't difficult. He had the kind of panther-like elegance that made it easy to imagine him indulging in any sport. She went through a series of costumes. Polo, with its tight, white trousers and glossy boots lingered in her mind. She already knew what he would look like in motorcycle racing leathers.

She thought about him swimming, climbing out of the pool, his tanned body glistening with water. She knew his shoulders were wide and his stomach flat. She knew his buttocks were tight and there wasn't an ounce of spare flesh round his waist or his hips. She had never seen him naked, but she was certain he would look good. She imagined his swimming trunks reduced to the barest minimum. It was an attractive picture. She stayed with it. Her hands would be on his hips, moving downwards, snapping his waistband. Then she imagined him stripped. She would be clothed and he would be naked. That would make him vulnerable. It would give her the advantage. She would run her hands over his body, exploring. Over his chest, his flat stomach. Her hands would slide down and grasp his balls. She would feel his cock swell as she played with it, rubbing and caressing. She would listen to the sounds he made as she excited him. She would feel his body trembling, slipping out of control.

Exactly as she was feeling at that very moment. Damn it, she thought, even thinking about him turns me on. But she doubted that he felt the same. The more she thought about him the more convinced she became that he didn't see any kind of long-term relationship as part of his future. Ninety days were all she was going to get. And a career advancement when she signed him on as a client.

Or, she thought, was it really *if* she signed him on?

However, despite feeling sure that he saw her only as a casual sexual companion, she still experienced a thrill of excitement when she answered the phone and heard his voice.

'How do you fancy an afternoon in the country?'

Outdoor sex, she thought. Sex in a haystack. Did they still have haystacks these days? 'Do you want me to dress up as a milkmaid?' she asked.

'Dress smart, but casual,' he said. 'There's only one rule: I want you to shave.'

That surprised her. If he preferred his women shaved why hadn't he asked her in the first place? 'I thought you liked proof that I was a natural blonde?' she said sweetly.

'I like variety,' he said.

'Aren't you going to send me a clothes parcel?'

'Not this time.' He sounded relaxed. The sexy authority that had coloured his voice when he had arranged their previous meetings was missing. He could have been any attractive man ringing her up for a date. 'I'll trust your good taste. Wear something you think an Arab millionaire would like.'

'Diaphanous harem pants?' she suggested, not really believing him.

'You're not auditioning for a Hollywood musical,' he said. 'This Arab went to Eton. He likes beautiful women, and he has impeccable taste.'

'Why have I got to attract him?'

'I didn't say you had to attract him. I said wear something you think he might like.'

'Same thing,' she said. She had a feeling he was playing a game with her and it made her angry. She did not want to dress up to attract someone else. 'If you want me to undress for this Arab, or make love to him, I'm not sure I like the idea.'

'You want to back out?'

The question came a little too fast for her peace of mind. Was that what he was planning? To force her to break their agreement? If she did, no doubt his conscience (if he had one) would be clear. He could take his account to Lucci's – and to Jade Chalfont. Or was she being paranoid? Jealous? Insecure? 'Just explain,' she requested.

His voice changed. 'You know better than that. I don't explain. I just give the orders. You agreed, remember?'

'Well, all right,' she said. 'But if you don't give me some idea of where we're going, how can I choose appropriate clothes?'

'To a private antiques fair,' he said. 'Invitation only.' His voice was charming again, the perfect gentleman. 'Do you like antiques?'

'I don't collect them, if that's what you mean.'

'It isn't,' he said. 'Do you think you'll be bored?'

'If you mean do I want to back out,' she said sharply, 'no, I don't. I like museums, so I'll probably enjoy an antiques fair too.'

'Maybe you will,' he said softly.

'When is it?'

'Saturday,' he said. 'I'll come for you at one-thirty.'

She suddenly remembered her promise to Mike Keel. 'Not this Saturday?'

'You've got a date?'

'Yes,' she said. When he did not say anything she added: 'I'm helping at the sports centre open day. It's for the hospice.'

Why am I explaining? she thought. Why didn't I let him think some other man was going to take me out? Would he care? Would he imagine how she would behave in bed with someone else the way she so often found herself fantasising about him? She rather doubted it. Did he ever think about her when they were apart? And if he did, was she just one in a long list of females he could use to satisfy his mental picture show? Did he even need to use his imagination when he seemed to find it easy enough to bribe women into making his fantasies real?

'Lucky for you,' he said, 'it's next Saturday. The twenty-fourth.' He paused. 'Would you have backed out of your charity engagement?'

'Of course,' she said.

'Business comes first?' His voice was slightly mocking.

She thought that was unfair. He had already reminded her that she risked terminating their agreement by refusing his orders. She did not think the sports centre would lose any money if she did not turn up, but she was glad that she would be able to keep her promise to Mike Keel. 'We have an agreement, remember?' It was a pleasure to throw his words back at him.

'Yes,' he said, in a neutral voice. 'We have, haven't we?'

She could not decide what to wear for the charity demonstration. She was not going to play a serious match so she thought she could afford to look a little more glamorous than usual, even if she did not intend to take up Mike's suggestion and wear a bikini. In the end she chose a tight white top and a short tennis skirt. She twisted her hair into a pleat and applied a little more make-up than usual. She refused to admit that she was doing this for anyone else's benefit but her own. If people were going to watch her she wanted to look good. If the audience included Jade Chalfont, looking good was even more desirable.

Mike met Genevieve in the entrance foyer. 'We've got John and Frank Bernson here. If you play a demo game with Frank, John says he'll give a commentary. After that anyone who wants to can come onto the court and ask questions, or maybe have a go. If there's enough people interested in learning we'll start a beginner's session.'

The balcony overlooking the squash court was crowded but Genevieve was used to spectators watching her play. Once John began his talk she concentrated on trying to perform the moves he was explaining, and to keep the game fairly slow until the end, when she heard John explaining that squash was one of the fastest racket games in the world – as Genevieve and Frank would demonstrate. For a few moments the two of them obliged, and the squash ball rocketed from the wall like a noisy bullet as they each tried to score. When they had finished, Genevieve was surprised to hear the crowd applaud.

More people than she expected came down to the court and Genevieve partnered some of them in a slow demonstration.

Several others claimed to have played squash at school or college and wondered if they were too old to take it up again. By the time she and Frank had finished answering questions and explaining points, Genevieve realised that she had been on the court much longer than she intended.

'Fancy a drink?' Frank asked, mopping his face with a towel.

'I rather wanted to see one of the martial arts demos. I hope they're not over.'

'Shouldn't be,' Frank said. 'It's only quarter past three. I think I saw karate down for three o'clock. It's in the main hall. If you change your mind about that drink, I'll be in the bar.'

Genevieve could hear shouts coming from the sports hall as she approached it. The centre had been turned into a demonstration area and there was quite a crowd watching younger members of the local club going through their paces. The commentator was explaining that karate was a disciplined sport that improved coordination, strength and flexibility.

The children were demonstrating the basic moves – punches, blocks and kicks – that everyone had to learn before they could progress to the more spectacular freestyle fighting. They looked serious and determined as they went through their paces, yelling with martial enthusiasm as they completed each set of moves. After they left the area to a round of applause, a young black belt demonstrated a *kata*. This, the commentator said, might look like a fancy gymnastic exercise but it was actually a series of defence and attack moves, woven into a pattern, and used for training purposes.

Although she knew nothing about karate, Genevieve was impressed by the young boy's speed and the sharp strength of his movements. When he followed his performance by showing how each of the *kata* moves worked against four opponents attacking him from different sides, she was even more impressed. The attackers – all youngsters of his own size – were obviously enjoying themselves pretending to be muggers and falling to the ground in make-believe agony as they were despatched. Genevieve joined in the applause when the demonstration was over.

'If that little bugger had a go at one of my boys I'd knock his head off,' a man said aggressively behind her.

'He wouldn't ever do that.' A woman next to Genevieve turned angrily. 'Unless your son attacked him.'

'My son wouldn't attack anyone,' the man said. 'But this stuff just encourages kids to be bullies.'

'It certainly doesn't,' the woman said. 'My children train with this club. They're taught self-control and respect.'

'By hitting people?' the man sneered. 'Teaching kids it's big to kick someone's head in? I prefer my kid to kick a football. We don't need all that kung-fuey junk over here.'

He stalked away and the woman turned to Genevieve, lifting her eyebrows in mock despair. 'Some people just don't know what the real martial arts are all about.'

'Your sons do karate?' Genevieve asked.

'My daughters,' the woman said. 'They're not here today because they're staying with my ex this weekend. But getting their black belts did them the world of good. It's given them confidence, and that improved their school work. But they're not silly enough to think a black belt makes them super-human.'

The crowd on the other side of the demonstration area parted and Genevieve saw six adults, five men and a woman, step forward. They all wore elaborate samurai-style armour protecting their chests, legs and arms and carried masked helmets and bamboo-bladed swords.

'The next martial art we are going to see is the kendo,' a cool voice announced. 'The Way of the Sword.'

Jade Chalfont was standing almost directly opposite Genevieve, a microphone in her hand. She was wearing a white karate-style jacket tucked into a long black *hakama*, the traditional Japanese 'skirt', usually worn by males. Her black hair was pulled back into a severe bun. Coupled with her pale skin and the red gloss of her mouth, it made her look like a combination of samurai and geisha. Genevieve was certain she had chosen the look deliberately. It was both sexy and aggressive. Jade Chalfont, Genevieve thought, would make an impressive dominatrix, uniformed in black leather.

While Jade described the different parts of the protective armour and explained that bamboo swords were used in early training, her six students wound scarves round their heads and then donned their helmets. They bowed and picked up their weapons. All their moves had a ritual slowness about them which gave an impression of calm control. They demonstrated various attack and defence moves, and then the woman and one of the men fought together while Jade's cool voice explained the methods of scoring used in competition bouts.

Genevieve was just wondering why Jade had not shown off her own skill when she saw one of the students take the microphone. Jade bent down and picked up a sword that Genevieve had not noticed before. It had a long blade that glittered in the sports-hall lights.

'You may have already seen a young *karate-ku* demonstrate a *kata*,' the student announced. 'We also have *kata* in kendo. Sensei Chalfont will now demonstrate one for you. As you can see she will use a genuine Japanese sword. In the hand of an expert this sword can sever a man's neck with one blow.'

He did not need to add that Sensei Chalfont was such an expert. It was obvious from the way Jade moved forward, bowed, and took up her starting position. Her movements were calm and economical but there was a quiet arrogance about her. When she began her *kata* she moved with fluid grace and speed. It looked effortless but Genevieve sensed the hidden power behind the ritual actions. She had no doubt that Jade's sword would slice through flesh and bone with ease.

Jade completed her demonstration, hesitated for a brief moment, and then bowed. The crowd applauded and moved towards her. Genevieve turned away. She did not want Jade Chalfont to know that she had been watching.

'Not going to join the kendo class?'

She spun round, startled. James Sinclair was standing by the entrance doors. 'Aren't you?' she responded, concealing her surprise.

He grinned. He was wearing a crisp white shirt, the sleeves rolled up to his elbows, pale combats and trainers. He looked stylish and relaxed.

'I might. Were you impressed?'

She decided that it was pointless and silly to lie. 'Yes. Miss Chalfont was very good.'

That shows you I know exactly who you came to watch, she thought. And I'm damned if I'm going to call her Sensei.

'She's been doing it a long time,' he said.

All right, Genevieve thought. Now you've made certain that I know you've met, and you've talked about hobbies. What else have you discussed? Taking your advertising account to Lucci's? Have you also suggested that Miss Jade Chalfont might like to be stripped and tied to your specially adapted door, and then tongued into the kind of climax that you gave to me?

The thought made her angry. Angry and jealous. She noticed that the top buttons of his shirt were undone. The white cotton contrasted with his dark tan. He wore a watch made of dull metal that Genevieve guessed was platinum. He was certainly attractive, but then so were a lot of other men. What was it that made her think of sex – want sex – whenever she looked at him? At least it's *only* sex I think about, she told herself. I'm not in love with him. It's purely physical. An obsession. When our ninety-day agreement is over I'll forget all about him.

So why did the idea that he was interested in Jade Chalfont's hobbies annoy her? The woman was a business rival, that was all. A rival in a competition that she was going to lose. Genevieve glanced across to the demonstration arena. Jade Chalfont was standing in the centre of a circle of people, answering questions. She noticed that Sinclair's eyes were gazing in the same direction. Then he turned to her. 'Can I buy you a drink?'

She would have loved a drink, but she had a feeling he might ask Jade Chalfont to join them. 'Is that an order?' she asked coolly.

'No. A civilised request. Orders come next week.'

'I have to get home,' she said. 'I've got some work to finish.'

'Housework? Can't it wait?'

'Business,' she lied.

His expression changed. 'That's all that matters to you, isn't it?'

'It's the basis of our relationship,' she replied.

He grinned crookedly. 'If you say so, Miss Loften. See you next Saturday.'

Despite her apparent cool Genevieve had spent the rest of that Saturday wondering if Sinclair had taken Jade Chalfont for a drink, and then back home, or to a restaurant or even for a pillion ride on his motorcycle. Somehow she could not imagine the super-cool, sword-wielding *sensei* wearing a mini-skirt and no knickers just to please a man.

But then, she had to admit, she would never have thought she would agree to play that role either. Not that she did it to please Sinclair, she told herself. It was part of the agreement. If she enjoyed it too, that was a bonus. And yet here she was trying to work out how to please him again. What did you wear to an antiques fair hosted by a millionaire Arab – providing that really was where they were going.

She decided that as Arabs were supposed to like their women demure and ladylike (at least in public), she would dress as conventionally as possible. She pleated her hair into a knot, just loose enough to look neat without being too severe. She chose a pale-grey suit with a jacket that was feminine without overemphasising her figure, and a straight skirt that skimmed her knees. Worn over a plain silk blouse she felt it gave the right impression of chaste femininity.

Since the Arab was not going to see her underwear – and Sinclair probably was – she wore a white lace basque with a detachable bra top and briefs, a narrow garter belt and pale stockings that sheened her legs discreetly in silky grey. She had already chosen a pair of matching court shoes but when she came to put them on she hesitated. She felt she needed something to imply that she was not entirely demure. After a moment's thought she discarded the court shoes and picked out a pair of higher, much sexier grey stiletto heels. They had been an impulse buy in a sale and she had only worn them a few times, not because she did not like them but because they rarely seemed suitable for the few social events she attended.

Now, combined with her ultra-respectable suit, and coupled with her lacy underwear, she felt suitably dressed for a meeting with a presumably conventional, Eton-educated Arab millionaire with impeccable taste, and for any later activities with the decidedly unconventional and educated goodness-knows-where James Sinclair.

He arrived promptly, sounded his horn and waited for her

at the kerbside. He was wearing a beautifully tailored dark suit and a silk tie. She saw him give her a swift visual inspection and treated him to a frosty smile as he opened the passenger door for her.

'Do I get a Grade A, or do you want me to go back and change?'

'You look fine,' he said. And surprised her by adding, 'As always.'

'You don't think my shoes will shock your Arab friend?'

He laughed. 'Nothing shocks Zaid. He'll love them.'

She settled in the passenger seat and fastened her safety belt. Sinclair sat beside her. The car moved smoothly away from the kerb.

'Want some music?' She nodded. He pressed a button and a drawer full of tapes slid open. 'You've got a choice.'

She chose a selection of film music and the sounds of the Hugo Montenegro orchestra filled the car. Sinclair let her enjoy it, occasionally commenting on the various tracks and the films they had accompanied. They soon left the suburbs and headed for the M25 where the Mercedes eased into the fast lane and stayed there until Sinclair turned off at Junction 8 and headed south.

After that Genevieve lost track of their direction. Sinclair drove confidently. The main roads became country roads. They passed through small villages and the Mercedes twisted and turned until it suddenly slowed and Genevieve saw large wrought-iron gates on their left.

The house was a surprise. It looked as if several Victorian architects had formed a committee to discuss its design but had never come to a unanimous decision. Its sprawling walls and balconies were thickly covered with ivy. Its massive entrance doors looked more suited to a castle, and were reached by an impressive flight of steps. A castellated tower had been added to one corner, making the whole building look slightly off balance.

'A millionaire lives here?' Genevieve was amazed. 'If I had money this isn't exactly what I'd buy.'

'Zaid doesn't own it, he rents it,' Sinclair said. 'I think it appeals to his sense of humour. And it's rather an appropriate venue for an antiques fair. Wait until you see inside.'

There were other cars parked near the entrance steps, all of them sleekly expensive. Genevieve noted three Rolls-Royces, one of them a gleaming Silver Cloud. A uniformed chauffeur sat in the driver's seat leafing through a magazine.

An impressively large gentleman who looked slightly uncomfortable in his smart suit and tie stopped them at the door. Sinclair produced a small card. The security guard glanced at it briefly, pressed a button and waited. After a moment the doors swung open and Genevieve followed Sinclair inside.

The entrance hall was oak panelled and the walls were hung with an assortment of hunting trophies. Dead stags and dead foxes stared at Genevieve. There was a massive stone fireplace and a central flight of stairs that rose to a balcony and then branched both left and right. Several people stood in small groups, talking. A waiter moved about silently with a tray of drinks.

'James, I'm delighted you could make it. I thought you'd back off and claim pressure of work.'

The man who stepped forward was slightly taller than Sinclair and a few years older, but equally slim and elegant. His jet-black hair was fashionably cut and he had a neatly trimmed beard. Combined with his darkly tanned skin it gave him a slightly satanic look. He was dressed casually in an immaculately tailored jacket and trousers, with a silk cravat tucked loosely into his open-necked shirt.

His eyes fixed on Genevieve. They were dark eyes, darker

than Sinclair's. There was humour in them, and obvious appreciation. He held out his hand.

'I am Anwar Zaid ibn Mahmoud ben Hazrain. But please just call me Zaid. You must be Miss Genevieve Loften.' Genevieve shook hands. His grasp was warm and firm. He smiled, and again she was reminded of Sinclair. 'James has told me a lot about you,' Zaid added.

Genevieve glanced sideways at Sinclair. He raised one eyebrow and shrugged. But there was the trace of a smile on his lips and she immediately felt suspicious. Why had he found it necessary to tell this undeniably attractive man anything about her? She was supposed to be just a visitor, viewing the antiques.

'James will show you everything,' Zaid said, 'and afterwards, I hope we'll see each other again.' He turned to Sinclair. '*Everything*, James. You understand?'

'If you say so,' Sinclair said. 'And I thought you would.'

Zaid laughed. 'You know me far too well. Better than my own brother. And certainly better than my wife.' He gave Genevieve another charming smile and then turned to greet another guest.

Sinclair took Genevieve's arm. 'What would you like to see first? China? Glass? Paintings? Toys?'

'Obviously I'm going to see *everything*,' Genevieve said pointedly. 'Whatever that means.'

'You'll find out what it means,' Sinclair said. 'Later.'

'And where's Zaid's wife?'

'Where all good wives should be,' he grinned. 'At home.'

'So your friend has a Western education, and medieval ideas?'

'Zaid probably thinks our idea of marrying for love is medieval. He sees marriage as a commitment to the future. His sons will take care of the family fortunes. His wife will ensure that they are properly prepared for their place in the world. In return she has a luxurious lifestyle. She has respect. She has children. She also knows that her husband would never do anything to disgrace the family name. It means too much to him. The arrangement suits both of them.'

Genevieve remembered the obvious appreciation she had seen in Zaid's eyes when he first saw her. 'And I'm sure he's completely faithful, too,' she said coolly.

'Zaid isn't celibate when he's abroad,' Sinclair said. 'His wife wouldn't expect it. He's permitted his sexual indulgences. He's a man, after all.' He glanced at her. 'And an attractive one, wouldn't you say?'

'Yes,' she agreed, in a neutral voice. 'Very nice.'

He looks a lot like you, she thought, but I'm damned if I'm going to tell you so. She remembered the slight pressure of the Arab's hand on hers. She knew he had found her attractive. Was that what Sinclair was planning? Was he going to offer her services to his friend? And if he did, would she agree?

'Don't feel sorry for Zaid's wife,' Sinclair said. 'It was an arranged marriage, but they both agreed to it, and I doubt if they were pressured. You might say it was a business agreement.' He smiled at her, and again she was reminded of Zaid's smile. 'You should appreciate the logic of that.'

I'm sure Zaid does too, Genevieve thought. It gives him respectability and the right to play the field. She followed Sinclair up the wide stairs. A couple passed them and smiled, the woman glittering with jewellery that Genevieve instinctively knew was genuine. She also knew Sinclair was planning something, and she was equally certain it involved his Arab friend. But what was it? And what had Zaid meant when he insisted that Sinclair show her 'everything'?

She soon realised why Sinclair had told her that the house was a suitable venue for an antiques fair. Each room was decorated in a different style or historical period, and the antiques on display had been chosen to suit the decor. In every room smartly dressed purchasers were politely haggling or writing cheques.

The Victorian nursery housed a toy collection. A flamboyant Chinese room had a display of silks, fans and screens. The Regency room contained furniture. A twenties-style music-room held a collection of instruments and music boxes. One, in a beautiful, polished-wood box, chimed 'Danny Boy' when Genevieve opened the lid. 'This is lovely,' she said. She looked unsuccessfully for a price tag. There was only a small number attached to the box. 'I think I'll buy it. How much is it?'

'Go and ask,' Sinclair said. 'The gentleman at the table over there will give you all the details.'

'This box?' The discreet, soft-spoken salesman glanced at the number. 'I'm sorry, madam, I believe this one has been sold.' He checked with a small laptop computer. 'Yes, it has. My apologies. I should have removed the number.'

Genuinely annoyed, Genevieve was about to argue when she heard an unexpected and familiar husky voice.

'James, darling. I didn't know you were interested in music.'

She turned in time to see Jade Chalfont kiss Sinclair affectionately on the cheek, brushing back her heavy fall of dark hair as she did so. In a figure-hugging black dress with her usual chunky jewellery she looked as self-confident as a top model posing on the catwalk. Her bright red, sensual mouth smiled insincerely as Genevieve walked towards her.

'James, you're with a friend. I didn't realise.'

'Miss Genevieve Loften,' Sinclair said.

Jade Chalfont's smile turned frosty. 'Oh yes. You're a Barringtons rep, aren't you?'

'An account manager,' Genevieve said, equally frosty.

'Do Barringtons still call them that? How quaint.' Jade Chalfont kept the smile fixed on her glossy red lips. 'You like antiques too, do you?' Her eyes looked briefly at the box Genevieve was holding. 'You collect little music boxes. That's very sweet.'

Because she was furious at Jade Chalfont's patronising tone, and well aware that Sinclair knew it, she fell into the trap Jade had set without thinking. 'What exactly do you collect, Miss Chalfont?' She felt like adding 'apart from men'.

'Japanese swords,' Jade Chalfont said. 'I'm just going to look at some.' She turned to Sinclair. 'Shall we go together?'

'Good idea,' Sinclair said, and Genevieve could have cheerfully slapped him. Instead she glared at him as he walked past her to the door, and he treated her to his most charming smile. 'Jade's an expert on oriental weapons. And a high-ranking kendo *sensei* too.'

'I know that,' Genevieve said. 'I was at the sports-centre open day, remember?'

'Oh yes, of course you were,' he said, still smiling. 'You were demonstrating squash, weren't you?'

'Squash?' Jade Chalfont repeated. 'I tried to play that at college, but it didn't intrigue me enough. No depth. The martial arts require a great deal of mental as well as physical discipline. I find that challenging.'

Inwardly seething, Genevieve followed them both into the Japanese room. It contained a stunning display of weapons, armour, pottery and paintings.

Genevieve inspected some ivory netsuke, picking up one that was shaped like a curled-up cat, its eyes closed.

'Beautiful, aren't they?' Jade Chalfont's voice sounded huskily in her ear. 'I have a collection of my own. The Japanese made even simple things into works of art.'

'And swords?' Sinclair said. 'You once told me you thought the sword was the height of Japanese artistic workmanship.'

Jade laughed delightedly. 'Darling, you remembered my impromptu lecture. And I thought I was boring you to tears.'

'I remember everything,' Sinclair said, softly.

All right, Genevieve thought. So now I know that you've had a nice tête-à-tête with Miss Chalfont. You flattered her shamelessly, and let her prattle on about the only thing she probably knows anything about, so she thinks you're marvellous. Which is more than I do at the moment.

'Come and look at these.' Jade went to one of the sword stands and started to lecture Sinclair on its merits. He leaned over her, nodding, and seemed fascinated by her monologue.

Genevieve turned back to the netsuke. She examined a few more of the intricately carved toggles, used by the Japanese in traditional costume, and the samurai, to hang items from their wide sashes.

'I can show you something more interesting than that.' Sinclair's voice startled her. She turned to find him standing closer than she expected. Over his shoulder she saw Jade Chalfont deep in conversation with the salesman.

'Both of us?' she asked frostily.

'Just you,' Sinclair said.

'You can't walk out on your *friend*,' she said acidly. 'It's not polite.'

'Jade will be in here for hours,' Sinclair said.

'And she'll go home with a nice new sword. How sweet.'

He laughed, quietly. 'She won't. Unless Zaid buys it for her. She couldn't possibly afford one of these.'

Was he telling her Jade and Zaid were lovers? 'Do you mean Jade is one of Zaid's – er – sexual indulgences?'

'Zaid is one of Jade's students,' Sinclair corrected. 'He practises kendo. I'm told he's very good.'

He took her arm and guided her out of the room, towards a flight of stairs that took them to an upper landing. Two security guards loitered in the corridor, trying, unsuccessfully, to look inconspicuous. They moved towards Sinclair and Genevieve as they approached. Sinclair produced a small card, which one of the guards scanned with an electronic device that blipped. 'Go right ahead, sir,' the guard said politely, handing the card back.

'How nice to have contacts in the right places,' Genevieve murmured as they walked on down the corridor and up another short flight of stairs. 'What are we going to see down here that needs extra guards?'

'The guards are as much to protect our privacy as the antiques,' Sinclair said. 'Although some of them are valuable, at least to specialised collectors.'

He pushed open a door. Genevieve walked into a dimly lit Victorian bedroom. Shaded lamps glowed. The wash-stand and chest of drawers, and several small tables, were set out with display items. The bed was turned down and a beautifully embroidered nightdress lay waiting. Genevieve went to inspect it. Sinclair watched her. 'Pick it up,' he said. 'You're allowed to handle the merchandise.'

She did so and held the garment against her body.

'Turn it round,' Sinclair instructed.

There was a circular hole cut in the back of the prim-looking nightdress, which would probably have left the wearer's bottom exposed. 'It's damaged,' she said.

To her surprise Sinclair started to laugh. 'Look closer,' he said.

Genevieve did so and realised that the hole was delicately hemmed. Sinclair came and stood beside her. 'Provided by a thoughtful Victorian husband for his new wife,' he said softly. 'Just to make sure she understood what position he wanted her in.'

Genevieve looked at the nightdress with less enthusiasm than before. and placed it back on the bed. 'I'm not sure I like that idea. Didn't the woman have any choice?'

Sinclair shrugged. 'Who knows? She may have approved. But from what I've read about Victorian marriages, she probably had to do as she was told.' He walked to a corner where a selection of canes stood in a tub. Taking one out, he sliced it through the air a couple of times. 'Or maybe the husband would have a different idea? Especially if he thought his wife had misbehaved during the day.' He slapped the cane gently against the side of his leg. 'These are genuine too.' He ran one finger down the length of the cane. 'Collectors can get a great deal of pleasure out of speculating how these have been used.'

'Is this Zaid's idea?' Genevieve asked. 'Pornographic antiques.'

'A specialist collection,' Sinclair corrected her. 'For the discerning buyer.'

'There don't seem to be many buyers,' she remarked.

'This is a private view,' Sinclair said.

He guided her into the next room. She was surprised to see that it was furnished like a schoolroom. There were desks, a blackboard on an easel, and something that looked like a small vaulting horse with a padded top.

She opened a desk. Its top was stained with ink and carved names. There were books inside. Picking one up she looked at the title: *The Story of Elizabeth*, she read. A brief glance through the text and pictures showed that Elizabeth's story consisted of a catalogue of demands that she bend over any available piece of furniture and be punished for her disobedience. Schoolmasters, school-mistresses and even other pupils administered the spanking. She put the book back and closed the desk.

She walked over to the padded horse. When she got closer to it she saw that there were wrist and ankle restraints fixed to its sides.

'It's genuine,' Sinclair said. 'A lot of Victorians believed flogging was good for the soul, and the earlier you started the better.'

'A lot of people must still think so,' she said, 'if they buy this sort of thing.'

'The people who buy this stuff probably only use it with consenting adults. It can give some people a thrill just to know they've got a genuine item.'

Genevieve walked over to a table where a large postcard album was on display. She turned the pages. Victorian beauties, tubby by modern standards, and with frozen smiles, posed in a variety of acrobatic sexual positions. The men, with curled moustaches and often still wearing their shoes and socks, looked serious and unexcited. The sepia photographs seemed to have been designed by someone intent on making sure everyone displayed their genitalia. They had a static, clinical quality about them. Genevieve found them boring rather than arousing, and said so.

Sinclair peered over her shoulder. 'I agree,' he said. 'They remind me of pictures of the old Windmill theatre nudes. No excitement. The women aren't interested in pleasing men, they're just doing their job. Take your clothes off, pin on a smile and collect your money at the end of the week.' He was standing very close to her now. She could feel the warmth of his body. 'If a woman doesn't enjoy it,' he said softly, 'it doesn't turn me on.'

'How can you be certain your partner is enjoying it?' she asked coolly. 'Lots of women are good actors.'

'Are you?' he asked.

'Of course,' she said.

'You've fooled me,' he grinned. 'Up until now.' He turned towards the door. 'Come on, if you don't care for these, have a look at the print-room.'

The next room was full of pictures. Paintings, drawings,

etchings, framed and unframed. The pictures on the walls, in heavy, gold lacquered frames, were mostly classical scenes of rather tame debauchery: tangled limbs and satyr's hooves, and drunken gods chasing plump nymphs. They might have been daring in the Victorian era but, Genevieve thought, they would hardly raise an eyebrow in the 1990s. One or two were more explicit, with erect penises and athletic couplings, but once again Genevieve found them unarousing.

She asked herself why, and had to admit that Sinclair's comment about the participants enjoying themselves was valid. She remembered Ricky Croft's pictures. There had been very obvious erotic pleasure on the faces he had drawn. Most of these Victorian paintings had a mechanical look about them. The artists were clearly interested in showing 'naughty' positions rather than sensual, physical pleasure.

The drawing she liked the best depicted Leda and the swan. A swooning Leda lay entwined in the coiling neck of the swan. The picture was erotic because of what it implied rather than what it showed. Leda had the look of a woman who was happily exhausted after an energetic sex session. The swan simply looked enigmatic. The premise was ridiculous, Genevieve thought. There was no way a swan could please a woman, but its very ambiguity made it interesting.

'Very classical,' said Sinclair.

Genevieve looked at the price and put the drawing back. 'And ridiculously expensive. Do people really pay these absurd prices for this sort of thing?'

'Of course they do. That's an original.'

'Would you?' she asked.

'No,' he said. 'I don't collect Victoriana.' He paused. 'Or dirty pictures.'

She wondered if that was a reference to Ricky Croft's drawings. 'But you'd accept them as a gift?' she hinted.

He shrugged, and turned to the door. She followed him. 'Maybe,' he said. 'It depends on why the gift was being offered. And what I was expected to give in return.' He glanced at her and smiled. 'Are you thinking of buying me a present?'

'No,' she said. 'I don't need to give you pictures. I'm giving you the real thing.'

'You're right,' he said and added coldly, 'Thanks for reminding me.'

Once they were back in the corridor Sinclair pointed to a door. 'In there,' he said.

It was a large room with one main piece of furniture. At first she thought it was simply a couch, padded with green leather, but then she realised there were padded loops and levers fixed to its sides, although she could not see their purpose. The room was lit by subdued lamps. Heavy curtains were drawn over the windows. A large Victorian armchair stood near the couch.

'Take your jacket off,' Sinclair said.

She did so, slowly.

'And the blouse,' he said.

Even slower she unbuttoned the silk blouse, slipping it back over her shoulders. His dark eyes watched her. 'Skirt,' he said, flatly.

She stepped out of her skirt and stood in her lacy white underwear, the brief panties, the garter belt, the pale silky stockings and the stiletto heels.

He looked her over slowly, and once again she felt a rush of mixed emotions as she felt her body respond. Her nipples actually tightened under their thin, white lace covering. No other man had been able to turn her on simply by inspecting her. The fact that Sinclair could do so both excited and angered her. It gave him a power that she did not quite want him to have. Luckily, she thought, he probably doesn't know it.

But the amusement that showed in his eyes as he watched her prompted her to wonder if she had not misjudged him. He moved forward and stood in front of her. His eyes held hers, unreadable, dark brown. He reached out and expertly removed the clips from her hair. It tumbled to her shoulders and he ran his fingers through it, tousling it lightly into disarray. The touch of his fingers on her scalp sent a shudder of pleasure through her.

He was so close she thought he was going to kiss her mouth, but instead his lips brushed her ear and his fingers ran along the edge of her bra. He found the fastening that clipped it to the basque and tugged. The bra peeled away. He closed his hands over her breasts and massaged them gently, his lips still whispering at her ear. She rocked on her feet. A moan began to form in her throat. Her hips moved to push against him. She could feel her clit begin to throb.

She had a feeling he was going to lift her up and carry her to the leather-padded couch, but instead he suddenly stopped handling her and stepped back. Her moan turned to one of frustration, which she managed to cover with a little cough, a subterfuge that she did not think fooled him for a moment.

'Tighten it,' he said. For a moment she did not understand what he meant. 'The corset,' he said. 'Tighten it. You can take a couple of inches off your waist.'

'This isn't a bondage outfit,' she said.

'It'll pull tighter,' he said. 'So do it.'

She struggled with the laces while he watched her. Tightening the basque pushed the lightly wired top up hard under her breasts, forcing them to a provocative fullness.

He smiled slowly. 'That's much better. Doesn't it feel better?'

'It feels uncomfortable,' she said.

He stepped towards her again. His fingers brushed her nipples.

'You're a liar,' he said softly. 'It feels good. Admit it. It feels sexy, and it feels good.' The tips of his fingers moved to and fro, lightly. 'Let's hear you say it,' he murmured. 'It – feels – good.'

She closed her eyes and gave in to the sensation. 'It feels good,' she repeated, obediently.

He took his hands away. 'You like being watched, right?'

The sudden change of tone startled her. 'Watched?' she repeated.

'You enjoyed it, playing a biker's tart. You enjoyed the idea that those men were getting their kicks from watching you.'

'I didn't have a choice,' she began.

'I wish you'd stop wriggling,' he said. 'Stop making excuses. You enjoyed it. Right?'

'Well – yes,' she admitted.

'But they couldn't see your face,' he said. 'Did that make it easier?'

'Maybe.' She thought about it. 'I'd be embarrassed if I thought I'd be recognised. I don't think I could handle it.' She paused. 'All right, it's more than that. I'd be petrified to think that someone would recognise me.' She reminded him quickly: 'You promised me it wouldn't happen. I have my career to think of.'

'Why does it always come back to your damned career,' he said sharply. 'If you knew your audience would be discreet, would you still perform?'

She brushed her hair back and stared at Sinclair. 'Just what are you leading up to?' she asked.

'You know what I'm asking you,' he said shortly. 'And I think you know who your audience will be.'

She nodded. He wants to make love to me in front of Zaid, she thought. Or maybe he wants Zaid to join in?

'I'm just interested to know why you're actually asking,' she said. 'I thought you gave the orders and I obeyed them.'

'Zaid wants you to agree,' Sinclair said. 'He doesn't want any arm twisting. You have to be happy with the arrangement. When it comes to discretion, it would probably damage Zaid's reputation more than yours if you did a kiss and tell act.'

'I'm not going to do that,' she said. 'Obviously. But why me? Surely Zaid can afford to buy the best professionals you can get? Women a lot more experienced than I am.'

Sinclair smiled. 'He can. That's not what he wants.'

'Then what does he want?'

'Why don't you let him tell you himself?'

She nodded. 'All right.' She had to admit that she was intrigued, and the idea that Zaid wanted her approval gave her a sensation of being in control. It was almost as if both of them were asking her permission to make love to her. 'I'm listening.'

Zaid came into the room almost immediately. He carried a small, black leather case. Genevieve suspected that he had been waiting outside the door and had probably heard all of her conversation with Sinclair. His first remarks confirmed this.

'It's true I can buy the most beautiful whores in the world,' he said. 'I can buy a woman who will do absolutely anything.' His eyes moved over her body and again she realised how much he reminded her of Sinclair. 'Have you any idea how boring that is?' He turned, went to the armchair and sat down, putting the leather case on the floor next to him. 'These women can act like Hollywood film stars, but all the time you're watching them you know their pleasure is fake. They're thinking about the money you're paying them. Or their next assignment. They're thinking about their boyfriends, or their girlfriends. If you make love to them, their moans and cries are lies. Even their orgasms are probably phoney. And making love is not really my kick, as they say. I like to watch. I like to see beautiful women being slowly brought to the point at which she loses control. But I want it to be real. Professionals bore me. You aren't a professional, Miss Loften.' His almost black eyes moved slowly over her half-naked body. 'I want to watch you. I want to watch James making love to you.'

'How do you know I won't be faking too?' she asked.

'I trust James,' Zaid said, with a quick smile.

Sinclair was standing behind her now. She felt his hands rest lightly on her waist. 'Well, of course, Mr Sinclair is an expert,' she said, with light sarcasm.

Zaid laughed softly. 'So I believe.' He leaned back in the armchair, once again reminding Genevieve of the way Sinclair had sat and watched her during their first session together. 'She's far too self-assured, James. Make her lose control. But take your time.'

Sinclair pushed her forward until she was standing close to Zaid's chair. The pressure of his hands turned her round, slowly, until she had her back to Zaid.

'Didn't I tell you I'd bring you a woman with a sexy arse? Was I right?'

'She's got too many clothes on, James.'

Sinclair laughed. He slid his hands under Genevieve's lace panties and pushed them down, his mouth following them, taking them slowly to her ankles, his lips brushing her thighs as he did so. Genevieve stepped out of the panties. Sinclair stood up slowly, his palms stroking up her legs again to her bottom.

'Turn her round,' Zaid said.

Sinclair turned her, unhurriedly, his hand parting the folds of her pussy. Genevieve saw Zaid's eyes move from her face, over her breasts and down to her now obviously aroused clit. 'Beautiful,' he said. 'Why don't all women shave themselves? Beautiful.'

Genevieve felt Sinclair's hands move to the top of the basque, and cup her breasts. His fingers found her nipples and he rubbed them gently, circling them with his thumbs. She leaned against him, her legs slightly parted, revelling in the sensations he was giving her.

'Do you want her stripped?' Sinclair asked.

'Yes,' Zaid said, after a moment's thought. 'Everything except the stockings and shoes. Roll the stockings down to her knees.' Sinclair tugged at the basque laces and Zaid added suddenly, 'No. Wait. Let her do it, James. You carry on exciting her. She has lovely nipples. I want them to stay hard and erect.'

Genevieve managed to unfasten the basque, but it took her some time. Sinclair's caresses were distracting her. The garter belt was easier. When she bent forward to roll down her stockings, he moved with her, his fingers still busy.

'Now,' Zaid said softly, 'put her on the couch.'

Before she realised what was happening Sinclair had lifted her effortlessly into his arms and carried her over to the padded couch. She felt the leather, cool against her skin.

'Tie her wrists,' Zaid said. 'And her ankles.' He leaned down and picked up the case. 'Here, I brought some scarves. Silk, you see? Nothing but the best for a beautiful lady.'

Sinclair took the scarves. 'Do you want her on her front or her back?'

'On her back,' Zaid said. 'For the moment.'

Genevieve closed her eyes, drowsy with pleasure. She let Sinclair lift her arms above her head and fasten her wrists to the padded loops on the couch. He wrapped the scarves round her ankles. She wriggled deliciously. Then she felt her legs parting. Surprised, she opened her eyes again.

'Do you approve of our equipment, Miss Loften?' Zaid asked softly. 'This is a genuine antique. I believe it came from the home of a titled Victorian gentleman. It was specially made.

By using the levers we can move you into any position we like. James, a little demonstration, please.'

Sinclair moved a lever and Genevieve felt her legs being lifted into the air until they formed an upright V. Another touch on the lever and her knees bent as the leather supports pressed against them. The couch tipped backwards, and then forwards. It forced her into a sitting position so that she was balancing on her bottom with her legs in the air.

'I'm afraid you look uncomfortable, Miss Loften,' Zaid said. 'The Victorians had some strange ideas. The owner of this couch obviously derived satisfaction from bending helpless women into strange positions, but I think a lady looks much better lying comfortably with her legs apart. James, make Miss Loften comfortable. But on her front this time.'

Sinclair adjusted the couch, slipped the scarves from Gene–vieve's wrists and ankles and turned her over.

'A slight adjustment, James,' Zaid said. 'Lift that deliciously rounded bottom into the air a little.'

Once Genevieve was in position, Zaid pulled the armchair forward until he was near to her head. 'Now, James,' he said softly, 'let me see some genuine reactions. Let me hear a woman moaning in pleasure. Let me hear her begging you to make her come.'

Sinclair's eyes met Genevieve's. He smiled. 'That won't take long.'

'Maybe the lady has more self-control than you think.'

'She hasn't any self-control at all,' Sinclair said. He ran his fingers over Genevieve's shoulders and lightly down the soft inner skin of her lower arms. She shivered. 'Not where I'm concerned.'

Zaid looked at Genevieve. 'What do you think of that boast, Miss Loften?'

Genevieve thought there was a lot more truth in it than

she wanted to admit. 'Mr Sinclair has an overinflated opinion of his own abilities,' she said, hoping her voice sounded steady.

Zaid laughed. 'We'll give him a handicap. Or maybe it will be an advantage.' He reached for the case, opened it, and tossed something to Sinclair. 'Use this, James. It switches on at the side.'

Genevieve saw Sinclair inspect the gadget Zaid had given him. It was a vibrator. When he switched it on, it made a faint humming sound. Unlike some of the cruder versions of this sex toy it was not designed to look like a penis. It was ivory coloured and tapered to a blunt point.

Genevieve had only seen vibrators in advertisements and had certainly never used one. She remembered with embarrassment how the subject had once been discussed in the sports centre changing-rooms, and she had expressed the opinion that only frustrated women used such things. Two young women had turned on her quite angrily and told her in no uncertain terms that they both used vibrators for solitary fun and games and insisted their boyfriends included them in their love-making too. They weren't frustrated, just adventurous. By the time they had finished lecturing her, Genevieve felt like a Victorian granny out of touch with reality.

Now she felt the tingling sensation of the vibrator on the skin of her thighs. It was light and pleasant, without being overtly sexy. She wriggled comfortably and sighed. Sinclair smoothed the sensitive skin behind her knees, just above the tops of her rolled-down stockings, ran the vibrator tip down her calves to her feet. Removing her shoes he touched her experimentally, until he found that she was not ticklish, then adding more pressure, he outlined her toes, one by one, unhurriedly, the vibrator sliding over the silk stockings. She sighed again, stretched and relaxed.

The vibrator moved back up her legs, lingered behind her knees again, and then travelled up to her bottom. Now the feeling began to get more erotic. Sinclair stroked her buttocks, forced the tip of the vibrator gently and briefly into the cleft between them, and then moved on to her spine.

Genevieve turned her head and saw Zaid watching her. She smiled drowsily as Sinclair reached her neck and caressed it gently, then combed the vibrator through her tousled hair. It was a strangely arousing sensation.

'Golden hair,' Zaid murmured. 'I love it. But don't send the lady to sleep, James. Not yet.'

Sinclair laughed. 'She'll wake up in a minute.'

The vibrator began to buzz faster. The tip fondled the nape of Genevieve's neck, then after lingering for a tantalising moment, the base of her spine. Because it was strangely warm and felt almost like a thick human finger she felt herself responding. With her bottom raised in the air it was easy for Sinclair to insert the vibrator between her thighs.

Now his movements were becoming more insistent and more erotic. He probed her masterfully, and she moaned involuntarily. He parted the cheeks of her buttocks and she felt the vibrator slide between them, its tip reaching for her clitoris, touching it lightly, and then withdrawing. After a few minutes of this treatment she was beginning to thrust her hips forward in an attempt to prolong the contact.

'Be careful, James,' Zaid said. 'She's going to come.'

'Stop worrying,' Sinclair said. 'When I promise you a show, you get one. Miss Loften has a long way to go yet.' He put his hand on Genevieve's back. She felt the warmth of his palm and the steady pressure, holding her. 'We haven't tried this yet,' he said softly. 'Let's see if you like it.'

The vibrator pushed between her buttocks, seeking her anus. She had never been entered this way before, and for a moment she panicked and tried to pull away. She felt Sinclair hesitate.

'Nothing that she doesn't approve of, James,' Zaid warned. 'I want to see pleasure, not fear.'

The vibrator tip moved to the base of her spine, tracing patterns, moving lightly over her buttocks. Genevieve relaxed. When Sinclair probed her again she let the tingling tormentor have its way. Sinclair was surprisingly gentle and she parted her legs to let him explore. It was a strange sensation. She did not find it as exciting as the clitoral stimulation he had provided earlier, but when she opened her eyes and saw Zaid watching her with obvious delight she felt it was worthwhile. His reaction aroused her more than the vibrator's moving pressure. But Sinclair did not continue. He noted that her response was not wholly enthusiastic and slowly withdrew it.

'You're stopping, James?' Zaid sounded disappointed.

'Miss Loften isn't quite sure about this treatment,' Sinclair said. 'And this isn't the time to teach her how to appreciate it.' Genevieve felt her body returning to its original horizontal position and then her hands and feet were untied. 'I know what you want to see, Zaid. Trust me.'

'I want to see this beautiful woman begging for an orgasm,' Zaid said softly. 'The most exciting sight in the world. English women are usually so cool and self-possessed, I love to see them lose control. Show me this, James. Show me now.'

Genevieve felt strong hands turn her over, and re-tie her wrists and ankles. The couch was adjusted so that her body was almost flat and her legs bent and apart. The spiky tips of her pale-grey heels dug into the dark green leather.

Through half-closed eyes Genevieve stared up at Sinclair. It was impossible not to be aroused by his expression. Possessive, slightly mocking, and totally self-assured. Even before he touched her she felt her body respond. When he moved his hands over her breasts and rolled her half-erect nipples between his fingers, the combination of discomfort and erotic pleasure made her gasp.

He worked on her silently, using his fingers, the palms of his hands, and his lips and tongue. He moved from her breasts to her stomach, circling her navel, and then to her thighs. One hand reached for a lever and the couch forced her legs still further apart, allowing him to kneel between them. His hands moved under her buttocks, lifting them, pulling her towards him. His tongue found the swollen bud of her clit; his lips sucked her.

Looking down and seeing the top of his head moving between her thighs was almost as arousing as the sensations he was giving her. She strained against the scarves, not because she wished to get free, but because it was impossible to lie still while he held her so expertly on the brink of release. Her hips pushed towards his face, but he simply moved back, dug his fingers harder into the firm flesh of her bottom, and teased her with more activity from his tongue.

She groaned in frustration and twisted her head sideways towards Zaid. She realised in surprise that he was not looking down at Sinclair. He was watching her face, watching her expression as she fought for control, enjoying the inarticulate noises she was making as Sinclair continued his delicious torment.

Sinclair's tongue moved faster. Genevieve thrust her body upwards, trying to force him into applying the pressure needed to trigger her response. As her head threshed from side to side she saw Zaid smile.

'Beg him.' Zaid's voice was hoarse with excitement. 'Beg him. Let me hear you. Beg him.'

'Please ...' Genevieve moaned, as much for herself as to please Zaid. 'Let me ... make me ... please.'

She felt her body shuddering, slipping out of control, and knew she was going to come, whether Sinclair intended it or not. Her back arched and she strained at restraints that held her.

'Oh . . . yes,' she cried. 'Oh . . . yes, please, now . . . !'

Her orgasm was intense and prolonged, subsiding gradually so that she was still panting and shivering with pleasure long after Sinclair had moved away from her. With her eyes half-closed she looked drowsily up at his tall figure standing over her, and then turned her head sideways to glance at Zaid.

He was relaxing back in his chair, smiling contentedly. She realised that she did not know if he had masturbated while watching her, but she had a feeling that he had not. His pleasure seemed to come, as he claimed, from watching her facial reactions, from seeing her metamorphose from a cool, self-possessed woman into a sexual creature frantic for orgasmic release.

Strange, she thought. You would think this would be the easiest erotic fantasy to fulfil, and yet it was probably one of the hardest. His money could buy him a hollow performance from professionals, but how many women could he trust to behave as naturally and uninhibitedly as she had just done? Clearly Zaid had to be careful with whom he allowed himself to be involved. His need for discretion was probably greater than hers. He had to be certain he could trust both the woman and the man.

She hardly felt Sinclair untie her hands and feet. She lay drowsily on the couch, her body relaxed, almost unaware of her nakedness until she realised Zaid was staring down her.

'Do you realise how beautiful you looked, Genevieve?' he asked softly.

She smiled up at him. 'I never thought about it.'

'Don't you enjoy seeing a man lose control? Don't you enjoy knowing that you've given him this pleasure?'

She saw Sinclair standing behind Zaid. 'Sometimes,' she said. Her eyes held Sinclair's for a moment. 'It depends on why I'm making love to him.'

'A woman like you only makes love because she wants to,' Zaid said. 'That's why it's such an intense pleasure for me to watch you. I know it's genuine. Believe me, I'm an expert. I know you were not faking.' He smiled, and again she was reminded of Sinclair. 'I shall not forget you. If you ever need anything I can supply, you have only to ask. James will tell you how to contact me. I don't pretend to be of any particular importance, but I do have some influence in certain spheres. You won't forget? There is no time limit on this promise.' He ran his hand over his jet-black hair and tugged at his immaculate jacket. 'And now I must go back to my guests. There is a bathroom and also some food and wine if you need refreshments.' His dark eyes lingered on Genevieve's face for one last moment. 'Don't forget, beautiful lady. Anything within my power. Any time.'

After a quick shower Genevieve dressed and followed Sinclair into an adjoining room, simply furnished, where a gourmet buffet had been laid out for the two of them. As she sampled the delicacies, Sinclair poured her a glass of wine.

'You impressed Zaid,' he said. 'But I knew you would. I know his tastes.'

'You've done this before?' she asked.

'No,' he said. 'Zaid and I had talked about it, though.' He glanced at her. 'It isn't easy to find the right woman.'

'I'd have thought under certain circumstances it would have been harder to find the right man. I know you kept your clothes on, but what if your friend had asked you to provide a more basic form of stimulation?'

Sinclair shrugged. 'Fuck you properly you mean? I'd have

done it.' He grinned faintly. 'I'm quite capable of it, you know.'

'I thought men didn't like performing in front of each other.'

'Whoever gave you that idea?'

'I read it somewhere. Something to do with masculine pride.' She sipped her wine. 'I mean, you might be embarrassed because yours isn't as big as his.' She saw Sinclair begin to grin. 'Or something,' she added.

Sinclair's grin turned into a smile of genuine amusement. 'There aren't many men as big as me,' he said smugly. 'You should know that.'

'You really are a conceited bastard,' Genevieve said.

'It's true though, isn't it?'

'I wouldn't know,' she said. 'I'm not a connoisseur.'

'A modern woman like you?' he mocked her, gently.

'I'm just an old-fashioned working girl,' she said. 'And I don't do it for my health.'

His smile disappeared. 'That's right. I forgot. Anyone who presses the right buttons can get a reaction. Or should I say, anyone who offers you a good business deal?'

She kept her temper. There was no way she was going to admit that no one had ever given her as much pleasure as he had. What would he make of an admission like that? She had an idea that he probably wouldn't believe her.

'You suggested the deal,' she said, coolly.

'And you accepted.' His smile returned. 'I'm not complaining. So far you've met all my expectations. Let's hope you continue to do so in the future.'

A few days later two parcels were delivered to her door, with a letter. She opened the largest first. It contained the music box she had recently admired. She lifted the lid and listened to the delicate chiming notes of 'Danny Boy.' The letter said: I CONFESS! WHEN I KNEW YOU LIKED THE MUSIC BOX I SIGNALLED TO THE SALES ASSISTANT TO SAY IT WAS SOLD. BUT ZAID INSISTED ON PAYING FOR IT. MY PRESENT IS SMALLER BUT MIGHT GIVE YOU JUST AS MUCH PLEASURE. She opened the second package. It contained the ivory-coloured vibrator.

4

'When are you going to play in the league again?'

Genevieve turned and saw Bill Hexley standing behind her. She smiled. 'Bill, I'm a working woman. I simply haven't the time.'

'Lots of us work,' Bill said. 'We make time.'

'Maybe next season,' Genevieve said.

Bill walked beside her. 'It's such a waste. You're a damned good squash player.'

'For a woman?' she teased.

He laughed. 'You're never going to let me forget that, are you? All right, I was a male chauvinist pig a few years ago, but I've changed. My wife has reformed me. Everyone knows that.'

Genevieve remembered the amazed gossip that Bill's marriage had generated. For a start no one could understand what a woman as pretty as Jackie Harwood saw in the paunchy Bill. The archetypal bachelor, Bill had degenerated from a fairly fit squash player to a very unfit smoker and drinker. His house, friends told Genevieve, was like a rubbish tip. He only washed up when he had ran out of clean crockery. He spent most of his evenings in the pub and he boasted that his main exercise was switching the television set on and occasionally watching a league squash game. It was on one of these occasions that he had made his disparaging remark about Genevieve.

Then, within a few months of meeting her, he married Jackie Harwood and slowly the overweight beer drinker had turned into a health-conscious vegetarian who took up squash again and bored any smoker he could find with the story of how he gave up instantly, with no ill effects and knew that anyone with an ounce of self-control could do the same.

'You ought to get married,' Bill said. 'All work and no play, you know? And it's a waste of talent too. Find some lucky man and make him happy.'

'It's not that easy,' Genevieve said. 'You and Jackie were lucky.'

She suddenly realised that walking with Bill she had taken a wrong turning. 'Hey, I don't want to go to the ice rink. I'm going home.'

'Sorry,' Bill said. 'Jackie's skating. I said I'd meet her.' He stopped Genevieve as she turned to go back. 'Here, cut through the fire exit. It'll take you past the fitness centre and you can get to the car park that way. But don't let the staff see you.'

'I never knew that,' Genevieve said.

'Legacy of my lazy past.' Bill grinned. 'I know all the short cuts. And while you're passing, take a look in the weights-room. It's ladies' night. There's a couple of women in there who give me an inferiority complex.' He mimed a body building pose. 'You won't believe it.'

There was rock music beating out of the weights-room when Genevieve approached. Curious, she pushed open the double doors and looked inside. Most of the women using the various fitness machines were working with looks of intense concentration. A couple were standing talking. Over by the mirrored wall, Genevieve saw two women whose bodies, if they hadn't been wearing stretch Lycra that accented their breasts, could well have been taken for men. Muscles bulged in their arms and thighs as they worked out with free weights. Their veins stood out like cords. Their skin glistened with sweat.

It was the first time Genevieve had actually watched women body builders working out. She was surprised to see that both of these women were conventionally attractive. They had strong, muscular bodies, but their faces would have not looked out of place in a cosmetic advertisement. As she watched them straining to lift weights that would have given some men problems, she wondered why they wanted their bodies to look so unfeminine.

'Awful, isn't it?' a male voice said.

She half turned to see a young man she did not know staring into the weights-room. 'Why do they do it, do you know?'

'The same reason that men do it,' Genevieve said. 'They think it makes them look good.'

'I think it makes them look grotesque.'

'That's because you've got a stereotyped idea of what women should look like,' Genevieve said.

The young man looked slightly shocked. 'You'd like to look like that, would you?'

'No,' Genevieve said. 'But that's my choice. Developing muscles is theirs.'

'Lezzies,' the young man said, contemptuously.

A woman standing near to the door had obviously heard their conversation. Now she looked up and grinned. 'Don't let Tess's boyfriend hear you say that. He's a body builder too.'

The young man shrugged and walked quickly away. The woman smiled at Genevieve. 'They can't handle it, can they? If you don't look like their ideal woman they just don't know how to react. Tess has won lots of competitions. She wants to compete in America. They really appreciate women's body building over there. And you can win big money, too. Do you do weight training?'

'No,' Genevieve said.

The woman glanced at Genevieve's sports bag and the

protruding handle of her squash racket. 'It would improve your game.'

'I just don't have the time,' Genevieve said.

She had been looking round the weights-room while she was talking. The two body builders had stopped working out. One of them posed in front of the mirror, flexing and twisting, while the other watched critically. A woman on the lat machine stopped her work-out, paused for a moment and then got up and walked over to them. Something about the imperious way that she moved made Genevieve look at her more closely. She realised with a shock that it was Jade Chalfont.

With her glossy hair tied back and her body covered by a dark cat-suit she looked lithe and fit. She started to chat to one of the body builders. As Genevieve watched, Jade Chalfont threw back her head and laughed. The sound made other women in the room look up with curiosity.

That's right, Genevieve thought cattily, make sure you're the centre of attention. She had to admit that the woman looked good in the figure-hugging suit. It was made from shiny black Lycra and reminded Genevieve of one of Georgie's leather outfits, although it lacked the sexy appeal of Georgie's well-placed zips.

Would Jade Chalfont wear an outfit like that? Genevieve looked at her again. She had the body of an athlete, shoulders broader than normal tapering to a narrow waist, and quite small breasts. Genevieve could not help wondering if this was the kind of figure that appealed to James Sinclair. It was more angular, and harder, than her own. Squash had made Genevieve strong, but she had never lost her rounded curves. Jade was built more like a boy. Maybe Sinclair found androgyny some kind of turn-on. She had a sudden and unwanted image of Jade Chalfont on her hands and knees as Sinclair entered her from the rear. The picture conjured up a memory of her own session with the vibrator, and its partial entry. Was that what he really liked? She had a feeling that it was not. She felt certain that he had performed that particular trick mainly to please Zaid.

She looked at Jade again. She seemed such a dominant type, Genevieve found it difficult to believe she would let any man give her orders, in bed or out. But she knew that appearances could be deceptive. How many people looking at her in her business suit, coolly elegant, would believe that she would not only submit to, but thoroughly enjoy, the kind of sex games Sinclair had initiated her into? She hardly believed it herself.

Jade Chalfont was still chatting to the body builders and as Genevieve watched she reached out and traced long fingers down one of the women's legs. The woman bent the leg and the muscle stood out. Jade nodded appreciatively.

'See the one with the black hair?' The woman was still standing next to Genevieve. 'She does some kind of martial arts thing with a sword.'

'Kendo,' Genevieve said, absently. She thought Jade seemed to be running her hands over the female body builder's muscles rather more than was necessary.

'Something like that.' The woman nodded. 'I'm not into martial arts. All that yelling puts me off. Aerobics and swimming are enough for me.'

Not wanting to be recognised, Genevieve backed away from the weights-room door, smiled goodbye to the woman she had been talking to and walked quickly down the corridor towards the exit.

She was annoyed to discover that she could not get the image of Jade Chalfont out of her mind. There was a hard edge about her that she realised could be seen as both sexually attractive and challenging to many men. She gave the impression that she would enjoy a fight, too. Did she see

Sinclair as a trophy to be won, both on a personal level and for Lucci's?

Up until then Genevieve had felt fairly sure of herself. But now doubts were beginning to creep in. She suspected that Jade Chalfont was her equal in ambition. She felt certain that Jade would have accepted any kind of sexual contract that Sinclair offered her. Had he offered her one? Was he playing with both of them for reasons of his own? Because he wanted Randle-Mayne to come to him cap in hand and ask to settle their differences? Sinclair's account was worth a great deal of money. If a large agency like Randle-Mayne lost him, it would not look good at their next shareholders' meeting.

Or was Jade Chalfont simply another challenge for Sinclair? Another chance to discover just what she would do to achieve her ends? To advance her career? A chance for him to discover how easy it would be to control her? Was James Sinclair just an erotic adventurer using women as pawns in his fantasies? Could she really trust him to keep his word? She was not sure.

But here was one thing she could be sure of: if she backed out now, she would never know.

Genevieve was watching a video when her mobile rang. She had recorded this particular programme several weeks before and had been looking forward to watching it. It was a potted history of popular music, with clips from original recordings, but as the pictures flickered hypnotically and the soundtrack evoked memories of songs she had liked when she was at school, she had slipped into a far more interesting fantasy in which she imagined a naked Sinclair tied to the Victorian green leather couch. She would manipulate the levers to arrange him in a series of interesting positions, and then question him about his relationship with Jade Chalfont. Any answers she did not like would result in his legs being pushed even further apart. And then, she thought seductively, maybe I'd use a vibrator until he begged *me* for relief.

It was a pleasant fantasy and she was not too pleased when her phone interrupted it. And even less pleased when she heard her brother's voice. She reluctantly banished her mental picture of Sinclair's tanned body and the impressive erection she had already decided he would be experiencing after just a brief session with the vibrator.

'Hi, big sister.' Philip's voice sounded cheerfully in her ear. 'Hope I haven't interrupted anything?'

Genevieve switched the video off.

'What was that background music?' Philip enquired. 'Didn't sound like your thing, sis.'

'A video,' she said.

'Thought you might be having a party.' He laughed to show her that he didn't think anything of the sort and for some reason Genevieve found his assumption annoying. There was a ten-year difference in their ages, but that didn't mean she was too old, or too stuffy, to know how to enjoy herself.

'Why shouldn't I be having a party?' she asked, more sharply than she intended.

'Hey, don't bite my head off,' Philip said. 'You never have parties. Too busy working, that's what you always say.'

Genevieve had to admit that he was right. Her social life had suffered because of work.

'I just thought I'd tell you that I took your advice,' Philip added. 'And it worked.'

For a moment she could not remember what she had told him.

'In fact,' Philip went on, 'I sat down with Jan, my new girl-friend, and spelled out exactly what I wanted. We both agreed that being tied up wasn't really politically incorrect as long as

I respected her and only used scarves and things, and not chains. She wasn't overenthusiastic, but she feels that equality works both ways. If I respect her wishes she'll respect mine. She's pretty broad-minded. We decided that I could do it twice a week, maximum.'

There was a long pause while Genevieve digested this. 'Well,' she said at last, 'that's fine. I'm happy for you both. Did you put it in writing and both sign?'

This time the pause was on Philip's end of the phone. 'You're taking the piss, big sister. I thought you'd approve.'

'Oh, for God's sake!' Genevieve said. 'It's so cold-blooded. You'll be telling me next you've drawn her a diagram.'

'Excuse me if I've got it wrong,' Philip said, 'but you were the one who told me to make sure my next girlfriend knew exactly what I wanted.'

'I didn't expect you to turn it into a business arrangement,' Genevieve said. 'I meant you to sort of suggest things romantically.'

'Don't be so old-fashioned, sis. What has romance got to do with it?'

'You're in love with this girl, aren't you?' Genevieve asked.

'Of course not,' Philip said. 'I don't want to get emotionally involved until I've finished college and seen a bit of life. I fancy her, that's all. And before you start on me again, I've explained that to her as well. I've been completely honest. I want sex, and I'm willing to buy her drinks and so on, but that's all.' He paused and then added, 'We have relationships without all that lovey-dovey stuff these days, you know? Modern women actually prefer it. Sorry if it shocks you, but this is the 1990s.'

Did it shock her? she wondered. And if so, why? Was it only because she really could not accept that Philip had grown up? She still saw him as her little kid brother. It was difficult to accept that he was now a young male with sexual needs. Was his arrangement with his girlfriend really very different from hers with James Sinclair?

After she rang off, she suddenly she felt like giggling. Whatever would Philip think if he found out the details of her recent erotic adventures? Dear politically correct Phil, who thought scarves were all right but chains were kinky. Thought you'd shocked me, did you? She stretched out her legs, tensed them, then relaxed, remembering. You don't know me at all, little brother. And perhaps it's just as well.

And how well did Sinclair know her, she thought, lazily sinking back in her chair and recovering her previous mental picture of him helpless on the green leather couch. What would he think if he could share that fantasy? Would he be excited? Horrified? Angry? She realised that she did not know. She knew so little about him.

She was not even really sure if he would keep the unorthodox agreement they had made. She could hardly take legal action against him if he backed out. This whole thing could be his idea of a rather unkind joke. An exercise in personal power. She would not know the truth until the ninety days had ended.

When her phone rang early on Wednesday morning she picked it up with a sense of expectancy, guessing that it was Sinclair. He surprised her by asking how she was, and she suspected that he was phoning from a more public place than usual.

'Are you free this Saturday evening?'

That surprised her even more. 'You're *asking* me?'

'I certainly am. I'd forgotten about this invitation to the Fennington and I really need a partner. It's an annual do, and if I turn up on my own I'm going to get collared by some terrible old harridan or the resident bore.' He paused. 'If you come with me I can promise you a really splendid dinner, and a rather traditional dance.'

'Well, all right,' she agreed, trying not to sound too enthusiastic. A dinner in the Fennington Hotel? How could she refuse? They had a reputation for expensive excellence.

'It's very formal,' he added. 'You're expected to glitter. Diamonds would be nice.'

'I haven't got anything very formal,' she said. 'Just the usual little black dress. And I haven't got any diamonds either.'

'I'll arrange something,' he offered. 'I'm rather good at choosing clothes. Maybe you noticed?'

'If you think I'm going to turn up at the Fennington wearing a leather miniskirt and a plunge-neck top, you can think again,' she said coolly. 'Agreement or not, that is definitely *out*.'

He laughed. 'Don't worry. If you don't like my choice you can buy something else, at my expense. Expect a delivery tomorrow evening.'

It sounded absolutely genuine, but she knew Sinclair better by now, and the first thing she did was check with the hotel. She was amazed when they confirmed Sinclair's story. They were booked for the annual dinner and dance of the Grand Order of the Knights of the Banner. Invitation only. A few more enquiries confirmed that the Knights were a well-established charitable Order and had been discreetly doing good for over a hundred years.

When the promised clothes arrived they provided further confirmation that this invitation was genuine. The dress was a classically tailored, off-the-shoulder design in heavy, dark-green satin with a long, hidden zip down the back. It reminded her of the gowns worn by film stars in the twenties, and although the skirt reached her ankles and the neckline was hardly deep, she wondered if some of the ancient and venerable Knights of the Banner would find it daringly modern. It hugged her figure, but not tightly enough to look tarty or display the lines of her underwear. She did not own a strapless bra but the boned front of the dress made it unnecessary. Sinclair had also sent her matching gloves, green silk-covered shoes with respectable heels, and a pair of silk camiknickers. There were no stockings. She thought the knickers were a nice touch, in keeping with the period style of the dress.

A small box came by another courier. It contained a heavy diamond choker and matching bracelet. They glittered convincingly but she knew they had to be fakes. If they were genuine she was holding a fortune in her hands. The five-stranded choker made her hold up her head in an imperious, slightly uncomfortable, position. The wide bracelet, worn over her glove, felt like a manacle. But, she thought, I'll certainly glitter.

She admired herself in a full-length mirror, and experimented with her hair, deciding to pin it up in an approximation of a twenties' style to complement the dress. She turned, smoothing the green satin against her thighs with her palms. She could not remember when she had last worn a full-length dress. It made her feel both sexy and elegant. And, she thought confidently, it makes me look that way, too.

When Sinclair arrived to collect her, elegantly formal in black, she noted the instant approval in his eyes and felt a thrill of pleasure. She posed, turning slowly, majestic in the dull-sheened satin.

'Very nice,' he said. 'I like the hairstyle.'

'I'm glad you approve. Do you want to check that I'm wearing knickers for a change?'

'No.' He smiled. 'I think you've learned the first lesson of our agreement by now.' He paused. 'But I might check later.' He reached forward and touched the heavy choker. 'I couldn't resist this. It looks like a fancy dog collar, doesn't it? That's why I bought it. Maybe I should have bought a leash as well.'

'I knew it,' she said. 'We're really going to a bondage club.'

He laughed. 'We're going to the Fennington,' he corrected. 'To a very formal dinner and dance.'

The Fennington was a glittering blaze of light. In the foyer, heavily encrusted with gold leaf and dark wallpaper, a distinguished elderly man greeted new arrivals and discreetly checked their invitation cards.

For Genevieve it was like taking a step into the past. She was introduced to a variety of middle-aged guests, the women corseted into their exclusive dresses, the men full of old-world charm. She danced with several of them, a stately whirl. It was unreal and theatrical. Once again she felt as if she was acting in a play. Time passed swiftly. The touch of Sinclair's hand on her arm brought her back to reality. He said, simply, 'Upstairs.'

So, she thought, this isn't just a straightforward night out after all. He's planned something. She experienced a sudden tingle of excitement. The formality of the evening made her feel like doing something deliciously wicked. Something that would shock these conventional and worthy old people if they knew about it. Sinclair placed his palm under her elbow, and guided her. They threaded through the crowd and she felt his hand tightening as yet another acquaintance stopped them to exchange pleasantries. He's getting impatient, she thought. The super-controlled Mr Sinclair, master negotiator, is probably beginning to feel distinctly uncomfortable. The thought pleased her.

They were very near the door when an old lady stopped them both with an imperious gesture. Judging by the fine bones of her face and her large, still bright-blue eyes, Genevieve guessed that she must have been a stunning beauty in her youth.

'James, how lovely to see you.' The eyes assessed Genevieve. 'Keeping up the tradition, I see?'

'Of course,' Sinclair said smoothly. He introduced Genevieve.

The old lady smiled. 'Nice to see some new young faces. Enjoy yourself, my dear.'

'Margaret is the daughter of one of the Order's founders,' Sinclair explained, when they were on their own again.

'What would she say if she knew what you were planning right now?' Genevieve asked.

He gave her an amused glance. 'She might be jealous,' he murmured.

Once up the wide flight of deeply carpeted stairs they turned into a long corridor with numbered doors. Gilt-framed mirrors hung on the walls, and plush-seated chairs were placed at intervals. In case the old dears who stay here can't make it to their rooms without sitting down, Genevieve thought.

Sinclair stopped halfway down the corridor. He turned, and put his hands on her shoulders. They lingered there for a moment and she felt their warmth. She waited, curious, expecting him to pull her towards him, wondering if he intended to kiss her. She imagined his mouth moving over her neck and throat, down towards the boned edge of her dress. Well, she had no objection to kissing him, she thought, as long as he was quick. There was no one here to see them.

His hands slid behind her back and grasped the zip of her dress. Before she fully realised what was happening, the zip opened and her dress peeled apart like the skin of a ripe fruit. Then it fell into a satiny pile round her feet. It was so sudden, and so unexpected, that she stood frozen with shock. She could hear the sound of the dance band floating up the stairs.

'I knew you'd wear the knickers,' he said softly. 'Sexy, aren't they?' His fingers hooked in the elastic and he tugged downwards, running his thumbs along the inside of her thighs. 'But this is better.' The knickers ended up on the carpet with the dress. 'You're still shaving,' he noted. 'Good. I like it. It makes it even easier to see what I'm getting.'

She came to life with a gasp and bent down, frantically scrabbling for her clothes. He moved just as quickly, caught her wrist, and forced her to stand up. She stood there, naked except for her diamond jewellery, gloves and shoes.

'Pick up the clothes,' he said. He sounded amused. 'But don't put them back on.'

'Are you mad?' She was both furious and horrified. 'There might be guests in these rooms. Someone might come out. Someone might see me like this.'

He laughed. 'But you like being seen, sweetheart. You like being watched. You certainly didn't object to Zaid watching you.'

'That was different,' she protested. 'We were in a private room. I knew we were safe.' He was grinning. Furiously she rounded on him. 'You know what I mean. I can't be seen by anyone here. You promised me.'

'If you're so bothered about it,' he said, 'do as you're told. The quicker you do, the quicker we move on to the next act.'

She stepped out of the dress and the knickers and picked them up.

'Walk,' he ordered.

'Which room?'

If only she could get inside a room she might even begin to enjoy this. They were next to one of the chairs. She hurried past, trailing the dress behind her, desperate to find a refuge from this all too public corridor.

'Who said anything about a room?'

She turned and saw that he was sitting down, his legs

stretched out in front of him. He looked totally at ease. 'Come here,' he said.

She considered making a dash for one of the doors in the hope that it would be unlocked and the room empty. But what if it wasn't? And he was definitely not going to sit there and let her make a bolt for it, was he? Her eyes flicked nervously to the doors again. Who was behind them? Sleeping guests? Guests dressing for dinner? Guests who any minute would come out and see her wearing only a diamond choker and a bracelet, a pair of gloves and shoes? Guests who might recognise her?

She went back to him, stood in front of him, feeling like a slave at a public market.

'Drop that damned dress on the floor,' he said. 'And turn round. Slowly.'

She turned, knowing that if she did not do exactly as he said he would keep her there even longer. While he did not seem at all bothered about the possibility of discovery, she saw each closed door as an eye waiting to open. But although she feared discovery and recognition (how could she look any of her colleagues in the face if they heard about this?), she felt her body begin to respond to the sexual danger of the situation. She was moist and her nipples were already hard. She completed her slow spin.

'There's something about diamonds and naked flesh,' he mused. 'Something very sexy. It makes you look like a whore and a lady, both at once.'

'Can we go into a room now, please?' she pleaded. 'I'll do anything you like. But let's go *now*.'

'You'll do anything I like anyway, sweetheart,' he said. 'That's the deal, remember?' He sat up straight in the chair. 'Come here.' She took a step forward. 'Closer,' he said. 'Spread your legs, each side of mine.'

She knew it was useless to argue. She stood astride him, aware that the physical evidence of her arousal was quite obvious as she straddled his lap. He slid one hand round her waist, stroked it lower and began to massage her bottom. The chair creaked and she jumped nervously, her eyes darting along the corridor.

'Relax,' he said. His other hand travelled up her inner thigh and his finger began to stroke her, intimately. 'Stand still.'

By now she was thoroughly aroused and it only needed a feather-light touch to make her gasp. 'I can't stand still,' she muttered. 'Not when you're doing that.'

He laughed softly and rubbed her swelling clit, gently at first then harder, trying to discover the speed and pressure that turned her on. Her reactions taught him how to please her. Waves of pleasure shuddered through her. The fear of discovery was drowned in a surge of sexual need.

His fingers stroked and teased expertly. He made her dance to his tune. Her legs bent, her knees pushed outwards and she leaned back, making herself even more accessible. She could see from his face that he was enjoying the sight of her, the inarticulate sounds she was making, enjoying the knowledge that he was causing her to lose control.

Once he had discovered exactly how she liked to be handled, he tantalised her by refusing to oblige and bring her to orgasm. He prolonged her excitement by sliding his finger very lightly over her clit, making it ache for more pressure.

She tried to stifle the noises of desire that rose in her throat. Her body moved in rhythm with his hand. Her feet slid on the floor and her passionate writhing deposited her in his lap. She felt the smooth cloth of his suit against her flesh, reminding her that he was fully clothed and she was naked.

Somehow the image intensified her excitement. She reached out for him, without thinking, and pulled his head closer. His mouth touched her erect nipple and he obligingly sucked her, first gently then with unexpected roughness. 'Yes,' she gasped. 'Oh, yes ... please, yes.'

His hand matched his mouth in urgency and the twin sensations of his lips and his fingers brought her to a point of no return. She climaxed suddenly with a cry of relief and delight.

As her body relaxed she became aware of her surroundings again, and of how she would look if anyone appeared in the corridor. Considering the noise she had been making, she was surprised that no one had come out to see what was going on. She reached for her dress, intending to put it back on as fast as possible and then find a ladies' and freshen herself up.

Sinclair stood up gracefully and took a tagged key from his pocket. 'Over there,' he said. She noticed with satisfaction that his voice did not sound completely steady. 'Number 32.'

It was a double bedroom, with a vase of fresh flowers on each bedside table. The lighting was diffuse. An inner door led to a bathroom. He caught her arm, spun her round and all but threw her on the bed. 'Now,' he said hoarsely, 'it's my turn.'

He knelt over her and unzipped his trousers. His erection was so huge that she was surprised he had controlled it for so long. She was still moist and relaxed from her own orgasm and when he entered her she felt a deep satisfaction in the knowledge that she could still get pleasure from his body. Despite his obvious need he thrust slowly, and she moved against him languorously.

'That's it,' he murmered. 'Relax. I can make you come any time I like. This time we'll do it nice and slow.'

Then she realised that this was a way of showing her that he was still calling the shots. He was still in control, the master and not the slave. She decided to alter the relationship. She tightened her muscles and pulled him in strongly. He groaned.

She held him, her hands on his taut buttocks, feeling his muscles tensed hard under her fingers. She flexed her hips in a series of thrusts that increased in speed as she sensed him losing control. His climax came much faster than she expected and probably, she thought with satisfaction, faster than he intended.

As he relaxed and withdrew she felt a delicious warmth flood over her. It was a gentle orgasm but every bit as satisfying as the violent climax he had given her in the corridor. She stretched out on the bed and sighed drowsily. She heard water running in the bathroom and closed her eyes. The next thing she knew, his hand was on her shoulder, shaking her gently.

'Go and have a shower,' he said. 'It's nearly time to eat.'

There were some younger faces at the candlelit dining table. Genevieve sat between Sinclair and a military-looking, middle-aged man who was surprisingly knowledgeable about modern rock music. Opposite her she noticed a woman in her thirties, imperiously beautiful, who caught her eye once or twice and smiled. Genevieve smiled back.

'Who's the woman in the blue dress?' she asked, when she next turned to Sinclair.

He shrugged. 'I've no idea. I've never seen her before.' But a little later he commented: 'That woman seems to know you. She keeps looking over here.'

'Perhaps she's looking at you,' Genevieve said demurely.

'I wouldn't blame her if she was,' he drawled. 'But I know when a woman fancies me, and that one doesn't. She seems far more interested in you.'

Genevieve did not think any more about the woman, or Sinclair's comments, until after the meal was over and the ladies began to wander out of the room.

'This is where we get a little traditional,' Sinclair told her. 'Most of the Knights stay at the table for a cigar and a brandy, the ladies are expected to go and freshen up. Old-fashioned, but that's the way they do it here.'

'And you're staying for a cigar?' she guessed.

'It won't be for long,' he said. 'It gives us a chance to talk about next year's charitable work.'

Left on her own Genevieve went back into the ballroom. The band was playing softly. Guests who obviously knew each other were forming into chattering groups.

'Hallo.' Startled, Genevieve turned and found herself facing the woman who had been smiling at her at the dining table. 'Are you at a loose end too?'

'A bit,' she admitted. 'I don't really know anyone here.'

'Neither do I,' the other woman said. 'I came to oblige a friend. He needed a partner at short notice. I'm Bridget.'

Genevieve introduced herself. Bridget looked round, rather like an unenthusiastic princess surveying her subjects. 'I'm sure all these old dears are terribly worthy,' she said, 'but most of them are also terribly boring. Why don't you come up to my room? We'll relax and have a drink and watch TV or something.'

It was better than standing in the ballroom like a wallflower, Genevieve thought. She followed Bridget up the wide stairs to the first floor, glancing slyly at a familiar chair as she walked past.

Bridget's room was very similar to the one she had already seen. Although there was a double bed, she could not see any evidence that Bridget was sharing with her friend. Once in the room Bridget lost her haughty manner. She opened a cupboard and took out some bottles. 'Let me mix you something.'

Genevieve accepted the drink. It was potent, and made her feel light-headed. Bridget came and sat beside her, and refilled her glass. They chatted casually. Then Bridget reached out and touched the diamond choker. 'That's beautiful.'

'Fake,' Genevieve said. 'And on loan.'

'Can I try it on?'

Genevieve nodded. She fumbled with the clasp and safety catch.

'Here,' Bridget leaned forward, 'let me.' She smelled enticingly of an expensive perfume. At close quarters her skin was flawless. She undid the choker expertly and held it round her neck. 'It doesn't suit my dress,' she decided.

Genevieve agreed. Bridget's gown was prudishly high necked. 'You need one like mine. Off the shoulder style.' She hiccupped suddenly and giggled. 'You've put something in my drink.'

'I have not.' Bridget sounded offended. 'Come on now, let me see what I'd look like in the choker and your dress.'

Well, why not? Genevieve felt in an obliging mood. She stood up. The bracelet clasp was easier than the choker. She removed it and dangled it in front of Bridget, finally dropping it in her lap. She began to peel off her gloves, slowly.

Bridget found a remote control and suddenly the room was filled with a rhythmic slow beat. 'Let's do it properly.' Bridget laughed. 'D'you think you'd make a good stripper?'

'You tell me,' Genevieve invited.

She had never stripped to music before, and normally she would have been embarrassed to try. But now she felt confident and relaxed. She let the music talk to her and it affected her in a surprising way. She felt sexy and liberated. She reached for the back zip and pulled it down. The dress opened, falling to her waist. Genevieve put her hands over her breasts in mock modesty but the movements of her hips, gyrating to the drum beat, sent the dress slithering to the floor. Stepping out of it, she waited for an appropriate moment in the music to hand it, with a flourish, to Bridget. The music stopped, almost on cue.

'Well?' she asked. 'Have I passed the audition?'

'Let's say, you're promising.' Bridget stood up. 'But much too fast. If you had a male audience you'd have finished before most of them had a chance to get a hard-on. You've got to tease. Wind them up, make them wait. And never stand still. You could have done something better with the gloves, too. A good stripper will make everything she takes off sexy. She doesn't need any of that crude stuff with snakes or bananas to turn her audience on.'

Genevieve was not sure whether to be annoyed or amused that Bridget was taking her performance seriously.

'All right, expert,' she challenged. 'Show me.'

Bridget pressed the remote control again. The music that came out of the speakers this time was harder and more insistent, a real stripper's beat. It seemed so appropriate that Genevieve wondered if Bridget had prepared the tape in advance.

And Bridget was a sensation as a stripper. Genevieve could not believe that this was the same haughty beauty she had smiled at across the dining table earlier that evening. Dancing with professional grace, Bridget made every move erotic. She removed her dress as if she was making love to it. She strutted in her dark-blue lacy underwear. She rolled her stockings down to her knees.

Genevieve felt her own body moving in time to the beat, and her feet tapping. The thought of watching another woman undress had never excited her before, but now she felt a distinct tension waiting for each item to be removed and tossed away. She realised how a man must feel, wanting to both prolong and end the teasing.

Bridget's naked breasts were firm and round and, Genevieve

thought surprising herself, really rather attractive. Standing close to Genevieve's chair, Bridget worked on her panties. She turned her back and began to rotate her hips suggestively, pushing the flimsy lace garment down to her knees, stepping out of one leg, then the other, tossing the panties into the air on cue to a crash of cymbals. Naked except for her rolled-down stockings and high-heeled shoes she reached out to Genevieve. 'Come on, darling, show me what you've learned. Dance with me.'

It was then that Genevieve knew she could say no and leave, and that would be that. If she stayed, she was committed. She would experience what would be for her an entirely new way of sex. Did she want to stay? Bridget was still swaying in front of her, smiling – her rounded body an unknown territory, but not a threatening one.

Yes, Genevieve decided, she wanted to know what it was like to feel those smooth curves, to know how a man felt when he caressed a woman. To know how James Sinclair felt when his hands explored her. She stood up and began to move to the music, closer to Bridget. They were together and yet separate, deliberately avoiding contact to begin with until Bridget put her hands on Genevieve's shoulders, pulled her close, and kissed her full on the lips.

It was a long kiss and it left them both a little breathless. Their bodies were touching now, in unexpected places. Genevieve felt Bridget's hard nipples brushing her skin. Felt her own touch Bridget. Bridget's mouth moved lightly over Genevieve's neck and travelled downwards. The music stopped.

'Let's make love,' Bridget said softly.

She bent down and picked up the remote control, and a different kind of music flowed from the speakers, gentle chords and a dreamy saxophone. Genevieve thought it was too convenient to be accidental.

'You planned this,' she accused, smiling.

'Well, sort of,' Bridget admitted. 'You never know if you're going to meet someone you like. Do you mind?'

'I've never been seduced by a woman before.'

'There's a first time for everything,' Bridget said. 'And this is yours, darling.'

Stretched out langourously on the bed, Genevieve kicked off her shoes. Bridget's fingers hooked under the elastic top of her knickers, gently slid them down and tossed them on the floor.

'Oh,' Bridget murmured, 'you shave. That's nice. I like that.'

Her mouth traced lingering patterns from Genevieve's neck to her breasts, drawing circles round the hardening peaks with the tip of her tongue. Genevieve felt warm tremors of pleasure course through her.

Bridget worked slowly on her body, seeking out all the special places that women know but men often can't be bothered to discover, licking and stroking unhurriedly, watching Genevieve for indications of sexual excitement. If Genevieve moaned or sighed Bridget lingered there. She seemed content to give pleasure rather than receive it.

But Genevieve also wanted to give, and the gradual arousal of her body was making it difficult for her to simply stay passive. She reached out and found the softness of Bridget's breasts. Giving in to an uncontrolled urge she fastened her mouth on a nipple and sucked gently, coaxing the pink tip into an even harder peak with light flicking movements of her tongue. Bridget groaned deep in her throat, offering herself to Genevieve, and Genevieve surprised herself by responding fully to the invitation.

They explored each other in an uninhibited orgy of sensation. Genevieve revelled in discovering new erotic pathways on Bridget's supple body, delighted in the small noises she drew from the other woman, shivered with delight as Bridget's mouth and fingers traced patterns over her own skin. Then Bridget's hand stroked gently between her legs.

'Darling,' Bridget murmered, 'you're so wet.'

She slid downward and suddenly Genevieve felt a warm tongue lapping her with soft caresses. The effect was instant. Bridget knew exactly how to tease her clit into full erection, how to prolong the intense agony of pleasure, and how finally to release it. Genevieve's back arched as the delicious spasms of her orgasm shook her, mounting to a climax and then subsiding gently.

She lay on the bed for a moment, recovering, feeling that she should offer Bridget the same pleasure, but for a hesitant moment she wondered whether she could actually use her mouth on another woman. She had never had any reservations about performing this service on a man. In fact the way she felt now she could have cheerfully taken James Sinclair's cock in her mouth and given it the full treatment, forcing him to the brink of release and then torturing him by refusing to oblige. She wondered how long he could control himself then, how long it would be before he groaned for relief. The thought excited her. Her encounter with Bridget had made her feel incredibly sexy.

Then she realised that Bridget had taken matters into her own hands, literally. With her eyes closed and her face tense with delight, Bridget brought herself to a manual climax that seemed every bit as satisfying and tumultuous as Genevieve's own. Opening her eyes again she smiled at Genevieve. 'Sorry, darling. Couldn't wait.'

They lay for another ten minutes in sleepy companionship, then Bridget sat up. 'We can't stay here forever. Duty calls. I'm going to have a shower, unless you want one first? You can use any of my things. Try the body spray, it's gorgeous.'

Showered and dressed, Bridget became once again a glacial

and haughty beauty. She helped Genevieve zip up her dress and fix the diamond choker round her neck.

'Playtime's over,' she said. 'Let's go and find the men.'

Genevieve found James Sinclair more quickly than she expected. He was waiting in the corridor, smoking a thin cheroot. Bridget looked at him archly.

'Not dancing, Mr Sinclair?'

'You've got my partner,' he said.

'Not any more,' Bridget replied.

Sinclair smiled slowly. 'Playtime's over, is it?' he drawled, from behind a blue curtain of smoke.

'For now,' Bridget said. She smiled at Genevieve: 'Maybe we'll get together again sometime, darling?'

She swept regally down the corridor. It took a minute for Genevieve to realise what the brief conversation implied.

'You bastard!' She turned on Sinclair, furiously. 'You've been watching us.'

'Well, of course,' he said. 'Didn't you guess?'

'No, I didn't.' She knew now that she should have. No wonder Bridget's hi-fi played such appropriate music.

'When I pay for something I expect to get full value.' He paused. 'And Bridget doesn't come cheap.'

'Do you mean she's a – well – a professional?' Genevieve stumbled over her words, more from disbelief than embarrassment.

'A whore?' Sinclair smiled. 'But of course. And a very expensive one. She used to be a dancer, Royal Ballet I believe, but the pay was terrible, so she took up stripping. Then she found that selling sex was a good way to make a lot of money fast. She won't be doing it for much longer, though. When she's saved enough she's going to open a riding school.'

'What kind of a hotel is this?' Genevieve demanded. 'Are there two-way mirrors in all the rooms?'

'Not in any of them,' he said. 'There are other, less obvious ways of accommodating voyeurs. This is a Victorian hotel. The Victorians were quite subtle about their spy holes.' He drew on the cheroot and blew a cloud of pale smoke into the air. 'I hope you remember those tips Bridget gave you about stripping. That wasn't just for fun. I like to get full value on my investments. Practise at home. You're going to give me a private performance before too long, and I expect it to be good.' He stubbed out the cheroot in an ashtray. 'Come on, let's try a different kind of dancing.'

She enjoyed the rest of the evening, its formality contrasting strangely with the sexual adventures she had participated in, but at the back of her mind anger was smouldering. She was not worried about Bridget. A professional of her standing would certainly be discreet, but Sinclair had put her in a dangerous position in the corridor. If anyone had seen her and recognised her the publicity could have ruined her. He had broken the rules of their contract. She was determined to have it out with him.

The last waltz finally came and went and Sinclair guided her off the dance floor. Genevieve saw the stately Margaret coming towards them. Her blue eyes were bright and enquiring.

'Did you enjoy yourself, my dear?'

'Very much, thank you,' Genevieve admitted, wondering what Margaret would say if she knew exactly what kind of enjoyment she had experienced that evening.

'Everything went very well,' Sinclair said. 'Thanks to you, Margaret.'

'I may be old,' Margaret said, 'but I haven't lost my touch.'

They both laughed, and Genevieve suspected they were sharing a private joke, but she had no idea what it could be. She waited until she was in Sinclair's car before confronting him.

'You broke the rules of our agreement.'

He slipped the Mercedes into gear and moved smoothly away from the kerb. 'I never break agreements.'

'You promised that whatever you made me do no one would recognise me,' she reminded him. 'And then you stripped me in a public corridor and – well –' She faltered, remembering that she reached a point where she had all but forgotten the chance of discovery. 'You know what you did,' she finished lamely.

'Gave you one of the best orgasms you've ever had,' he agreed. 'Made even better because you were so tensed up about being seen. Because secretly you wanted to be seen.'

'I did *not*,' she snapped back angrily.

'Oh, not recognised,' he admitted, 'but seen. That really turns you on. Admit it.'

She was not going to admit anything of the sort, although she knew it was true. 'You promised I'd never be put in that position,' she accused.

'I kept my promise,' he said. She started to protest but he silenced her. 'There was no chance of you being seen or recognised. The whole first floor was booked for members of the Order and their guests.'

'And I suppose you'd asked them all personally not to appear in the corridor while we were there?' she challenged acidly.

'I didn't,' he said. 'Margaret arranged it. And made sure no one came up the stairs until we were safely in our room.'

'*Margaret?*' Genevieve could hardly believe it.

He smiled. 'Didn't you get her reference to tradition?'

She stared at him. 'What exactly *is* this Grand Order of the Knights of the Banner, Mr Sinclair?' It was her best boardroom voice.

He slowed down at a set of lights and stopped. 'A genuine

charitable order that does a lot of good work,' he said. 'The story is that when the Order was founded, over ninety per cent of its members were so straight and conventional you could have drawn squares with them. The others,' the Mercedes slid forward again, 'were maybe a little less so. When these particular Victorians grew bored with too many long meetings, they arranged to slip away for some fun and games upstairs. All very discreet. The girls were well paid if they were pros, and those that weren't just had a good time. Over the years it became a tradition. It still is. We always use the first floor and all the little conveniences that those Victorian adventurers arranged for their personal entertainment.'

'Like the spy holes?' Genevieve kept her voice cool and disapproving. 'I just can't believe Margaret approved any of this, let alone helped you.'

'You've misjudged Margaret,' Sinclair said. 'She loves to be involved. She's the one who recommended Bridget.' He turned his head slightly and grinned. 'She also thought you might make a pretty good stripper, with practise. She loved your other performance, too. And don't worry,' he added quickly when he sensed she was about to protest, 'Margaret's the soul of discretion. She's had a lifetime's practice. She was a star performer on the first floor in her youth.'

The package that fell through Genevieve's letterbox the following morning contained a single cassette tape with two words printed on the cover: REHEARSAL MUSIC. When she slipped it into the hi-fi the first tune to beat out from the speakers was the David Rose classic: 'The Stripper'.

5

Alone in her flat, Geneviere was practising her striptease. Pictures of Sinclair filled her mind, and when her phone rang, she was certain that it would be him. The thought of speaking to him while she was stripping made her feel sexy. She picked up her mobile abruptly, one hand behind her back searching for the hook on her bra.

'Hallo, big sister. How's life?'

'My life's fine,' she said, taking her hand off her bra and making an effort not to sound disappointed. 'What's the problem?'

There was a pause. 'Why should I have a problem?'

'Why else do you ring me?'

'Well, that's charming,' Philip said. 'I think I'll ring off.'

'OK,' she said. And waited.

'It's my girlfriend,' Philip said. 'She's ditched me.'

'The one you had the nice cut and dried sex contract with?'

'Well, I wouldn't put it like that. The one I thought I'd squared things with, yes.'

'What was wrong this time? Not politically incorrect again?'

'Worse.' Philip paused dramatically. 'She said I was boring.'

'But I thought you agreed on a programme of fun and games?'

'That's why she said I was boring. She said it was like having sex to a timetable. She said I wasn't spontaneous.' Philip sounded genuinely hurt. 'And I thought that was what she wanted. To be consulted. I respected her opinions.' He added accusingly: 'What exactly *do* you women want from men? You're a woman. Tell me the secret.'

'If I could answer that I'd write a book and make a fortune,' Genevieve said. 'We're all different, little brother. You have to play it by ear.'

'That's a great help,' Philip said. 'How do I get some decent sex, that's what I want to know?'

'Pay for it,' Genevieve suggested.

'You're joking!' Philip sounded horrified.

'I'm sorry,' Genevieve said innocently. 'Is that politically incorrect too?'

'It's disgusting. That's what dirty old men do. Or wimpy nerds who can't get a woman any other way.'

'Actually it isn't,' Genevieve said. 'It's often what men do when they've got a special need that they can't find anyone to satisfy. Which sounds a bit like you.'

'You make me sound like a pervert,' Philip said. 'All I want is a no-strings relationship with a girl who's willing to lie there and let me do things to her while she's helpless. Or pretending to be helpless. I'd even tie her hands very loosely so she could get away easily if she wanted to. And I don't want someone who's doing it for money, or playing "let's pretend". I'd actually like her to enjoy it too. I'm sorry if you find that a bit shocking, but I don't think it's too much to ask.'

'I don't find the tying-up bit shocking,' Genevieve said. 'It's the fact that you seem to be more interested in sex than a loving relationship that bothers me.'

'Don't get all old-fashioned on me, sis. I know women have got minds and feelings and all that. I'm surrounded by female students all day, for God's sake, and most of them are feminists. But there are times when I don't want to discuss political theory or environmental problems. Or be a shoulder to cry on. Or be good friends. There are times when I just want to – well – have sex.'

'Perhaps when you want to make love,' Genevieve said, 'you'll have better luck.'

'A lot of help you are,' Philip said. And rang off.

Genevieve put the phone down and smiled. But she did wonder if she was really a hypocrite to lecture her brother on love. What would he say if he knew the kind of relationship she was currently involved in? Sinclair had already accused her of selling herself, and she supposed that it would look like that to Philip too. The fact that she now felt comfortable with Sinclair, and couldn't imagine indulging in any of the sexual adventures that he arranged with anyone else was a bonus. She had been lucky. Her business arrangement had turned into a pleasure-filled adventure.

But would it last beyond the ninety days?

The morning had dragged on longer than normal. Genevieve had been closeted with a particularly argumentative client who disagreed with virtually everything she suggested and whose ideas seemed to Genevieve to be 50 years out of date. She sighed with relief when he had gone, and went to get herself a cup of coffee.

On the way back she passed two colleagues gossiping about their holiday. Snippets of conversation followed her.

'. . . there were bare tits everywhere . . . so I thought, why not? I felt silly with my top still on.'

'My boyfriend didn't want me to strip off with all those gorgeous Latin types around, the jealous sod! So of course, I did . . .'

Genevieve continued on down the corridor, trying not to spill her coffee. Would she go topless? Before she met Sinclair she would have known her answer to that. But he had given her a strange new of confidence in her body. Because he was turned on by her, she felt powerful and sexy.

When she reached her office and sat down again she carried on her fantasy. She was on a golden beach, wearing only an indecently tiny white triangle of cloth held up by narrow ties, one round her waist and the other pulled between her buttocks. She was walking, confident strides, her feet sinking into the warm sand, her breasts jiggling provocatively, her hair loose. She was walking towards Sinclair.

He was lying down, watching her, wearing black briefs made of silky material that accentuated the shape of his balls and his semi-erect prick. His briefs were held together by tiny silver buckles on each side. As she drew closer she saw his cock move and swell, straining to be free.

There were other men on the beach, all wearing bathing trunks as tight (but so not well filled) as Sinclair's. They whistled at her as she passed, told her in detail what they'd like to do to her, reached out for her. She ignored them. She knew where she was going. When she reached Sinclair – and she took her time – she stood over him, astride him. The other men gathered round, silent now, forming a circle, watching.

Genevieve loosened the thong, removed it, tossed it away. She ran her hands down her thighs, then smoothed them over her buttocks, palms flat. Below her, Sinclair released the buckles on his briefs, and when he peeled the cloth away his erect prick was every bit as excitingly massive as she remembered. He slowly got to his knees, the muscles in his slim and powerful body moving under his tanned skin. He knelt in front of her, reached out to touch her. She knocked his hands away and pointed. She wanted his mouth, his lips, his tongue. She reached out and grasped his head, pulling him forward.

The image in Genevieve's mind was so arousing that she

almost groaned. She felt moist and uncomfortable. On an impulse she got up and locked her office door.

Back in her chair again she let her mind return to the fantasy. Her hand slid along her thigh. She had always preferred stockings to tights and now her fingers moved from their silky smoothness to her warm skin, and under the elastic of her panties. She touched herself, gently at first, then urgently, rubbing her wet sex, her finger sliding, finding the rhythm she wanted. It wasn't as good as Sinclair's tongue, but it was good. She groaned again.

The picture in her mind changed. Now Sinclair was standing over her. He watched her, smiling that exciting, possessive smile, his eyes travelling over her body, taking their time, down to her open thighs. She rubbed faster, imagining the pleasure and sexual excitement that would show in his eyes. She caressed her swollen clit, and then her body shuddered as the orgasmic spasms rolled over her, claiming her, for a moment making time stand still.

Afterwards, she lay relaxed and limp in the chair, wishing Sinclair was with her, and wondering exactly where he was, who he was with. She did not want to think about Jade Chalfont, but deliberately trying not to do so was like being told not to think of a pink elephant.

She pictured Sinclair with other women. She pictured them dancing for him, and stripping. She pictured them tied to the door in his study while he tortured them to a frenzy with his tongue and his hands. She pictured women lying beneath him, or on top of him; women moaning in sexual delight as his strong, slim body forced them to new heights of pleasure. She groaned softly. The pictures were infuriating, but arousing.

She told herself she was not jealous. There was no future in getting serious about a man like James Sinclair. It was ridiculous to be jealous. She knew she could please him sexually, but their partnership was a business deal. And she also knew that if she was sensible she would keep it that way. If he knew her feelings were starting to get personal he would either drop her or take advantage of her. Either way she would get hurt. She would lose control.

She stood up, smoothed her skirt and went down to the washroom. When she returned George Fullerton was sitting on the edge of her desk.

'I brought you a coffee,' he said.

'Thanks, George, but I've just had one.'

'You haven't,' he said. He pointed to her cup. 'It's gone cold.'

Genevieve felt herself blushing. 'Oh, yes. I forgot it was there.'

'Thinking about work?' Fullerton asked.

'In a manner of speaking,' she said.

'Thinking about Mr Sinclair?'

A warning bell began to ring in Genevieve's mind. She knew George too well not to realise that this was leading up to something. 'Why should I be?' she countered, lightly.

'I heard you'd been seeing him,' Fullerton said. 'Socially, that is.' He paused. 'An antiques fair? Am I right? Rather an exclusive one. Something to do with one of Sinclair's super-rich pals?'

'You're ahead of me, George,' Genevieve said. 'I met the man who arranged the fair, but I didn't know he was one of Sinclair's friends. We didn't talk much. It was just a rather nice afternoon out.'

'Did Sinclair mention going to Japan?'

This time Genevieve was genuinely surprised. 'No, he didn't. But we didn't really talk business.'

'Well, it could be just gossip,' Fullerton admitted. 'But there's a strong rumour that Sinclair is planning to expand into Japan. If he does, and we get his account, we'll expand with him.'

'George,' she said, 'I'm certain Sinclair is going bring his account to us. If he really does have his eye on the Japanese market, he'll probably wait until his plans are finalised before he makes a move.'

'I agree,' Fullerton said. 'And it would explain why he's taking so long, and playing the field.' He paused and smiled at Genevieve, but his eyes were shrewd and hard. 'Don't forget that Lucci's have Jade Chalfont, and she's something of an expert on Japan.'

'She does kendo,' Genevieve said. 'That hardly makes her an expert.'

'She's lived in Japan,' Fullerton said. 'Trained there. She even speaks the language. That makes her a pretty useful contact.'

'You seem to know a lot about her,' Genevieve said.

'I make it my business to find out,' Fullerton replied.

'Who from?'

'That's classified.' He smiled, and walked towards the door. 'But people gossip. I've found there's nearly always some truth in rumours. If I was you, I'd check out this Japanese thing. Otherwise Miss Chalfont might end up one step ahead of you.'

Genevieve relaxed in her bath trying to think about Japan. The idea conjured up pictures of dark-suited businessmen bowing formally to each other. Businessmen who would later relax in the intimate privacy of the geisha houses, drink saki and be entertained by the highly trained and beautiful geisha who worked there.

She knew the geisha claimed not to be prostitutes, and maybe this was true for some of them, but for others surely the entertaining of their rich clients did not just stop at plucking the *koto* and singing a few songs. She remembered reading somewhere that the geisha's traditionally stiff-collared kimono was designed so that when the women knelt submissively at her lord and master's feet, the garment stood proud of her neck and formed the entrance to a tunnel that gave the man an uninterrupted view down the sweep of her spine to the cleft in her buttocks and the shadowy hint of what was beyond.

From there he would presumably lean forward and maybe caress the white smoothness of the girl's neck. Or perhaps make her sit up so he could open the kimono front wider to inspect her breasts. Or maybe unwind the stiff sash and strip her there and then. And she would bow her head and smile, Genevieve thought. And maybe even say thank you as her gentleman stroked and fondled. The perfect uncomplaining female, ready and willing to play. Would Sinclair enjoy that kind of hospitality if he went to Japan? Would his Japanese business friends make sure he experienced all the traditional sights of their country? A visit to a Zen monastery or a Shinto shrine by day; a geisha house at night?

The thought of Sinclair enjoying a submissively beautiful Japanese woman made her angry. Would the geisha be trained to use special erotic tricks? Would she find it exciting to practise them on Sinclair? Genevieve imagined the contrast between Sinclair's lean and muscular body and a delicately tiny Japanese girl. Imagined the geisha's expert mouth and hands turning him on. She had read that Japanese women did not find large Westerners particularly attractive, although she was sure a geisha would hide her personal feelings and give good value for money. Would Sinclair find the geisha desirable? Genevieve thought so. There was something subtle and erotic about their pale faces, their glossy hair, their traditional costumes – and the idea that their purpose in life was to please men.

Sinclair would love that, she thought crossly. Any man

would. The idea that women were actively trying to turn them on was both flattering and arousing. That was why they liked watching a striptease, wasn't it? They were pretending that the performer was doing it just for them. Genevieve had played the tape Sinclair had sent her many times, and had even tried dancing to it, but somehow she always felt awkward. Even swallowing several glasses of wine and imagining Sinclair watching her did not help her to loosen up.

In her imagination she could perform like a shameless sexual tease, pirouetting and posing, peeling away her dress and underwear, flouting her semi-naked body, writhing to the music's beat. In her imagination Sinclair watched her with increasing discomfort and finally had to unzip his trousers and drag her towards his lap before her dance had ended.

But when she tried to translate her imagination into action her body refused to behave in the way she wanted. Her stripping routine was awkward and amateur, very far from the fluid eroticism of Bridget's apparently effortless performance. A performance that he had found exciting.

She realised that she wanted to please Sinclair. She suspected that he did not think she was capable of performing with Bridget's professional aplomb. She wanted to prove him wrong, partly because she wanted him to find her sexy. At least, sexier than Jade Chalfont, or any of the other women he knew.

The idea of having dancing lessons came to her as she picked at her lunch the following day. Obviously she could never hope to compete with a trained dancer but she felt certain that she could benefit from the advice of a teacher. The problem was that dance teachers did not advertise themselves as striptease instructors. She decided she would pretend to be an amateur actress looking for private lessons to help her prepare for the part of a stripper in her next play. Giving a false name she phoned several addresses, meeting with a variety of responses, from some bemused but kindly meant suggestions that although the school did not deal in striptease dancing they were sure that something could be worked out, to a snooty 'we only teach ballet' and an avaricious 'sure we can teach you, but it's not on our curriculum so it'll be expensive'.

She finally decided on the Academy of Dance and Mime, where the response was first to ask her some questions about her age and experience and then to suggest that although the school did not exactly teach striptease they could probably work out a routine for her, or help her polish the steps she was already using.

Dressed casually in jeans and a loose shirt, her hair tied back, and her costume in a bag, she drove out to the suburbs to find the dancing academy she had chosen. It turned out to be a large Victorian house set well back in its own grounds, once grand but now slightly seedy, its woodwork in need of a new coat of paint. The drive was neatly kept though, and when the front door was opened she was pleasantly surprised by the smiling, middle-aged woman who greeted her.

'Miss Jones? Please come in.'

The woman had a slight foreign accent and, although she was older than Genevieve had expected, her dark, smooth-fitting dress revealed her figure to be supple and elegant. If she did not dance much now, Genevieve thought, she had certainly danced in the past. Her hair was swept back in a bun, ballerina style.

She led Genevieve into a studio that had obviously been formed by knocking out several of the ground-floor walls. There were practice bars and mirrors, and the floor was beautifully polished wood. A piano stood in one corner.

'I'm Theodosia Solinski,' the woman said. 'Please call me simply Thea. You must tell me exactly how I can help you.' She smiled. 'Usually I teach little girls whose mothers believe they will surely soon be world-class ballerinas.'

Genevieve smiled back. 'I take it for most of them it's just a dream?'

'For all of them,' Thea said. 'But I sympathise. Even for me it proved to be so. Therefore, I teach. But it is good to dream.'

'All I want', Genevieve explained, sticking closely to the story she had made up for herself, 'is to look convincing when I play the part of a stripper in this play I'm in. I've tried dancing to the music we're using, but I know it doesn't look right.'

'Stripping is an art,' Thea said, surprising Genevieve, who had imagined a teacher as traditional-looking as Thea might have treated her request for advice with some disdain. 'Many women, even the so-called professionals, do it very badly. They are in love with themselves. They strip for themselves. They care nothing about their audience. Their performance lacks passion. Or else they are bored. They run from one seedy club to another and perform for ten minutes while they think about their shopping list. Which one are you?'

Genevieve was startled for a moment. Then she remembered her cover story. 'Oh, you mean in the play? I have to strip for a man I love, or rather someone I want to fall in love with me.'

'A seduction?' Thea nodded. 'You have your music?' She took the tape Genevieve gave her. 'I will listen. While it plays maybe you will show me what you have already prepared? You don't have to take off your clothes. Just go through the moves.'

When the music started Genevieve tried to obey, but she felt repressed and awkward knowing that Thea was watching.

'Relax, please,' Thea instructed. After a few minutes she added: 'Would you prefer to strip properly? Have you brought your costume?'

Genevieve suddenly felt embarrassed at the thought of undressing in front of this elegant woman.

'I ... er ... well ... maybe later,' she mumbled, blushing. 'It's just the steps I want to learn, really.'

Thea gave her an uncompromising stare. 'I think the idea of performing for another woman disturbs you. But there will be women in your audience, when you perform your play. And this is not a real striptease. I do not expect to see you naked. Just dance. Dance!'

She turned the music up. The sexy beat throbbed out. Genevieve tried to obey. She did not really understand what was the matter with her, but she felt clumsy and tense. Maybe this dancing lesson had not been such a good idea after all. Thea switched the tape off.

'I think it would be better if you put on your costume,' she suggested. 'It will put you in the correct mood. Perhaps it is difficult to feel sexy in jeans. I will show you the changing-room.'

But coming back into the studio in her dress, seamed stockings and high-heeled shoes did not make Genevieve feel better. She still had to perform under the sharp professional eyes of Thea Solinski. That was what was bothering her, not her clothes. She tried to dance again, and stumbled.

'Maybe my shoes are too high,' she commented.

'Your shoes are fine,' Thea said. She switched off the music. 'Your attitude is the problem. Have you ever made love to a woman?'

Totally thrown by the question, Genevieve could only stammer: 'No, of course not.' She knew she was blushing.

Thea smiled. 'That answers my question. You have had an affair, or maybe just a single encounter. And you are ashamed of it. Why?'

'I'm not ashamed,' Genevieve objected. 'It was just something that happened. I prefer men.'

'As I do,' Thea nodded. 'But I have had two affairs with

women. They enriched my life.' She smiled briefly. 'My sex life, too. I think you are afraid to let yourself relax in front of me because you remember your encounter and you feel guilty. Maybe you think you encouraged the other woman, or maybe you are just ashamed that you enjoyed it. But these things are part of life. I do not believe anyone is completely heterosexual. Many people do nothing physical about their desires, or even want to, but nearly everyone can appreciate the beauty of their own sex. Is this shameful? I think not. It's natural.' She switched the tape on again. 'Forget about me. Think about your own man, or if you do not have one think of someone you like, an actor, anyone. Pretend he is watching. Perform for him.'

Did she really feel guilty? Genevieve wondered. Before her encounter with Bridget she had always believed that lesbian relationships were rather silly, and definitely inferior to sex with a man. Now she knew that women could give each other intense sexual pleasure. And this made stripping in front of this elegant woman – or any woman – difficult. It was no longer an innocent bit of play-acting. She would never be sure if another woman was looking at her with secret lust. And she would never be wholly sure that she did not welcome those thoughts.

Suddenly her inhibitions left her. Why shouldn't women enjoy their own bodies? Bridget had made her feel desirable. Was that so terrible? Sinclair made her feel the same way. Like Thea, she knew that she would always prefer the sexual company of a man, but she decided she was not going to go through the rest of her life nursing secret feelings of guilt because she had enjoyed an erotic adventure with a woman. So maybe Thea would find it exciting to watch her? What did it matter? It was a compliment. She should feel proud, not embarrassed.

She relaxed, and danced. She imagined Sinclair watching

her, but she was aware of Thea too. Sometimes she was rolling down her stockings and unhooking her bra for Sinclair, sometimes for Thea. It did not seem to matter. The music climaxed and Genevieve stood wearing only her high-heeled shoes and her lacy black suspender belt.

There was a long silence. Then Thea switched the tape to rewind.

'Well,' she said at last, 'you have more talent than I expected.'

'I thought about my boyfriend.' Genevieve wondered if Thea believed this half truth.

'I envy your boyfriend.' Thea's eyes wandered over Genevieve's body in frank admiration. 'But surely you will not end up like this on the amateur stage?'

For a moment, as Genevieve responded to Thea's visual caress, she had forgotten her original story. 'The stage?' She came back to the present. 'Oh, yes. I mean, no. I'll still keep a G-string on, or turn my back or something. But what I want is to dance properly. That is, sexily. To look professional.'

'Well, you won't fool a real professional,' Thea said, with brisk honesty. 'It's quite obvious you're not a trained dancer, but you will probably fool most of the audience, and the men will not be critical. They will just enjoy. But you are too quick, you do not tease enough. Let me demonstrate.'

She undid the buttons of her dress and slipped out of it. Underneath she wore a leotard and tights. Genevieve hoped that when she reached Thea's age she would still have a figure as neat and well toned. Switching on the music, Thea began to dance. As she danced, she demonstrated and talked. She did not strip. It was not necessary. She mimed, and her trained body spoke the language of seduction with every move she made.

'You see? When you take the stockings off, don't remove

them at once. Go so far, then turn like this. Show them your derrière. It's a very nice one, so display it. Then turn out your knee, bend the leg. Let them guess what they could see if you were facing them.' The first number on the tape ended. Thea beckoned to Genevieve. 'Now, you try.'

Genevieve danced again, and Thea corrected her. Her hands were light and gentle, touching an arm, a hand, sometimes sliding intimately over Genevieve's body as she guided her into a new position. Only an hour before, this would have embarrassed Genevieve, but now she accepted it, even enjoyed it. She also knew instinctively that it would not result in any further intimacies unless she offered active encouragement.

When the lesson ended Genevieve suggested booking another session, but Thea told her with friendly honesty that she did not think it was necessary. 'All you needed was to relax. Lose your inhibitions. And I believe you have done that. Now it is simply practice.' The older woman smiled slightly, her dark eyes holding Genevieve's gaze for a moment. 'However, if you wish to return, I shall not discourage you. Perhaps as a friend next time? We can have hot Russian tea.'

It was more than just a social invitation, and both women knew it. But Genevieve also knew that she could not accept. It would have been dishonest to Thea. She did not feel able to enter a relationship that she guessed the older woman would want to be more than just a quick physical fling. She could not juggle two affairs. Not, she thought suddenly, that she could really call her present situation with Sinclair an affair.

'I have a boyfriend,' she said. 'But thank you.'

'So it is goodbye.' There was a note of regret in Thea's voice. 'But I am always here for you. As a teacher. Don't forget.'

'Heard the latest?'

Genevieve turned and found herself face to face with a

grinning Ricky Croft. She also noticed the small portfolio under his arm.

'Even if I have, I'm sure you're going to repeat it,' she said. She pushed past him, her lunch-time rolls in one hand and a glass of cola in the other. The pub was half empty and she found a seat easily. Ricky sat directly opposite her.

'"East is east, is home the best?",' he said smugly.

'If you're referring to Mr Sinclair,' she bit into her roll, 'it's a rumour, that's all.'

'He'll be taking a trip very soon,' Ricky said confidently. 'And you can bet he'll find some time for pleasure.' His slim artist's hands stroked the portfolio. 'The Japanese know how to enjoy themselves. Have you seen any of their erotic prints?'

'No,' Genevieve said. 'But I've a feeling you're going to show me yours.'

'You don't want to see what Mr Sinclair could be taking with him to please his new friends?' Ricky opened the portfolio. 'These are copies, but they'll give you the idea.'

Despite herself Genevieve looked at the pages as Ricky slowly turned them, and once again she had to admire Ricky's skill. The black and white line drawings mimicked the Japanese style. They were very explicit. Japanese ladies in, and half out, of their traditional kimonos, were shown stretched out, bent over, upended and even standing on their heads, being penetrated in every available orifice by men with impressively huge penises. The women's faces looked blandly unconcerned and the men looked inscrutable. Genevieve did not find the pictures particularly arousing.

'Like them?' Ricky asked.

'No,' she said.

'Women just don't appreciate erotic art.'

'Your models all look bored,' she said.

'It's Japanese tradition,' he said. 'Perhaps they think it's impolite to look enthusiastic when they're fucking. I copied the faces from original prints.'

'So why bother?' she asked. 'It's a bit like taking coals to Newcastle.'

'Well, my stuff's more imaginative,' Ricky said. 'I bet there are some positions here the Japanese have never thought about. But these are just for the traditionalists.' He turned the pages again. 'I've got other samples for the – er – less conventional.'

He displayed more pages. Drawn in realistic Western style and looking like monochrome photographs, these pictures showed Japanese men in modern clothes with Western women, often two or three men with one woman. Although the expressions on the women's faces seemed to indicate sexual excitement, they did not give Genevieve an impression of erotic desire, but of force. There was something unhealthy about the deliberately posed excesses and the smirks on the men's faces. She felt that these men were enjoying the women's humiliations rather than the idea that they were receiving any pleasure, and that they would have continued to pursue their fantasies even if the women had objected.

In the second set of pictures the women were clearly not enjoying themselves at all. There was revulsion and horror on their faces as the men – some in Japanese World War II uniform, some in suits – tied and twisted them onto various torture racks and benches, lashed them until blood ran, and assaulted them with a variety of crudely designed sexual implements.

Genevieve reached out and slammed the portfolio shut before Ricky had shown her the extent of his collection.

'You make me sick,' she said, coldly.

He grinned crookedly. 'The Japanese love this stuff. Especially if Western women are on the receiving end.'

'There are perverts in every country,' she agreed. 'I daresay you could find a market for it over here too.'

'Sure I could.' He smirked. 'But it's difficult to find clients who'll pay my price. It takes time to do these specials. They're real collector's items.'

The idea of Ricky closeted in his bedsitter, studiously working on these pathologically sadistic pictures filled her with disgust. 'Then go and find yourself a collector,' she said. 'And do it right now. I'd like to finish my lunch without your company.'

'You mean you won't help me?'

'Help you?' She was furious. 'What the hell do you mean, help you?'

'Give my name to Sinclair,' he said.

'That's the last thing I'd do,' she said. 'I told you that before.'

'Just drop a few hints.' He leaned over the table towards her. 'You don't have to admit to having seen my work, nothing like that. Just hint that you know an artist who can supply really special pictures. Sinclair'll know what you mean.'

'Why are you so sure of that?' she asked, her anger under control now.

'He's kinky,' Ricky said. 'Everyone knows that. People like him love this kind of stuff.'

'Well, I don't know who your sources of information are,' Genevieve said. 'But it looks to me as if you're the kinky one.'

Ricky's expression changed. 'I've got bills to pay. No one'll employ me.'

'That's your fault.'

He glared at her angrily. 'Get me into Barringtons. Then I won't have to draw dirty pictures.'

'No. I've given you a chance already. I'm not giving you another one. You're unreliable. You're argumentative. You've got an inflated sense of your own importance and the word deadline doesn't feature in your vocabulary. And furthermore,' she added, when Ricky stood up, obviously furious, 'if you mention my name in connection with those drawings to anyone at all, James Sinclair included, I'll have the vice squad round at your door, double-quick time.'

Ricky backed away from the table. 'They'd laugh at you. I haven't done anything against the law.' But he sounded uncertain, and Genevieve wondered if he had some other, even less savoury, pictures stored in his room.

'Just keep away from me,' she warned. 'I don't want to see you, or any examples of your so-called art, again.'

'You're a bitch, Loften,' he said tightly. 'A first-class bitch.'

'Just go away,' she said in an icy tone.

He went, muttering insults. The meeting had ruined Genevieve's lunch hour. The memory of the pictures lingered in her mind. She found it both sickening and sad that there were people who enjoyed seeing women hurt, and gained pleasure from knowing that they were being forced into sexual humiliation and pain against their will. She was even angrier at Ricky's suggestion that Sinclair was one of those men.

She wondered again if Jade Chalfont had really given Sinclair any of Ricky's previous drawings. At least the mock Regency scenes had shown two people enjoying themselves. She remembered that she had found them arousing, and could believe that Sinclair might have liked them too. But she refused to believe that he would want to see what were, in effect, pornographic torture scenes.

She had been surprised at her own easy acceptance of Sinclair's mastery during their sexual encounters, although she did sometimes think it might be fun to occasionally reverse the roles. She had to admit that she enjoyed the sensation of being tied up. Of fantasising that he owned her – at least for the duration of their erotic games. She had enjoyed the distinctly sexy pain of the spanking she had received while straddled across the motorbike. But she always felt safe in the knowledge that they both knew that these meetings were part of a fantasy world, with unspoken rules. However much she protested on the surface, she was excited by his assumption of power. It was fun.

There had been no sense of fun in the latest batch of pictures Ricky had shown her, and she doubted if the kind of men who would pay to see them would even know what the word meant. She shook her head as if to clear the last traces of memory from her mind, picked up her bag and left the pub.

'I want you at my house tonight at eight o'clock. I'll send a taxi.'

Genevieve felt a thrill of anticipation at the sound of James Sinclair's voice but made sure that none of her excitement showed in her voice. 'And what am I to wear?'

'Whatever you like,' he said. 'As long as it includes the fur coat I gave you. You change when you get here.'

'Into what?'

She knew he was smiling, although his voice did not alter.

'Into whatever I provide for you, sweetheart. You can bring your own things, if you'd prefer it. But just remember that the emphasis on this evening's entertainment will be on getting out of your clothes. I want to see if you've been practising your dancing skills.'

'And if I haven't?' she asked.

'I'll send you home,' he said, 'and you won't get the chance to sample an excellent meal.'

'You're going to cook a meal?' She was genuinely surprised.

He laughed. 'I wouldn't inflict my cooking on my worst enemy. The meal will be delivered here, if you deserve it.'

* * *

154

'Lights.' Sinclair clicked a switch and three spotlights illumin-ated the bare floor. 'Music.' Another click and the familiar introduction to 'The Stripper' growled out of the hidden speakers. 'Do you need anything else? A chair, maybe? A mirror? You'd be surprised at the props I can provide.'

Genevieve was tempted to say 'a python', but she wasn't sure he'd even smile. He had sounded pleasant enough on the phone but he did not greet her with any show of enthusiasm and she had the distinct feeling that he doubted whether this particular evening was going to fulfil his expectations.

When she first saw him in his elegant, dark suit and a white pleat-fronted shirt she thought he had changed his mind and intended to take her out. But a quick look round proved her wrong. The room was arranged for her performance. The three spotlights were not there as decorations. A large leather-covered armchair waited in the shadows. On the small table next to it there was a bottle and one glass. Sinclair switched the spotlights off, leaving a shaded standard lamp to provide a warm glow.

'Go upstairs,' he said. 'You'll see a room with the door already open. Take anything you think you could use. Clothes, props, whatever.'

'I've brought the things I've been practising in,' she said. 'I'm used to working in them.'

She was going to say 'dancing' but changed her mind. Maybe this really was going to be work. He gave the impression that he intended to be deliberately hard to please.

'You sound very professional,' he said. 'Let's hope you look it when the music starts.'

'And you sound doubtful,' she countered.

'I don't happen to agree with Margaret that you'd make a good stripper, Miss Loften.'

'And what do I have to do to prove you wrong, *Mr* Sinclair?'

'Give me a decent hard-on for a start,' he said.

'Well, you got one at the Fennington, didn't you?' she asked. 'Spying on me through some hole in the wall, or wherever it was.'

'I got one watching Bridget,' he corrected. 'Not you.'

It was hardly an encouragement, but instead of feeling insulted Genevieve felt challenged. He turned away from her and went over to the armchair. He poured himself a drink, and sat down. The half light shadowed his already dark face. He watched her over the rim of his glass.

'Don't take too long to change,' he said.

Upstairs she was tempted by the exotic, red lace basque, a matching bra, shiny red patent shoes that had been laid out on the bed, and by a choice of sexy dresses (all with convenient zips and fasteners), but in the end she decided to use her own clothes. She felt comfortable in them. She knew exactly how they would react to her touch. The rather severe black dress could have been worn to an office social and she felt that it both suited her, and the way she performed. It gave her act a touch of class. A feeling of being in control.

She retained this feeling when she went downstairs again. Sinclair had switched off the subdued light and now the spotlights blazed. It was like stepping onto an empty stage, with an audience of one.

'Get on with it.' His voice came abruptly from the shadows, and almost at once the music started.

The lights isolated her, and their harsh brilliance was hardly flattering. She was suddenly very glad she had gone to Thea for instruction. If she hadn't she knew she would have felt disorientated and embarrassed. Sinclair's attitude was aggressive. It was as if he was willing her to fail. But Thea had given her confidence. Instead of feeling intimidated, she let the music flood over her, eased her body into its rhythm, moved with it.

Legs apart, she ran her hands over her body. She was not going to hurry. This was not going to be a quick, amateur strip, with her ending up gyrating awkwardly, naked and exposed in the glare of the lamps. She was going to take her time. She was going to remove her clothes at her own speed, and she was going to display just as much of her body as she chose. She knew how many numbers there were on the tape, and she knew just how to react to each of them. She peeled her dress off slowly to 'The Stripper' making each movement deliberate, taking her time.

Free of the dress she felt liberated. She strutted in her lacy underwear. Her panties came off but she wore a tiny G-string underneath, the thin ties drawing erotic lines round her waist and seductively down into the cleft between her buttocks.

She moved nearer to Sinclair. He was lounging back in his chair, his legs stretched out in front of him, slightly apart. She could see the glint of the brandy glass as he twisted it in his hand. She stood as near as she could without leaving the floodlit circle formed by the lamps. She took her time with the bra, loosening the straps, peeling away the gossamer thin black lace, covering her naked breasts with her hands in mock modesty, fingers splayed to let the nipples peep through.

She took even longer with the suspender belt, turning her back, bending over, rolling her stockings down to just above her knees, turning back again. She noticed that his legs were wider apart now, and his hands were still moving, but they were stroking, and no longer holding the brandy glass.

She moved out of the light and close to his chair. She straddled his outstretched legs in a position that reminded her of their last encounter in the hotel corridor. But this time she was in control. She put one foot on the arm of his chair, her hips still rolling sinuously in time with the music. She ran her hand along her thigh, toying with the ties that kept the thong in place, but leaving them still fastened, leaving the black silk triangle barely covering the faint softness of her own blonde pubic hair, which was just beginning to grow back. When she turned to move away again she felt his fingers close round her wrist. He spun her round.

'That's enough,' he said, harshly.

She pulled against him. 'The music isn't finished, Mr Sinclair.'

'You've finished dancing,' he said. 'Kneel down.'

'I've been practising for all this time,' she objected, 'and now you don't even want to see ...'

'You talk too much.' He let go of her wrist and reached for her hips, twisting his fingers into the silky ties, snapping one of them roughly as his hands pushed her to her knees. The thong fell away. Naked except for her stockings and high-heeled shoes she knelt between his legs. He unzipped his trousers and she saw that he was already huge and erect. She glanced up at him.

'I'd say this qualifies as a decent hard-on.'

'Don't waste time admiring it,' he said. 'Do something with it.'

She reached for him, hoping to tantalise him a little more before giving him relief.

He pushed her hands away. 'Use your mouth,' he said thickly. 'I want to feel your mouth. And do it slow.'

She turned her head and smoothed her lips up the length of his erection, flicking the rounded end with her tongue. She sucked, gently at first, and then harder as she felt him respond. He groaned and shifted in the chair, opening his legs wider, his hand on her head with just enough pressure to make sure she did not move away and leave him unsatisfied. She slid her mouth up and down his cock, lightly tantalising him with the edge of her teeth, teasing, watching his response, wishing that he would let her use her hands as well. He groaned again. She moved her head and caressed his balls with her lips and tongue.

Suddenly he pushed his hands under her arms, lifting her up, her legs widely straddled across him. Pleasuring him had turned her on and she was already deliciously wet. His hand explored between her legs.

'You're ready for it, aren't you?' His voice was hoarse with excitement. 'Really turns you on, doesn't it, someone watching you. Can't wait to be fucked, can you?'

She caught his prick in her hand, and felt it hard and throbbing under her sliding fingers. 'How long do you think *you* can wait?' she asked.

He let her handle him for a few more moments, but she could feel his body begin to shake.

'Not much longer,' he admitted. 'God, you'll have to stop doing that. I don't want to come yet.'

She let go of him and waited as his breathing steadied. He put his hands on her bottom and pulled her towards him, guiding her onto his shaft, pushing his own hips forward. It wasn't the most comfortable position but she began to move with him.

'That's good,' he said, softly. 'That's really good.' His eyes were half closed and as she thrust towards him she was able to watch his face. His expression reflected the pleasure he was feeling, the pleasure she was giving him. She really felt like a stripper obliging a member of the audience. In her mind there were others round her, watching. The fact that she was naked and he was fully clothed made the mental picture even more erotic.

'Keep it slow,' he murmured. 'Make it last.'

She was willing to try and prolong his pleasure, but she could already feel his body begin to shake, and suddenly he cried out and pulled her closer. For once he did not consider her needs. He thrust into her, intent on his own satisfaction, but she found this lack of control arousing. It fitted her fantasy scenario. It was her job to give, not receive.

Nevertheless she was near to orgasm when he came. He cried out again, and she felt him plunge even deeper inside her, while his body convulsed in spasms of pleasure. Her own sensations, robbed of their climax, subsided slowly as he withdrew. His breathing gradually returned to normal. There was a sheen of perspiration on his face.

Genevieve eased herself into a standing position and watched as he zipped his trousers and pulled himself up in the armchair.

'I hope you're satisfied, sir?' she said, lightly.

'And if I'm not?' he asked. 'Are you going to get me hard and start all over again?'

'Your wish is my desire.' She bobbed a mock curtsy and he grinned.

'Be careful with your promises,' he said. 'I recover fast. But you needn't worry. Right now I'd like a drink.' He pointed to a cabinet. 'You can pour me another brandy and then get yourself something from over there.'

She obeyed, bringing a bottle of wine and a glass back with her. He watched her as she sat in a chair opposite him. He was staring at her intently and she felt strangely disconcerted, wondering what was going on in his mind.

'I think I'll keep you here,' he said, his eyes moving lazily over her naked body. 'Stripped and ready. While you're waiting for me to come home and fuck you, you can do the housework. Does that sound good to you?'

She realised, much to her own surprise, that she thought it

sounded fine. At least, as a fantasy. The idea of belonging to him was increasingly attractive, and this knowledge suddenly disturbed her. These fantasies might be fun, but this was still strictly a business deal. She was in danger of letting her emotions blur her common sense. If she was not careful she could end the ninety days by being badly hurt.

James Sinclair was obviously not a man about to involve himself seriously with any woman. He had the money, the contacts and the free time to indulge himself in his own particular brand of sexual play acting. He had probably arranged these adventures before, and would undoubtedly do so again when another woman either attracted him or needed something from him. There was no reason for her to suppose that she meant anything special to him. When he had finished with her, she could expect nothing more than what he had already promised: a signature. He would walk right out of her life without a second thought.

It was ridiculous of her to expect anything else. He was cultured enough to make their meetings civilised, but she had to accept the fact that to James Sinclair she was nothing more than an erotic toy, someone to be stripped for his pleasure and used in his fantasies.

Sometimes when he looked at her she thought there was more than just lust in his gaze, but looking at him now, lounging back in the leather armchair, she decided that it was simply her imagination.

'I hate doing housework,' she said.

He laughed. 'All right, forget the housework. Do the cooking instead.'

'I presume you like burnt toast?' she countered.

'Isn't there anything at all that you're good at, Miss Loften?' The tone of his voice was still light and teasing. 'Apart from servicing me?'

It was tempting to believe that he was really interested in learning more about her, but she discounted the idea. He was just playing games. She deliberately kept her voice cool, determined to remind him that she had not forgotten why they were together. To remind him that they were not lovers, seeking to learn more about each other. This was strictly business.

'I've been told that I'm very good at my job,' she said. She saw his expression change and knew that she had made her point.

'Of course,' he said softly. 'Your job. This is part of it, isn't it?'

'That was the arrangement,' she reminded him.

'That's right,' he said. 'I suppose I shouldn't complain. We're two of a kind, you and I. We both know what we want and we're willing to pay whatever it takes to get it.' He paused. 'Or that's what you'd like me to believe, isn't it?'

'I'll do whatever it takes,' she agreed.

'I wonder if that's really true?' His dark eyes surveyed her curiously. 'Would you really do absolutely anything I asked?'

The look on his face made her suddenly nervous. Was he planning to test her? To try and find something she would refuse to do? She knew that there were plenty of sexual games she would not enjoy playing. She remembered a friend once telling her about some activities she indulged in with her current boyfriend, and which she euphemistically described as 'water sports'. Genevieve had innocently believed this involved sex in a swimming pool, or maybe the bath, and had been genuinely repelled by her friend's unashamed account of the actual details. She had not found them remotely erotic, although her friend obviously did, and had even suggested that Genevieve might like to make up a threesome.

What would she do if Sinclair asked her to get involved in

something like that? She looked at him, relaxing in the armchair, elegant in his black suit. He looked infuriatingly self-assured. So far she had enjoyed everything he had suggested, but what if he asked her to do something she found, if not totally repugnant, at least unpleasant. Would she agree, if he insisted? Did the completion of her business deal mean that much to her? She was not sure. This was unmapped territory. How far would she really go to get what she wanted?

Sinclair seemed unaware of her inner turmoil. He surveyed her for a few seconds more, then smiled.

'I promised you a meal, didn't I? Do you like Chinese?'

'I love it,' she said, with genuine enthusiasm.

'Good.' He looked round the room. 'I think we'll eat in here.'

She went to pick up her dress. 'I'll go and get dressed.'

'No,' he said. 'You stay as you are.' He grinned suddenly. 'But you'd better keep out of the way when the caterers arrive. I wouldn't want Mr Ho and his friends to be shocked.'

She waited upstairs while the food was delivered, listening to the vague hum of voices in the room below. The upper corridor of Sinclair's house was deeply carpeted and pleasantly warm. She wandered about, pushing open doors and peeping into rooms. Two were obviously guest bedrooms, the others were clearly unused. Wherever Sinclair slept, it was not on this floor.

She wondered what his bedroom would be like. A huge water bed? A fourposter? Mirrors on the ceiling? Erotic prints on the walls? Her imagination began to run riot. A brass bedstead with chains so that he could spreadeagle his latest girlfriend and indulge himself in whatever sex play he fancied? She had surprised herself by enjoying the sensation of helplessness when he had tied her to the door during their first meeting. What would it be like tied to a bed? What would he do? Would he have a collection of exotic sex toys? Or a collection of whips?

When Sinclair called her downstairs again she was in a pleasantly aroused state of mind. Several small tables held a selection of bowls containing Chinese delicacies. He had placed two armchairs opposite each other and indicated that she should sit in one of them.

The act of eating, while dressed in nothing but her high-heeled shoes, was unexpectedly erotic, all the more so because Sinclair sat watching her with undisguised pleasure as he helped himself from the various dishes at his disposal, and entertained her with stories and gossip about the various theatre and television personalities that he had met.

She deliberately tried to tantalise him by moving into seductive poses, crossing and uncrossing her legs, squeezing her arms close to her body so that her breasts swelled out provocatively, hoping to tease him into losing some of his studied self-control.

She did not succeed. He remained the perfect host and did not touch her until it was time for her to leave and she had dressed again. As he helped her on with her fur coat his hand strayed to her bottom, stroking it with an insistent circular movement.

'I enjoyed your performance,' he said. 'All of it. You've got talent. It seems a pity not to share it. I think I'll arrange a professional booking for you. Keep practising.'

She did not believe him, although the idea intrigued her. She thought about it during the taxi ride home, remembering the warmth and glare of the lights, and the strange feeling of power the act of stripping had given her. What would it be like to have dozens of pairs of hidden eyes watching her as she performed? She thought she would enjoy it.

She wondered what professional strippers thought about

when they were on stage. Were they really reviewing their next shopping list as they gyrated to the music? Or did they imagine they were dancing for their husband or boyfriend or even, as Thea had suggested, a favourite actor or a pop star?

What would she think about? She knew the answer to that. She remembered the erotic thrill of knowing that James Sinclair was watching her every move, enjoying the slow exposure of her body. She would picture him lounging in his leather armchair, the bulge of his erection pushing against the zip of his trousers. She would think about the taste of him in her mouth. She would think about what he would do to her after her dance had ended.

Yes, she would definitely think about Sinclair.

The following day there was a large brown envelope on her doormat when she returned home from work. Inside was a letter headed Club Bacchus, with a London address, confirming that she was booked to appear on the tenth of that month 'as arranged'. The second letter was from Sinclair: AS YOU SEE, I'VE ARRANGED YOUR PROFESSIONAL APPEARANCE. TAXI WILL CALL AT SEVEN. BRING YOUR MUSIC TAPE. GEORGIE IS MAKING YOU A MASK.

6

The sports-club bar was crowded and noisy but Genevieve hardly heard the jumbled sounds of conversation and laughter until Lisa Hadley brought her back to the present with a snap of her fingers.

'Wake up, Gen. Your orange juice is getting cold.'

'Sorry.' Genevieve picked up the juice carton and toyed with the straw.

'Your mind's been wandering all evening,' Lisa said. 'It certainly wasn't on our game, otherwise I'd never have won. If I didn't know you better I'd say you were in love.'

Genevieve smiled. Love was certainly not the emotion occupying her mind at that moment. Sex, yes. But not love. 'I haven't time to fall in love,' she said.

An overweight man pushed past their table, his face bright red and sheened with sweat. Lisa watched him with undisguised amusement.

'He was in the weights-room, can you believe?' she said. 'I always thought the weights-room would be full of hard, young, male bodies, all glistening and muscular, and when I peek in, what do I see? Humpty Dumpty, puffing like an engine. Disgusting.'

'Perhaps you just picked the wrong night,' Genevieve suggested.

'Believe me,' Lisa said, 'I've tried every night. It's always the same. Middle-aged flab trying to turn itself into Schwarzenegger in five quick sessions.'

'Have you seen the two women who seem to have actually managed it?'

'Women? You're joking?'

'I'm not. These two had muscles a lot of men would envy.'

'Sounds horrible. Were they really hideous?'

'No,' Genevieve said. 'They were really nice looking.'

'I don't believe you.'

'Well, it's true. Take a look during the ladies session. See for yourself.'

'No thanks,' Lisa said. 'I prefer looking at men. But not the ones in our weights-room. Do you know, I think I'd actually pay money for a few hours of passion with one of those hunks you see in the body building mags, if I could ever find one.' She glanced quickly at Genevieve. 'Wouldn't you?'

'No, I wouldn't,' Genevieve said. The over-muscled bodies, their veins standing out like cords, skin gleaming with fake tan and oil, always seemed to her the ultimate turn-off. Sinclair's body had always felt lean and hard. His muscles were those of an athlete, sinewy and strong under his skin.

She realised, with a little shock of surprise, that although she could picture his body she had never seen him naked. He stripped her, but kept himself fully clothed, allowing her access only to his cock and balls, as if this was the only part of himself he was willing to share with her.

'You're doing it again,' Lisa said. 'You've got that faraway look in your eyes. Come on, who's the man?'

'Hasn't it occurred to you,' Genevieve said, 'that I might be thinking about work?'

'Knowing you, I can believe it,' Lisa agreed. 'Don't you ever get frustrated?'

'Certainly not.'

'You're weird,' Lisa said. 'I do.'

'But you've got a boyfriend,' Genevieve said, in surprise.

'Dear old Bart.' Lisa nodded. 'The original once-a-week man. I can tell you exactly how Bart's going to make love to me. He'll touch my ear and then kiss it a few times. Then he'll move down to my neck. After about a minute there he'll undo my blouse, or push up my T-shirt, or whatever. And if my nipples aren't hard enough for him he'll say "What's the matter? Aren't you in the mood?" and make it sound as if there's something wrong with me. Two minutes of foreplay and I'm supposed to be panting with lust!' Lisa grinned wryly. 'If you're telling the truth about not having a special man perhaps you're lucky. You'll be less frustrated with a vibrator.'

'But you've been with Bart for ages,' Genevieve said.

'I know,' Lisa agreed. 'That's the bit I don't understand. I *like* him. Maybe I actually love him. Sometimes I think I do. I certainly can't imagine life without him. I just wish he'd liven up in bed. I wish he'd surprise me for once. Tip a bottle of chocolate sauce over me and lick it off. Anything for a change.'

'Sounds awful,' Genevieve laughed.

'Perhaps not chocolate sauce,' Lisa said. She thought for a moment. 'How about wine?'

'Still sounds awful. And think what a mess it'd make of the sheets.'

Lisa grinned. 'You're just too conventional, Gen. You and Bart would make a good pair.'

Genevieve wondered what Lisa would say if she explained why she had not been concentrating on their squash game. She had checked the Club Bacchus by telephone and discovered that it was a genuine venue. But the receptionist's reaction to her suggestion that they were staging a strip show was distinctly frosty. Club Bacchus, the cool voice informed her, was for wine connoisseurs, and membership was by invitation only.

So, she thought, Sinclair had not been completely honest with her. Either the club was just the starting point in his plan or he had hired the venue for a private party. Would she be expected to strip in front of his friends? Was that his idea of a 'professional booking'? Was that why he told her to wear a mask?

She had already received an elegant, leather face hood from Georgie's workshop. It covered her hair completely and strapped round her neck, leaving only her nose and mouth free. The eye holes were outlined with tiny diamond studs. It was exquisitely crafted, comfortable, and disguised her completely.

It had given her a few temporary doubts about the clothes she normally wore for her striptease, but when she tried on the whole outfit she was surprised at the erotic contrast between the bondage hood and her conventional dress. She had a feeling that Sinclair had anticipated this. To complement the tiny studs she decided to wear her diamond choker and had to admit that the sharp glitter of the stones set against the dull sheen of the leather looked striking.

She stared at her reflection in her full-length mirror. Stripping was supposed to be a submissive act, the slave girl disrobing for her master's pleasure. But dressed in black, with the hood masking her hair and eyes, she looked far from submissive. She altered her stance and made it more aggressive. She imagined herself in thigh-high black boots, holding a whip. Mistress Genevieve, strict dominatrix? The idea amused rather than aroused her.

She took the hood off and put it with the other clothing that she had received from Sinclair. At the end of the ninety days, she thought, what would she do with these things? Would she ever wear them again? She realised that she could not imagine dressing up for anyone except Sinclair. For a moment the realisation frightened her. How had she allowed him to come to mean so much to her? It was ridiculous. Perhaps it would be a good thing when the ninety days were up, and their strange relationship ended. Maybe she would be miserable for a few weeks, but she would get over it. You always got over it. A few weeks missing him and then she could get on with her life again.

'We should see our moggie pictures up on the hoardings soon,' George Fullerton said, putting a cup of coffee on Genevieve's desk, 'and in most of the pet lovers' monthlies. If that cat's face doesn't double the sale of Millford's tasty cod morsels I'll run them another campaign for nothing.'

'Did you tell them that?' Genevieve asked, smiling.

'No,' Fullerton admitted. 'And if you do, I'll deny it. But you must admit we were lucky to find that animal. It has character. It even seemed to like posing.'

'She,' Genevieve corrected.

'Sorry, they all look the same to me.' Fullerton sipped his coffee. 'If it was female, no wonder it enjoyed all the attention.'

'That's a sexist remark, George,' Genevieve said.

'Maybe,' Fullerton agreed. 'And here's another one. How's your charm working on James Sinclair these days?'

'I've seen him socially,' Genevieve said carefully. 'He hasn't mentioned anything about Japan.'

'Well, he's keeping you in the dark then,' Fullerton said, 'because I know he's definitely going. He's been buying into multi-media, and he's got his own interesting little team of whizz-kids, the kind of brilliant dropouts who spent their college days listening to dreadful music and smoking illegal cigarettes. People who won't conform, and conventional firms won't touch with a ten-foot pole. People who sit there fiddling around with their electronic screens and then suddenly come up with ideas that make someone a millionaire. In this case Sinclair, if he's lucky.'

'I thought he was a millionaire already,' Genevieve said.

'I'm sure he is,' Fullerton said. 'On paper, anyway. But I don't suppose he'll say no to doubling his profits. The point is, if this Japanese visit is successful it will certainly involve a worldwide marketing campaign at some point. And it would be very nice if Barringtons were involved.'

'There's no reason why we shouldn't be.'

'That's what I thought,' Fullerton said. He paused. 'Jade Chalfont is also going to Japan with Sinclair.'

'*With* him?' Genevieve repeated, unable to keep the shock and anger out of her voice.

'That's what I heard.'

'Maybe you heard wrong.'

'Maybe,' Fullerton agreed. 'But don't forget she could be a very useful companion, and Sinclair has never been shy of using people. The fact that she's also with Lucci's might be pure coincidence.'

'You don't believe that, George. They must have given her time off.'

'She could have holidays due to her,' Fullerton soothed.

'Do you mean they're actually travelling together?'

'I really don't know their travel arrangements,' Fullerton said. 'I just know that Sinclair is going to Tokyo, and so is Miss Chalfont. At the end of next week. On the same flight.'

That evening Genevieve was tempted to phone Sinclair, and then suddenly realised that she did not know his private number. Angrily she contacted enquiries and a recorded voice confirmed what she had already guessed: he was ex-directory. She flung herself down in a chair, but she was forced to admit that phoning him would solve nothing. What would she have said to him? How dare you go to Japan with Jade Chalfont? How dare you go with an employee of Lucci's? How dare you go with any woman except me?

She knew she could not say any of these things. They would make her look jealous (which she knew she was), and they would also show the extent of his control over her. She had no intention of letting him know that. Her pride would not allow it. Perhaps it was a good thing she did not know his number. He would probably have answered her questions by telling her to mind her own business. She would have ended up looking not only jealous but stupid, because, she had to admit, it wasn't any of her business what he did in his free time, or who he did it with.

But she hated the idea of Jade Chalfont escorting him round Tokyo, impressing both him and the Japanese with her knowledge of the country, the food, the customs and the language. Sinclair would hardly travel out with her and not see her at all during his stay, business meetings or not.

And what else would they do? Genevieve wondered angrily. Jade Chalfont was a sexy woman. If Ricky Croft had been telling the truth, she had not been adverse to buying erotic pictures and offering them to Sinclair as a gift. Would she have sex with him? Genevieve drummed her fingers angrily on the arm of her chair. You bet she would! Anyone would. You'd have to be blind not to find James Sinclair attractive.

She tried not to imagine them together. She had seen Jade in a figure-hugging leotard so she knew the woman had a good body. Although she had never seen Sinclair completely naked, her imagination, and her memory of the many times his body had been close to hers, filled in any gaps in her knowledge. She could picture both of them, without any trouble. And the more she tried not to, the stronger the mental images became. What kind of fantasies would they play out? Would Jade, the kendo sensei, play the submissive role? Why not, Genevieve thought. *She* did, despite her strong belief in equality in everyday life.

Her anger prompted her into another fantasy. Suddenly the idea of acting as a dominatrix did not seem so ridiculous. Mentally, she dressed herself in her black leather corset, her boots, long gloves and the hood. She wore black leather pants, too. She was in control now. Sinclair would see only the parts of her body she chose to show him. She armed herself with a nice, pliable whip.

She imagined him waiting for her in a room containing just a bed. A brass bed with a plain mattress covered by a white sheet. He would wait there for her until she was ready. When she came in he would begin to apologise. He had not meant to upset her, to offend her. She would cut off his words with an imperious flick of her whip, and order him to undress.

He would strip while she watched, which, she thought, would make a nice change. Since he had never done it in real life, she took her time over her mental picture show. First the tie, then the jacket. He would have to fold everything neatly. She imagined a table where the clothes could be laid. The shoes and socks would be next. Then the shirt, slowly. The trousers, even slower. She pictured him wearing just his briefs. Black, she decided. He could keep those on. For now.

She pointed to the bed. He went over to it obediently and lay face down. He had done this before. She had taught him exactly what she expected from him. She walked over to him and ran the tip of the whip down his spine, enjoying the reaction it brought. She tapped his buttocks. He knew what that meant and began to wriggle out of the briefs, still lying flat on his stomach. It was a bit of a struggle. She knew he was already getting hard. Finally he tugged the briefs over his swelling erection and pushed them down to his knees, where they stayed, a black restraining band.

She admired the taut muscles of his bottom. Not an ounce of spare flesh here, or round his waist. His thighs were long and lean. She prodded him, stroked him, massaged his shoulders and ran her hands down to his buttocks, kneading them roughly. She heard his breathing quicken. Reaching between his legs she checked his erection. As soon as her fingers touched him, he groaned in frustration.

'I think you're ready,' she told him. 'You know what to do.'

He reached up and held on to the bed posts. She was surprised at the satisfaction it gave her to imagine the whip landing on his waiting bottom. The first blow would have cracked down hard, and made him yelp with surprise, and probably relief. The following strokes would not be so hard, but they would sting. She was not out to cause extreme pain. She wanted to arouse him, and to humiliate him a little. Each stroke was retribution for the women he had had before her. She was sure there were plenty. And the last five, a little harder than the others, were for Jade Chalfont.

By now the fantasy had aroused her as well. She even considered using the vibrator, but she did not want to break her mood by getting up. Instead she leaned back in her chair and imagined Sinclair turning over, his erection massive and upright, ready for her. She would sit astride and ride him, controlling the depth of his thrusting to suit herself. She would not let him touch her with his hands. She would not bother about his pleasure. And if he did not come in time with her, she would slide off him, maybe give him permission to obtain manual relief, or maybe do it herself. Perhaps she would make it a rule that he did not come inside her during these sessions, just to see how good his control really was.

Her own relief came faster than she anticipated. She had

barely started to touch herself, and was preparing to enjoy imagining tantalising him still further, when she felt her body shuddering with orgasmic tremors. She allowed the sensations to build up and flood over her. Her body stiffened and shook. She groaned, closed her eyes, and felt her hips thrust forward involuntarily. She wished Sinclair was there with her. She wished it was his hand that was pleasuring her. She forgot all about hating him because he was going to Japan with Jade Chalfont and not her. Or hating him because she suspected he was simply using her, and would never see her as anything other than a dispensable sexual partner. She simply wished she would see his face when she opened her eyes.

'Long time, no see.' Genevieve looked up and saw Ben Schneider standing in front of her, a can of beer in each hand. He put one can down next to her glass of cola. 'What's that rubbish you're drinking? Not on the wagon, are you?'

'No. I don't drink alcohol during lunch.'

'Since when?' Ben dipped a fingertip into her glass and tasted it. 'Good God, you're right. It's Pepsi or something. My stomach'll never stand the shock. I know you've turned into a real lady since you joined Barringtons, but you haven't gone teetotal, have you?'

'Not completely.' She smiled. 'Just at lunch time.'

Ben tapped the beer can. 'Good job I didn't open it. Take it back with you. Remind yourself of the good old days, when you did your drinking with the working classes.' He leaned back in his chair and smiled. 'I like the new hair-style, too. Makes you look older, though.'

'Thanks a lot,' she said. 'Time has not diminished your charm. Are you still drawing comic strips for a living?'

'Time has not diminished your charm either. They're graphic novels. Artistic stuff.'

'You're actually making a living?' she teased.

'I'm surviving,' he said. 'But the thing is, I've never been happier. Leaving advertising was the best move I ever made.' He let his deep brown eyes rove over her. 'And judging from the obviously expensive suit, and that ruinously expensive bag, *and* the smart hair-cut, joining Barringtons was a good move for you too?'

'I think so,' she agreed.

He swallowed a few more mouthfuls of beer. 'And do you still see our mutual pal, the frustrated genius, Ricky Croft?'

'Last week,' Genevieve said.

She was wary now. Ben Schneider had been a good friend and a drinking companion when she was just starting in advertising and he was fresh out of art school. Their paths had crossed several times since, but she had a feeling that this meeting was not pure chance. Ben had never been in this pub at lunch time before.

'Have you given him any commissions?' Ben asked.

'You're joking!' she said. 'You know what he's like. Totally unreliable.'

'I've been told he does some – private stuff. Have you bought anything off him?'

'No, I haven't,' she said. 'What's all this about?' She pushed the capped can of beer aside. 'If you want information, you don't have to bribe me with alcoholic drinks. But I'm sure I can't tell you anything about Ricky that you don't know already.'

'You can,' Ben said. He leaned across the table. 'Who damaged him?'

'Damaged?' she repeated. 'What do you mean?'

'Somebody beat him up.'

'When?'

Ben shrugged. 'I'm not sure. A couple of days ago. He's got a nice black eye and some nice big bruises. He says he was mugged, but no one believes him. Apparently he hasn't been to the police, and he doesn't want to talk about it, which is unusual for our Ricky.'

'What makes you think I'd know anything about it?' Genevieve asked.

Ben avoided her eyes, which made her even more suspicious. 'There was a rumour – just a rumour – that James Sinclair was involved. One of your clients, isn't he?'

'No, he isn't,' she said. She was going to add: not yet, but decided against it. 'And even if he was, how does that tie in with Ricky?'

'You know Ricky's been doing the rounds, trying to flog dirty pictures?'

'Yes,' she said. 'He showed some to me.'

'Rumour has it that he might have also offered them to Mr Sinclair.'

'You're not suggesting James Sinclair was so offended that he beat Ricky up?'

'Hardly,' Ben said, grinning. 'From what I've heard, he'd be reaching for his cheque book. Mr Sinclair does have what you might call a reputation, although a lot of it has probably been exaggerated. I take it he's never made a pass at you?'

'My relationship with Mr Sinclair is strictly business,' Genevieve said, demurely. And, she thought, truthfully.

'You're probably not his type,' Ben said.

'And what is – his type?'

Ben hesitated, considering. 'Slinky, sexy ladies, I'd guess,' he said. 'Rich women. Exotic types.'

'Politicians' daughters?' Genevieve prompted.

Ben grinned. 'You heard that story too, did you? I did as well, but I'm not sure I believe it. Well, not all of it, anyway.' He looked at her mischievously. 'I would have said Mr Sinclair was more likely to go for someone like – er – Jade Chalfont.'

Genevieve smiled. 'You may be out of advertising, Ben, but you certainly keep up with the gossip, don't you?'

'Well, I try to,' he said. 'I'm not having much luck with you though, am I?'

'I honestly don't know anything about this,' she said. 'I can't imagine Sinclair thumping anyone without a very good reason. Probably the rumours are wrong.'

'Maybe,' Ben said. 'But most people think they're true. Not that they feel sorry for Ricky. He's been a pain in the arse lately, pestering people for jobs or offering them his masterpieces.'

After Ben had left, Genevieve sat thinking about James Sinclair and Ricky Croft. Why had Ben Schneider come to her for information? He obviously kept up with all the latest advertising gossip, and would know that Sinclair was not yet a Barringtons' client. Were there any rumours going around about their private arrangements? If so, who had started them? Had Ricky been spreading gossip that, although he did not know it, might turn out to be uncomfortably near the truth? Everyone knew she had once given him a commission – although she had regretted it ever since. Had he mentioned her name as a referee, despite her warning? In fact, she realised, if he did go around telling people that she had recommended them as prospective purchasers of dirty pictures there was nothing she could do about it.

If he had approached Sinclair with such a proposition, and used her as a referee, would Sinclair really have punched him? It was a nice thought, especially when she remembered Ricky's last batch of sadistically pornographic drawings. Serve the little creep right. But was it likely? She had to admit that she did not think so. Why should Sinclair care anyway? As far as he was concerned she was also quite willing to use sex as a bargaining tool.

Perhaps the rumours were totally wrong. Maybe Ricky had simply got drunk and fallen down the stairs. Maybe someone had beaten him up because he owed them money which, knowing his lifestyle, was highly likely. Or maybe he really had been mugged.

The idea of Sinclair defending her honour was a pleasant one. What price equality now, she thought wryly. Here you are, a modern, independent businesswoman, in the upper wage bracket, and you're secretly delighted at the idea of a knight in shining armour riding out to do battle on your behalf.

But, she realised, she found the idea of her knight in shining armour stripped and stretched out submissively on the bed, even more appealing. She smiled to herself. No wonder her poor brother Philip claimed not to understood women. She wasn't sure she even understood herself.

A curt message on her answer-phone told Genevieve when to expect the taxi that would take her to the Club Bacchus. Wear your mask, it instructed her. You probably won't have time to put it on when you arrive.

She wondered if she was going to be pitched straight out onto a stage. She imagined a crowded room, men drinking, noise and smoke. Suddenly the idea of performing for an audience did not seem so attractive. But the Club Bacchus, she thought, was not a pub. According to the snooty-voiced receptionist it was a high-class, members-only venue for wine connoisseurs.

She dressed with a sense of apprehension. Black underwear, black dress, high-heeled shoes – and the leather face mask. She clipped the diamond choker round her neck and pulled on the long black gloves. She wanted to trust Sinclair. She *did* trust him. And yet a little voice at the back of her mind suggested that maybe he was now going to try and find assignments that she would not like. And eventually one that she would refuse. That would be his victory. And his excuse to transfer his interest totally to Jade Chalfont.

The taxi driver arrived promptly and gave a brief toot of his horn. She wrapped herself in the fur coat and went downstairs, once again feeling grateful that she lived in an apartment block where she very rarely met any of her neighbours on her way to the street.

The driver looked unsurprised at her appearance. Clearly he was used to picking up fares in strange clothing.

'Club Bacchus, isn't it? You performing, or watching?'

Genevieve felt nerves flutter in her stomach. 'Performing,' she said.

'You want the stage door, then,' he said, pulling away from the kerb.

Obviously he knew something about the Club that the receptionist had not admitted over the telephone. Genevieve wondered whether to question him, but her pride would not let her.

The taxi finally turned into a side street. Genevieve had a brief glimpse of the front of the Club, with its discreet illuminated sign, before the taxi stopped in a darkened alleyway.

'Have a good time,' he said.

He did not seem to expect any payment, but waited until she knocked on the anonymous-looking door and it opened, sending a shaft of light out to the pavement. Obviously satisfied that he had delivered her safely he accelerated away again. Genevieve saw a tubby man with a shock of black hair that looked like a toupee, gazing at her critically, but without surprise.

'Right,' he said. 'Which act are you?'

His voice was curiously high pitched. 'Striptease,' she said.

'You haven't brought a costume. Collecting it here, are you?'

'I'm wearing it,' Genevieve said. She opened the fur coat but he hardly bothered to glance at her.

'Right,' he said. 'You'll have to share a dressing-room. Don't mind that, do you?'

'No,' Genevieve began.

He turned and walked away. 'Right. Follow me.'

'Wait.' Genevieve was determined to make some sense of her predicament.

The tubby man stopped and turned.

'What exactly happens here?' she asked.

He stared at her. 'You do your striptease,' he said. 'That's what you want, isn't it?'

'I was told this was a club for wine connoisseurs,' she persisted. 'Obviously that's not true.'

He seemed to be trying to decide if she was serious. 'It's your first time, right? You've done a strip before?'

'Of course I have,' she said quickly. 'But not in a wine club.'

'They'll be drinking something stronger than wine tonight,' he said. 'Tonight the Club Bacchus becomes the Club Bacchanalia. Right? Tonight Mr Roccanski entertains his friends. Or rather, you do. You and the others. The other performers. Right?'

'Who's Mr Roccanski?'

'The owner. Most of the time this is a legitimate club. Members only. The best wine in London. But every so often Mr Roccanski likes to arrange something special for selected guests. Invitation only. Strictly private.' He smiled for the first time and winked. 'And uncensored. Right?'

Right! Genevieve thought. She was beginning to understand.

'And the entertainers?' she asked. 'Are they professionals?'

'Some are,' he said. 'Some are amateurs, like you. The main thing is, everyone enjoys themselves. Right?'

'Right,' she agreed. She followed him down the passage. Now she could hear the muted sound of a dance band.

The tubby man stopped by a door. 'In here,' he said. 'What about your music? You want the band to play?'

'I've got a tape,' she said.

He held out his hand. 'Give it to me. I'll make sure it's ready for you. You'll be called in good time. You want a drink – ring the bell. Right?'

She looked at the various doors along the passage. It reminded her of being backstage in a theatre.

'Is this really a wine club?' she asked.

'It is now,' he said. 'But it used to be a night club. Cabaret and all. Mr Roccanski didn't alter much. You'll have all the trimmings for your act.'

He pushed open the door. There were two naked men in the room. Genevieve stared at them in startled amazement. One was well muscled and shaven headed and, Genevieve had to admit after giving him a quick look, very well endowed. The other was reed thin, with a thick mop of curls. The rest of his body was devoid of hair, making him look delicate and vulnerable.

'Don't worry about Carl and JoJo,' the tubby man said. 'They wouldn't know how to do it with a woman, even if you fancied them.' He grinned at the two men. 'Right?'

'Wrong,' the curly-headed man said. 'Knowing and doing are two different things. And I wouldn't do it with you either, ducky.'

The tubby man blew a mock kiss and closed the door.

'I'm Carl,' the shaven-headed man said to Genevieve. 'The pretty one over there is JoJo.'

'I'm Marlene,' Genevieve used the first name that came into her head.

'What's your act?' JoJo asked.

'Striptease,' Genevieve said. 'What do you do?'

'We fuck,' JoJo said. 'To music.'

Carl slipped unselfconsciously into a black posing pouch, pulling it tight so that it gave him an impressive bulge, and then began to buckle on a pair of chrome-studded leather chaps held up by a wide belt.

'It's very artistic. A class act.' He picked up a white satin pouch and tossed it over to JoJo. 'Here, get dressed. We'll be on soon.'

'Is this how you earn your living?' Genevieve asked.

Carl laughed. 'It's how we pay our bills. I'm an actor. JoJo's supposed to be an artist.'

'Don't be bitchy,' JoJo said. 'I've sold two pictures this year.'

'To friends,' Carl said. 'That doesn't count.' He pulled on a pair of biker's boots and picked up a leather cap ornamented with chains. 'It's one way of earning some money. We fuck each other anyway, so we figured we might as well get paid for it.'

'Unlike you rich amateurs who do it for fun,' JoJo added.

'What makes you think I'm an amateur?' Genevieve asked.

'The mask,' JoJo explained. 'You don't want to risk being recognised, do you? Your husband might even be out there in the audience.'

'I'm not married,' she said.

'Boyfriend then.' JoJo shrugged. 'Or are you a dyke?'

'Ignore him,' Carl said. 'He's just jealous of your fur coat.'

'I know a man who'll buy me a fur any day,' JoJo pouted. 'And if you're going to be nasty to me, lovey, I'll pack my bags and go straight to him.'

They began to bicker and swop insults in a familiar way. JoJo tucked his cock and balls into the posing pouch, pulling on the side laces so that the pouch bulged like a padded codpiece.

'Don't tie knots,' Carl warned, watching him. 'You know I can't undo them when we're performing.'

'Rip them, macho-man,' JoJo said. 'You spend enough time in the gym. What are those muscles supposed to be for?'

Genevieve suddenly remembered Lisa's complaint about the kind of men she saw in the weights-room. Carl would have met her requirements, at least visually. She stifled a giggle. Poor Lisa, her charms would be wasted on Carl.

Carl rubbed his hand between his legs. 'I'll show you what *this* muscle's for when we get out there, pretty boy.'

'Oooh, promises!' JoJo mocked.

A bang on the door interrupted them. 'Two minutes,' a voice called.

'The bright lights are calling,' JoJo said. He turned to Genevieve. 'I bet you're on after us. Something for the gays, and then a treat for the boring old straights. That's the way they usually work it.'

They left the dressing-room together. Genevieve heard the music stop. There was a brief silence and then she heard a new, harder beat. She guessed this was Carl and JoJo's music. Suddenly she was curious. She had never seen two men making love.

She left the dressing-room and walked down the corridor towards the music. Once through a double door, she was standing by the side of a small, round stage, but hidden from the audience by heavy curtains. A man stood checking a printed list. He glanced at her briefly.

'What's your act?' he asked.

'Striptease,' she said.

He consulted his list. 'You're next. When the lads have finished.'

A spotlight swept the stage, catching and holding Carl and JoJo in its circle of light. They began to dance, both of them moving with professional grace and confidence. Carl strutted and posed, while JoJo was sinuous and yielding.

The act involved Carl pretending to force JoJo into sexual obedience. As Genevieve watched, Carl tugged the younger man's satin posing pouch and ripped it off. He twisted JoJo round, displaying him. JoJo now had a sizeable erection. Genevieve heard a murmur of approval from the darkness. Then JoJo reached backwards, and when the two them broke away from each other, Carl's black posing pouch had also been removed. The sight of Carl with a massive erection between his leather-clad legs brought more sounds of delight, and some applause, from the audience.

The action became more erotic. JoJo was forced to his knees in front of Carl. He used his mouth and his hands on his partner until Carl, apparently out of control, swung him round and brought the affair to its conclusion. Grasping JoJo round the waist and bending him forward, his dark leathers a stark contrast to JoJo's white skin, Carl entered his partner, and as both men shuddered to a noisy climax the lights went out.

The performance had not really aroused Genevieve, although she admired the men's dancing skill, but it was obvious from the audience reaction that they had thoroughly enjoyed the display. The prolonged clapping and cheering gave her a twinge of nerves. Would her striptease seem rather tame after such an explicit sex scene? The stage was still dark when the man with the list came up behind her.

'Give it a couple of minutes,' he said. 'Let the gays out there re-arrange themselves, then you're on. We'll put a spot on you and then start your music. OK?'

'Well, yes,' Genevieve said.

'Not nervous, are you?' He sounded sympathetic.

'Will anyone be interested in a striptease, after what they've just seen?'

'You bet they will,' he laughed. 'Not everyone gets turned on by two blokes making out. I don't, for a start. I'd much rather watch you.'

With that to boost her confidence, Genevieve stepped on to the darkened stage. It was an eerie experience. As she stood for a few moments waiting for her music to begin she could hear the sounds of the audience as they shifted in their seats; she heard the clink of glasses, and the low murmur of conversation. It was obvious that no announcements were being made. Each new act was a surprise.

When the spotlight picked her out with abrupt clarity, Genevieve was reminded of the last performance she had given for Sinclair. Was he watching? She assumed so, but there was no way of telling. She had a brief glimpse of the faces that surrounded her, like pale blobs in the darkness, then the first bars of her music beat out of the speakers, and before she even thought about it she began to dance.

Once again she blessed the day she decided to go to Thea for advice. Thea had given her the confidence she needed. Her body moved seductively as she strutted and turned. The audience were silent, but she sensed their tension as they watched each garment revealing more of her body.

It was a strange sensation, performing in front of a group of total strangers. She knew that stripping was usually considered to be degrading, but it made her feel powerful. The idea of all those unknown eyes watching her was exciting. They were captives, and she was their jailer. She was controlling them, controlling their reactions, controlling exactly what they would see, and when.

For the first time she really understood the teasing aspect of the strip. She understood what Thea meant when she said some women stripped for themselves and not for their audience. Genevieve was very aware of the audience, and what she was doing to them. She wished she could have prolonged her dance but she was limited by her music. When it stopped, she felt a brief stab of disappointment. She stood naked on the stage for a moment, wearing only her shoes, the leather hood and the diamond choker, and then the lights blacked out.

She felt someone touch her arm and guide her off the stage. Two people swished by in the darkness carrying something bulky. Genevieve thought it looked like an old-fashioned vaulting horse. A man and a woman followed, the man in an evening suit, the woman dressed as a maid. Curious, Genevieve lingered near the stage. The man guiding her tried to hurry her along.

'Wait,' she said. She noted that the woman was masked. 'What are they going to do?'

'Spanking scene,' the man explained. 'The maid drops a glass and it breaks. So she gets up-ended over the horse. It's a popular act.'

Genevieve remembered her own experience of an erotic spanking. The memory excited her. The idea of Sinclair administering the slaps excited her even more.

'Come on,' the man hassled her. 'Your client's waiting.'

'Client?' Genevieve forgot all about the act that was about to begin on stage. 'What client?'

'How do I know?' He sounded annoyed now. 'You made the arrangements, not me. Table five.'

'I don't know what you're talking about,' Genevieve said firmly. She suddenly realised that her companion was not carrying her clothes. 'And where's my dress and underwear?' she added.

'The instructions said you go straight to table five,' he told her. 'They didn't say anything about wearing clothes. You'll get them back later. Your client wants you as you are.' He grinned suddenly. 'I don't blame him, either.'

'Do you know who this client is?' she asked.

'No,' he said. 'Don't you?'

Did she? She assumed it would be Sinclair, but what if it was a stranger? What if Sinclair was planning some more voyeuristic fun? Would she mind? She had already made love to Bridget while he watched, even though she had been unaware of her audience at the time. But Bridget had been a woman, which somehow made a difference. And it had been her choice. She might have made love to Zaid, if that had been what he wanted – he had reminded her strongly of Sinclair. But that would have been her choice too.

Was she going to be given a choice this time, or was she going to be pushed into someone's lap? Could she make love to a stranger while he watched? Did the business deal really mean so much to her? Once again, at the start of the ninety days she would have said: yes. Now she was not so sure.

Her mind was so busy with these thoughts that she hardly noticed the audience reaction to her progress. On stage the erotic games were beginning but heads still turned as she passed the numbered tables, although no one made any attempt to touch her.

Tables on the side of the room were set back against the wall, in shadowed cubicles. She reached number five. And gave an audible sigh of relief when she saw Sinclair.

'Amazing, isn't it?' he said softly. 'I've stripped you quite a few times, but seeing you do it to music still turns me on.' He shifted to one side. 'Come and sit here.'

She realised that the seat against the wall was wide enough for two. When she sat down she felt the smooth cloth of his trouser leg against her bare skin. On stage the maid had dropped the wine glass and was being ordered to take her punishment. Protesting and struggling (although not very effectively), her black dress was pushed up to reveal silk stockings, suspenders and lacy knickers that were soon down to her knees. The man bent her over the padded 'horse'.

Genevieve found the performance arousing. She could identify with the girl, and she knew both performers were enjoying the situation. The girl was certainly there from choice, her mask proved that. When the man's palm smacked on her upturned bottom Genevieve felt a thrill of excitement.

Sinclair turned towards her. His hand slid along her inner thigh. He gently eased her legs apart. His palm stroked her flesh but his eyes were on the couple on the stage.

'You might have told me that you were planning this,' she said.

'Planning what?' His fingertips moved to her kneecap. 'This?' He drew light patterns on her skin.

'For me to meet you here,' she said. The last word ended in a stifled gasp. He had traced back over the curve of her thigh and ended up between her legs again.

'Why?' He pushed his other hand round her back and under her arm, cupping her left breast, rubbing his thumb over her nipple, playing with her for a few moments before moving his hand away. 'Did you expect to meet someone else?'

'I never know what to expect,' she said. 'You make the rules.'

He leaned over and circled her nipple with his lips. His tongue flicked insistently while his other hand continued to explore the warm centre of pleasure between her legs.

'Would you still have come, if you thought you'd be meeting a stranger?'

She wriggled involuntarily. His fingers were moving faster now, expertly. 'Do I have a choice?'

'You've always got a choice,' he said.

She leaned back and stretched out her legs under the table, one leg bent outwards to give him easier access. 'I wouldn't know who I was meeting – until I got here.'

'But if you did know? If I told you to come and allow a complete stranger to enjoy you?' He entered her fully with a finger, then with two fingers. His thumb excited her swollen clit. 'If I told you to let a stranger do this?'

She did not want these questions. She wanted to abandon herself to the sensations that were claiming her.

'Would you have come then?' he insisted.

'I'm coming now,' she groaned.

She writhed on the seat as her orgasm shook her, pushing against his hand, trying to stifle the noises of pleasure that rose in her throat. Then she realised she need not have bothered. The stage act had finished and the audience were clapping enthusiastically. The sound would have drowned any gasps and moans she made. By the time she had recovered, the stage was blacked out again. Her legs felt sticky against the cover of the seat.

'I'm wet.' She grabbed one of the paper napkins from the table and tried to make herself more comfortable.

'You haven't answered my question,' he said, taking another napkin to wipe his own hand.

'What question?' She screwed the napkin up.

'Would you have serviced a total stranger?' he asked.

Suddenly she was angry with him. She just wanted to relax in the warm afterglow of her orgasm. She didn't need a cross-examination.

'Of course I would,' she said, in an aggressive, clipped voice. 'This is *business*, isn't it?'

There was a pause. Then he smiled. 'Strictly business,' he agreed. 'I forgot.'

'And you've made me miss that act,' she added. 'I wanted to watch it.'

'You wanted to watch Miss X getting spanked, did you? Why?'

'I thought it would be a turn-on.' She turned away and peered at the darkened stage. 'Do you know who the girl was?'

He laughed. 'Yes.'

'Tell me!'

He shook his head. 'No way. But you'd be surprised if you knew.'

'If it's such a secret, how do you know?' she challenged.

'I'm a regular here,' he said. 'I can be trusted. And I can tell you that the mysterious Miss X really loves performing. Why shouldn't she enjoy herself?'

'Everyone should have a hobby,' Genevieve agreed lightly.

'Even if it's only squash,' he said dryly.

'Or collecting pictures,' she hinted.

He seemed unaffected by the reference. 'You collect pictures, do you?'

'No,' she said. 'I thought you did?'

'What makes you think that?'

She had a feeling he was going to be deliberately evasive, and decided to be blunt. 'There's an artist called Ricky Croft. He draws erotic scenes.' She waited for a response, but did not get one. 'He's always looking for customers. The last time I spoke to him he seemed interested in contacting you.'

'I know of him,' Sinclair said. His voice sounded cold. 'He deals in pornography. I don't need pictures.' His hand touched her thighs, stroked up between her legs to her moist pussy. 'I can always get the real thing.'

'So you've never met him?'

The fingers on her leg tightened.

'Why are you so interested, Miss Loften?'

She was tempted to say: because I want to know if you beat him up. And why. But she knew instinctively that even if she asked the question, Sinclair was not going to give her any answers. 'Just curious,' she said flatly.

'Well, stop being curious,' he said. 'You're not here to interrogate me.' His hand moved from her leg to her breast. He cupped it and squeezed gently. 'You're here to entertain me.' His fingers tightened. 'Agreed?'

'Agreed,' she said.

She felt the warmth of his skin against her flesh, and felt her nipple hardening in response to his handling. He relaxed his fingers and massaged her breast with his open palm. She leaned back against the wall and closed her eyes.

'Does this turn you on?' he asked softly.

'Yes,' she murmured.

His fingers caught her erect nipple and pinched it, firmly. Startled, she opened her eyes.

'And this?' he asked. 'A little bit of erotic pain?'

'Yes,' she said.

'You like it all, don't you?' he said. He withdrew his hand. 'Spanking, too. You enjoyed it when you were tied to my motorcycle. You loved it. You'd like it to happen again. Am I right?'

'Don't jump to conclusions,' she said. 'I simply said I wanted to watch that couple on stage.'

'I've ruined your evening, have I? I'll make it up to you. I'll show you some experts at work, people who'll make those two look like amateurs.'

'When?' she asked casually. 'After you've come back from Japan?'

'I thought I told you to stop interrogating me.'

'You might have told me about it,' she said.

'Why? I knew you'd find out anyway. It's hardly a secret. It'll only be for a few days, and it makes no difference to our arrangements.'

'So it's strictly a business trip?'

'What else would it be?' he asked lightly.

'I've heard that Japanese women are very beautiful.'

'So are English women. Are you trying to find out whether I'm going to sample any of them while I'm out there?'

'No, I'm not,' she said, quickly and untruthfully.

He laughed. 'For a moment I thought you might be jealous.' He ran his hands over her breasts, and down between her legs, touching her briefly and skilfully. 'Foolish of me, wasn't it? I'm just a business opportunity to you.'

'And I'm just an entertainment to you,' she countered.

'True,' he said. 'And the evening's not over yet. Get your coat. I'm hungry.'

'Can we eat here?' she asked.

'We can, but we're not going to. I've a good bottle of wine at home, and I've ordered a meal to go with it.' The stage darkened again.

'I'd like to watch the show,' she suggested.

'I'm tired of watching,' he said. 'And I call the shots, remember? Get your coat, but don't bother to dress. You'll soon be performing again.'

As she got out of the car and walked to the steps leading up to Sinclair's house, Genevieve wondered why it felt so sexy to know that you were naked under a perfectly respectable-looking fur coat. She hugged the fur to her, feeling the cool silk of the lining against her skin. She had already removed her head mask and shaken out her hair.

The hall felt pleasantly warm. Sinclair opened a door.

'In there,' he said. 'Pour yourself a drink. And take your coat off. You look over-dressed.'

It felt even more sexy to be naked in this masculine room, with its subdued lighting, polished-wood floor and leather-upholstered furniture. There were two large armchairs, and there was also a stool with a padded seat. It was smaller than the room they had used on her previous visit, and she noticed that the door was not drilled with holes. One wall was completely shelved with books.

She poured herself a glass of wine and went over to look at them, searching for the kind of titles Sinclair's reputation prompted her to believe she would find. The *Kama Sutra*, maybe? *The Story of O*? First editions of well-known erotic novels? Privately printed books on the byways of specialised sex? Instead she found poetry and astronomy. Books on ancient history, and a shelf of science-fiction paperbacks.

She finished her wine and moved round the room, looking at the framed prints on the walls, mainly old-fashioned hunting scenes and animals, and the occasional portrait of unidentified, grim-looking elderly men in high wing collars. She was standing in front of one of these, trying to work out who it was supposed to be, when she realised she was reflected from the waist upwards in the picture glass. She placed both hands under her breasts, lifting them until her nipples were in line with the portrait's primly disapproving mouth. She giggled suddenly, and wriggled provocatively. I'll bet this never happened to you in real life, whoever you are, she thought.

'What the devil are you doing?'

The sound of Sinclair's voice made her jump. She turned, her hands still under her breasts. He was standing in the doorway. He had taken off his jacket and his formal white shirt was now open at the neck, half-unbuttoned, the sleeves rolled up to just below his elbows.

'I'm just looking at your pictures,' she said.

'It looked as if you were dancing.'

She walked across to him, her hands crossed in mock modesty over her breasts. 'I thought the poor old boy needed cheering up.'

'Oh, did you?' He was standing close to her now. The subdued light shadowed his face and made his black hair gleam. He reached out and caught her wrists, pulling her arms down to her sides. He leaned forward as if to kiss her. She moved her face towards him but he dipped his head and his lips closed over her nipple instead. His tongue circled its tip briefly, lightly, and expertly enough to send a shudder of pleasure rushing through her. 'Well,' he said, after repeating the caress once more, 'I don't think that respectable old Victorian gentleman would have appreciated seeing a wanton woman flaunting herself in the nude.'

'Wanton woman?' She giggled again. 'Do you mean me?'

'Certainly.' Suddenly he spun her round. With her wrists held captive in his strong grip he pushed her forward towards one of the chairs. 'You would have been seen as a threat. A sex-mad female. You would have been punished. For your own good, naturally.'

They were standing in front of one of the armchairs now. Genevieve leaned back against Sinclair, relishing the warmth and strength of his body, enjoying the smooth feeling of his shirt against her bare skin. He leaned forward and placed his mouth close to her ear.

'The Victorians were great believers in punishment.' He shifted his grip to hold her wrists with one hand. His free hand roved over her bottom. She shivered. 'Corporal punishment,' he added softly.

Suddenly he spun her round, sat down in the chair and pulled her face down across his knees. The movement was so unexpected that she offered no resistance.

'He would have loved this,' Sinclair said. She heard a hint of amusement in his voice. 'He would have thought this was just what you deserved.'

The flat of his hand landed on her bottom and she yelled in startled surprise. She kicked out, but he moved expertly and trapped her legs between his own. His hand landed three more times in quick succession. They were sharp, hard blows and yet the stinging pain, and the uncomfortable position he had trapped her into, aroused her as much as a soft caress.

'And I agree,' he added.

Another flurry of slaps landed on her unprotected flesh. She struggled ineffectively. Even the movement of her body against the hard muscles of his thighs excited her.

'I'm beginning to see why the Victorians enjoyed this kind of thing,' Sinclair said. His hand landed again, harder this time.

'You pig!' she yelled. 'That hurt.'

He leaned over and she felt his breath against her tangled hair.

'And you love it,' he whispered. 'Admit it?'

Her answer was to struggle more violently.

'Admit it,' he repeated. 'It turns you on.'

'It doesn't.'

She knew it was a ridiculous lie. She did not expect him to believe it, and she was right. He reached forward and found her breasts, found her nipples, hard as berries. His hand explored her, his thumb rubbing, teasing her. Her body shuddered convulsively. When he stopped fondling her she gave a small gasp of disappointment.

His hand stroked over her tingling bottom and slipped between her thighs. This time her gasp was one of desire. Then he stood up, pulling her with him. With a strong push of his arms he spun her round and sat her down in the chair. He knelt in front of her, between her outstretched legs. He grasped both her wrists and forced her hands over her breasts. She felt her nipples pushing against her palm.

'Proof,' he said. 'Corporal punishment turns you on, Miss Loften. I'll bet that's something you never knew before.'

She had to admit that it was true, but felt like adding: it depends on the administrator. He moved her hands slowly, forcing her to massage herself.

'Now turn me on,' he said softly. 'Turn me on some more.'

She gazed at him through half-closed eyes, waiting for him to start pleasuring her with his tongue. But he did not move.

'I want to watch you,' he said. His voice was hoarse with suppressed excitement. She was about to move her hands from her breasts but he stopped her. 'Let me see you do it,' he murmured. 'Let me see how you do it when you're alone.'

She moved slowly at first, and then with increasing speed. She rolled her nipples between her fingers. She felt no embarrassment because she knew it was arousing him. She relaxed back in the chair.

'Make yourself come,' he instructed. 'You're ready for it. I'm not going to touch you. You're going to do it all.'

The excitement in his voice acted like a potent aphrodisiac. Again she felt in control and powerful. She opened her legs lazily and reached down to touch herself. The physical manhandling that he had given her had aroused her even more than she realised. She had barely begun to caress herself before she felt the sensations building.

'Make it last, baby,' he muttered. 'Nice and easy. Nice and slow. Make it last.'

But for once she was incapable of obeying him. She wanted to come, and the desire blotted out everything else. Her orgasm was intense and lengthy. She writhed in the chair, her body stiffening and shaking with pleasure. When it was over she sighed deeply and relaxed.

She felt his hands under her arms as he lifted her up and then a pressure on her head as she was made to kneel in front of him. He unzipped his trousers and pulled her towards him. He was so erect and so excited that her mouth had barely touched him before he came, his own release as violent as her own.

Later, when she had bathed and dressed again, and sat opposite him enjoying the delicious Chinese meal he had ordered, she reflected on how civilised they both looked: a lady in a neat black dress and a man in his dark dress-suit trousers and his formal shirt now loosely undone.

She felt warm and comfortable. Was that what good sex did for you? She wondered if he felt the same. Certainly he had gone out of his way to be charming and entertaining during the meal, and once again she was impressed by the range of his knowledge. He was informative without being pedantic, and his conversation proved that his interests were as wide as his choice of books implied.

She made only one effort to bring up the subject of Japan.

'Not that again?' He raised one eyebrow quizzically. 'Why are you so fascinated with my trip to the exotic East?'

Well, she thought, I can hardly say: because I want to know if you're going to make love to Jade Chalfont while you're out there.

'I'm not fascinated,' she said untruthfully. 'Just – mildly interested. Mounting an advertising campaign that appealed to a Japanese market would be quite a challenge for us.'

'Always the businesswoman, aren't you?' His voice hardened. 'And what makes you think you're going to get the chance to do a Japanese campaign?'

'If your negotiations are successful . . .' she began.

'I'm not your client yet,' he interrupted.

'I didn't think there was any doubt that you would be,' she said coolly.

'Obviously you can't count, Miss Loften,' he said. 'The ninety-day agreement still has some time to run.'

'Forgive me for saying so, Mr Sinclair,' she was icily polite now, 'but there are times when I suspect that you're just using me.'

'You're right.' The trace of a cynical smile touched his mouth. 'And very nice it is, too.'

'I meant, there are times when I doubt if you mean to keep your word.'

It was the first time she had really seen him angry. She sensed the tension in his body.

'I hope you don't mean that, Miss Loften. I've got plenty of faults, but breaking my word isn't one of them.' There was ice in his voice, and in his eyes.

She realised then that James Sinclair would be a very dangerous man to cross. 'I'm sorry,' she said. And meant it.

'Good,' he said, curtly. 'If anyone breaks our agreement, it'll be you.'

But only if you force me, she thought. And the way he was looking at her now she felt he was more than capable of it. The thought was not a comforting one.

'Maybe if I offered you a pound?'

Genevieve came back to the present with start. George Fullerton was standing in front of her desk, smiling.

'You didn't seem interested in a penny,' he said.

'A penny?' she repeated.

'For your thoughts. You were miles away. Thinking about work?'

'Well, yes,' she said. 'In a way.'

'Did you hear the latest about James Sinclair?'

'The Ricky Croft rumour?' She nodded.

'Do you believe it?'

She remembered Sinclair's brief, cold anger the night before. 'Mr Sinclair is quite capable of thumping someone,' she said. 'But I can't imagine why he should choose Ricky Croft.'

'Neither can anyone else,' Fullerton said. 'Have you heard anything more about the Japanese trip?'

'Only that it's definitely on,' she said.

Fullerton nodded. 'Mr Sinclair is fast becoming a very desirable property. And despite the fact that he's still flirting with Lucci's and their attractive swordswoman, I'm sure you'll win the battle of the sexes in the end.'

Genevieve wished she was equally confident. The brief glimpse of Sinclair's anger showed her that there was still a lot about him that she did not know. Was he really the manipulator that so many people claimed. A man who used others as a kind of hobby? Was he really just using her, confident that he could get her to break their agreement any time he chose? It had certainly sounded like it.

She was still not sure when she received a parcel of paper napkins with the message: I'M SURE YOU CAN FIND A USE FOR THESE. But she knew that she would find out before long. She was running out of time. The ninety days would soon be over.

7

Although she knew Sinclair would not ring her from Japan, Genevieve still half expected to hear his voice every time she picked up her phone. Instead the calls were routine contacts from friends, and one from Philip claiming that he was going to remain celibate for the duration of his college course.

'A group of us are doing it,' he told her. 'Women just aren't worth the hassle.'

'One minute you're frustrated because your girlfriends won't agree to a bondage scene,' she said, 'and the next minute you're planning to be a monk. It's the stupidest thing I ever heard.'

'You think I won't be able to keep it up?'

'I think you won't be able to keep it down,' she said.

'Really, big sister,' he said, crossly. 'I'm not a sex maniac.'

'No,' she said. 'Just a normal human male. You'll have another girlfriend in a week.'

'Like to make a little bet?' he asked.

'Of course not,' she said. 'You never pay up, anyway.'

'I'm really serious about this,' he said. 'You'll see.'

When Sinclair finally rang he sounded relaxed and friendly. He surprised Genevieve by asking how she was, rather than giving her instructions.

'I'm fine, thank you,' she said, hoping that she had managed to disguise the pleasure she felt at hearing his voice again. 'How did you find the Japanese?'

'Very cooperative,' he said.

'And the geisha girls?' she asked, sweetly.

'The same,' he said.

She was tempted to ask whether Jade Chalfont had enjoyed her visit, but pride forbade her to even acknowledge that she knew – or cared – that Jade had gone with him.

'Jade enjoyed herself too,' he added cheerfully, while she was still trying to think of something neutral to say. 'You remember Jade Chalfont, don't you? You met at the antiques fair.'

'Of course I remember,' Genevieve said icily. 'Miss Chalfont does judo, or karate, or something.'

He laughed. 'Nearly right. She also works for Lucci's. Or did you forget that, too? She was very useful to me in Japan.'

'You've obviously been working on this Japanese deal for some time,' Genevieve said. 'Why didn't you tell me about it when we discussed your future advertising requirements?'

'Nothing was confirmed,' he said. 'I don't believe in counting chickens. But things are certainly moving now.'

She suddenly felt apprehensive. She knew that Lucci's would be only one of the other agencies courting him. Would he really keep to the unorthodox agreement he had made with her? Was it naive of her to believe him when he insisted that he always kept his word? If he wanted to walk out of her life after the ninety days and never contact Barringtons again, he could do so easily. She was hardly in a position to offer any public objections.

'We'll look forward to the challenge of an international advertising campaign,' she said.

'You haven't got it yet,' he answered, smoothly.

'Is there some doubt?'

'There's nearly two weeks of our agreement to go,' he said. 'Or had you forgotten?'

Again she found herself wondering if he would find it

amusing to test her. To try and find something she would not do. When she first began their unusual agreement she had honestly believed that she would do anything sexual for him – and not necessarily with him – in order to get his cooperation. Even if she hated it, she would oblige him. But now things had changed. She had changed. He had changed her. He had changed her life, and her way of thinking.

'I hope you remember Georgie's address?' he said.

'Of course,' she said.

'I've asked her to make you a new outfit,' he said. 'But she'll need your measurements. She's not too busy at the moment, so I've made you an appointment for tomorrow lunch time. I hope that suits you?'

'You give the orders,' Genevieve said, with a coolness she did not feel. 'At least for a couple more weeks.'

She felt certain he was smiling.

'Yes,' he said, 'I do, don't I? Make sure you keep remembering it.'

Genevieve was glad to get out of the office the following day. Several people had expressed reservations about Barringtons' chances of gaining Sinclair's account.

'Why should he come to us now? This Japanese thing is going to put him in the big league.' Martin Ingrave, one of the account managers, perched on Genevieve's desk. 'I thought it was a bit odd when he approached us in the first place. We're small-fry compared to Randle-Mayne, and even Lucci's.'

'Sinclair likes Barringtons,' Genevieve answered.

'I reckon he must like Lucci's too,' Martin said. 'He certainly likes Jade Chalfont, anyway. I mean, he took her to Japan with him, didn't he?'

'Martin,' Genevieve said irritably. 'I know that.'

Martin leaned forward confidentially. 'She does this kendo

thing,' he said. 'I reckon Sinclair might find that interesting. I've heard he likes dominant women. The kind of women who kick men around. Kinky types, you know?'

Genevieve stared at Martin in genuine surprise. 'Well, that's not what I've heard,' she said.

'Lots of people think he's having a fling with Chalfont,' Martin said. 'And you couldn't get more dominant than a swordswoman, could you?'

'Lots of people don't know what they're talking about,' Genevieve snapped.

'Do I detect a little jealousy here?' Martin grinned. 'Fancy him yourself, do you?'

'He's a prospective client,' she said. And lied: 'I don't mix business with pleasure.'

'Sounds to me as if you'd like to.'

'Sounds to me', she said coldly, 'as if you're asking for a punch on the nose. And get your behind off my desk.'

'Wow!' Martin pantomimed a kiss. 'You're beautiful when you're angry. Why don't you try that approach with Sinclair? It might turn him on.'

But I do turn him on, Genevieve thought, as she made her way to Georgie's by taxi. I wonder why? I don't conform to any of the types believed to attract him. Why did he choose me? She remembered he had once told her she was a highly sexed woman waiting to be liberated. Looking back on the last couple of months she had to agree that he was probably right. But how did he know that? she thought. I didn't even know it myself.

Georgie answered Genevieve's knock. This time her T-shirt said: RECLAIM THE STREETS: TREES NOT TARMAC! Her workroom was still as cluttered and untidy as Genevieve remembered, and still smelled sexily of leather. The zipped suit had gone. Now the tailor's dummy wore a complex creation with narrow straps and buckles growing like a spider's web from a front-laced basque.

'Nice, isn't it?' Georgie noticed her interest and turned the dummy round. 'It'll look even better on a real body. This customer is turned on by straps.'

'How odd,' Genevieve said.

'It isn't odd at all.' Georgie traced one of the straps with a finger. 'This is really a sex map. All the lines actually go somewhere. Men love that. Why do you think they all like seamed stockings?'

Genevieve laughed. 'There's a world of difference between a man liking seamed stockings and getting turned on by a kinky bondage outfit.'

'Not so much of the kinky.' Georgie pretended to be annoyed. 'This is more normal than you might think. Let's face it, a plain naked body soon gets boring. It needs dressing up. And plain sex gets boring too. Fantasy helps to keep it fresh. You must believe that, or you wouldn't come here.' She added slyly: 'You liked the corset I made for you, didn't you?'

'It wasn't my choice,' Genevieve said quickly.

'That's what you say.'

'It really wasn't,' Genevieve protested.

'You enjoyed wearing it, didn't you? You enjoyed the idea that it was turning your fella on?'

'I had to wear it.'

'What do you mean "had to"?' Georgie grinned. 'Did someone point a gun at your head?'

'I have this sort of – agreement,' Genevieve hedged. 'With my – friend.'

'So you're into playing games.' Georgie nodded. 'Aren't we all? Fun, isn't it?' She searched for, and found, a tape measure. 'You'll have to take your jacket off. And your skirt.' When

Genevieve stared at her in obvious surprise, she added: 'The order was for a dress and boots. I'll need to measure your legs.' She watched as Genevieve unbuttoned her coat, and slipped out of her skirt. 'I can probably alter a standard boot for you. It'll be a bit cheaper than custom-made. You've got really nicely shaped legs.'

Genevieve suddenly remembered that Georgie was a lesbian. 'Thank you,' she said, rather more abruptly than she intended.

Georgie stood up and grinned at her cheekily. 'Don't look so worried. I'm not going to rape you.'

Genevieve blushed. 'I'm sorry. That wasn't what I was thinking.'

'That's the trouble with you straights,' Georgie said. 'You think gays are all raving sex maniacs.' She began to take measurements, with professional efficiency. 'I don't go around wondering what every woman I meet is like in bed. If it happens, it happens. Actually you're not my type. Too feminine.'

'I've got nothing against gays,' Genevieve said.

'Lots of your best friends are lesbians?' Georgie challenged.

'Well, I don't know,' Genevieve admitted. 'It's not something you go around telling everyone, is it?'

'That's the point,' Georgie persisted. 'People don't talk about it, and that's why everyone gets these peculiar ideas. I bet you'd be ashamed to introduce me as a lesbian to your friends. I bet you'd be ashamed to go into a lesbian club.'

Genevieve thought about Bridget. She was tempted to confide in Georgie about it, but wondered if Georgie would be discreet with the information. And was Bridget really a lesbian, or just a professional who would put on any kind of performance for money?

'I wouldn't be ashamed at all,' she said.

'You've been to hundreds of gay clubs!' Georgie mocked.

'I wouldn't even know where to find one,' Genevieve said, which was true. 'They don't put "Lesbians Only" on a sign outside, do they.'

'I'd take you to a club,' Georgie offered. 'Would you come? See how the other half lives?' When Genevieve hesitated she added: 'We don't dance around naked, prodding each other with big rubber dildos. And I wouldn't take you to The Cupboard. That's a bit specialised. Just a place with a nice friendly atmosphere and some decent wine.'

Genevieve smiled suddenly.

'All right. When?'

'I'll be working late for a few nights,' Georgie said. 'But I'll give you my number. You can ring me and I'll arrange something. If you don't ring, I'll know you've had second thoughts. No hard feelings if you do.'

'What about your girlfriend? Won't she be jealous?'

'She won't be there.' Georgie grinned. 'She's on a management course. But she wouldn't mind anyway. You're straight, aren't you? And like I said, you're not my type.'

When she first unpacked Georgie's outfit, Genevieve thought she had been sent a conventional dress, but when she held it up she realised that this beautifully crafted leather creation was certainly not a design you could wear in the street. It was sleeveless, with a scoop neck that curved well below her breasts. There were thin chains attached to rings across the neckline, and this time Genevieve knew exactly how this adornment was to be fitted.

The dress was almost literally backless. A leather strap formed a thin belt, another ran down between her buttocks, and two more looped under them, drawing black lines that emphasised her curves. The straps could be attached to studs on the front of the skirt, pulling in tight against her thighs.

The parcel also contained a pair of elbow-length leather gloves, and a pair of boots. They were close fitting and laced from the toes to high above her knees, and had stiletto heels so high that once she was wearing them she would be practically standing on tiptoe. The platform soles would make it even more difficult to balance. They were far more extreme than any previous footwear Sinclair had arranged for her. When she finally laced them and stood up she felt as if she was tipping forward. Georgie had thoughtfully included some padding in the toes, but Genevieve wondered if she would actually get down the stairs and into the car without falling over. She also wondered what her neighbours would think if they saw her. Once again she was thankful that she lived in an apartment block where most of the tenants returned to their country homes and their families at the weekends.

She practised wearing the boots and was surprised to find that once she adjusted the way she moved, she could walk without pitching forward or tripping over. She had to take tiny steps. Like a geisha, she thought. It was not a comparison she wanted to dwell on. When she thought about geishas, she thought about Sinclair enjoying himself in Japan.

She thought about him with a beautifully costumed Japanese girl kneeling at his feet, removing his shoes. She thought about him in a dark kimono following the girl to a deep bath. She thought about them together, naked, the girl washing his back, giggling. She thought about them later, stretched out on a futon, making love. Sinclair exploring the girl's body with his mouth. The girl working expertly on him with hers, sliding her lips up and down the length of his cock until his body jolted with an orgasmic shock. Then the geisha changed, and became Jade Chalfont, and Genevieve realised that her thoughts were no longer just fantasy. They were painfully near to possible fact. The thought both depressed and angered her, and even Sinclair's voice later on the phone, arranging their meeting time, did nothing to cheer her up.

He arrived outside her flat almost to the minute and hooted. She put on the fur coat over her dress and negotiated the stairs on her impossible heels without too much trouble. Sinclair watched from the driving seat as she walked towards the car.

'I hope you're dressed correctly,' he said. She opened the fur coat briefly. 'Very nice,' he approved. 'Turn round.'

At the start of their agreement she would have questioned him. Now she did not bother. The streets were empty. The Mercedes stood under a pool of light from a street lamp.

'Lift the coat,' he said abruptly. 'You know what I want to see.'

Once again she did not bother to argue. She turned, and gathered the skirt of her coat to one side, and stood with her legs slightly apart. She could almost feel the movement of his eyes stroking the curve of her buttocks.

'Very nice,' he said. He pushed open the car door. 'Get in.'

She settled beside him and the Mercedes moved smoothly away from the kerb. She glanced sideways at him. He was as immaculate as ever in a dark suit, but this time he wore a black polo neck instead of his usual shirt and silk tie.

'Why am I the one who always has to dress up?' she asked.

'Because I paid for your outfit,' he said. 'So I think I'm entitled to show it off.' He paused. 'Do you want to back out?'

'Certainly not,' she said sharply.

He laughed. 'Business comes first, doesn't it? As always.' He drove silently for a few minutes. 'And you're lucky,' he added.

'I was going to get Georgie to make you a real bondage corset. Then you would have had something to complain about.'

'I thought I already had one,' she said. She saw his teeth flash briefly white in the shadows.

'That was fancy dress,' he said. 'The real thing would have to be tailor-made. It would give you the kind of waistline you've always dreamed about. A real hourglass figure. It would have straps and buckles to truss you up, and immobilise you. You'd move only when I let you move. And it would be *very* uncomfortable. You'd love it.'

'What makes you think I like being uncomfortable?' she asked.

'You like feeling helpless,' he said.

'I most certainly do not.'

'You most certainly do,' he said. 'Not in real life. But here, with me. Haven't you learned to accept and enjoy your sexual nature yet?'

'I do as I'm told when I'm with you,' she said coolly, 'because that was our agreement. Enjoyment doesn't come into it.'

'And you haven't enjoyed any of it?' he mocked. 'Well, congratulations. You're a very good actress. You certainly fooled me.'

I'm acting, she thought. But not in the way you think. I'm acting all the time. Pretending I don't care. Pretending this is all strictly business. And it's fooling you. I'm a much better actress than I thought. Aloud she said: 'Where are we going?'

'I promised to show you some classy CP, didn't I?'

'CP?' she repeated.

'Corporal punishment,' he said. 'But don't worry, in fantasy land no one really gets hurt. Well, not much, anyway.'

The car stopped outside two darkened shops. Between them was a single door, with a small electric sign above it showing the outline of a whippet.

'Wait here,' Sinclair said. 'I'll park round the corner.'

He was only gone a few minutes but it gave her time to fix the hood. Once her face was obscured she felt more comfortable. Now she was unrecognisable. Free.

Sinclair inserted a card in a slot and the door opened. A steep flight of stairs led down, dully illuminated by lights designed to look like torches. She negotiated them carefully in her high-heeled boots. At the foot of the stairs was a surprisingly large foyer. The walls looked like stone, and were decorated with a variety of evil-looking implements that would have looked more at home in a torture dungeon.

A cheerful girl in a tight leather dress took Genevieve's coat. She hardly gave Genevieve's outfit a second glance, as if seeing half-naked women in a leather hood was an everyday occurrence. Which, Genevieve reflected, judging from the decor of this club it probably was.

She turned in time to see Sinclair give her one of his slow, admiring looks. He caught the chain that linked her breasts and pulled her towards him.

'You've got it right this time,' he said softly.

His mouth was very close to hers, but he did not kiss her. Instead his hand slid round and cupped her bottom. She felt it, warm against her flesh as he propelled her towards a set of double doors and into the club.

After her eyes had adjusted to the flickering light from the mock torches Genevieve realised why the girl in the foyer had not looked particularly surprised at her outfit. Compared to some of the club's patrons, her clothes were almost conventional.

Three women sat by the bar, talking. One of them wore a leather dress that exposed much more of her than it covered. Her two friends were wearing outfits consisting solely of thin straps wound and criss-crossed over their bodies. They wore shoes with heels as high as Genevieve's and none of them, she was amazed to note, had made any attempt at anonymity.

Sinclair leaned against the bar and ordered drinks. Two men in conventional suits walked over to the trio of leather-clad girls and began to talk to them. The girls laughed and chatted back. Apart from their extraordinary clothes they could have been three friends enjoying a drink on their way home from the office. One of the men edged closer to the girl in the revealing dress but, although he showed a definite interest in her, he made no attempt to touch her.

A man in a brief leather posing pouch and biker's boots wandered by, obviously looking for someone, followed by another man wearing a complicated harness that kept his prick strapped against his stomach in a position that Genevieve thought looked distinctly uncomfortable. He also wore nipple rings, a spiked dog collar and a hood similar to her own.

On the tiny dance floor, couples were moving languidly together, many of them dressed in skin-tight leather. One woman had chains joining her ankles. Despite this restriction she managed to sway and gyrate sensuously to the music. If she looked like stumbling, her more conventionally dressed companion put out his hand and steadied her.

In fact Genevieve was surprised at the number of men in suits. The women's costumes were far more adventurous. She was also surprised at the lack of any overtly sexual behaviour. Apart from the various way-out costumes this could have been the interior of any conventional, well-mannered London club.

'Madam's boots are magnificent.'

The voice behind her startled her. She turned and saw a good-looking, smartly dressed, middle-aged man standing near her, smiling.

'Would madam permit me to kiss them?'

Taken by surprise, Genevieve was lost for words. Was this a joke? But the man looked serious enough, almost anxious.

'Go ahead,' Sinclair said, easily.

'I need madam's permission,' the man stated.

'She'll give you permission,' Sinclair hinted.

'Well, of course,' Genevieve said, awkwardly.

'Thank you, madam.'

Kneeling in front of her, the man began to kiss the toe of her boot, twisting his head to run his tongue along the platform soles, licking the high heels. Vaguely embarrassed, Genevieve glanced round to see if anyone was watching. One or two people were glancing her way, but most of the club's patrons simply carried on dancing or talking. The man who had been chatting to the girl in the revealing leather dress had now moved with her away from the original group, and had his hand round her hips, his fingers probing the cleft of her buttocks. It was obvious from the girl's expression that she had no objection to his caresses.

Genevieve looked down at the man crouched in front of her. His attentions were too impersonal to be arousing. Clearly he was attracted to her boots, and not to her. But she did have a sudden vision of Sinclair kneeling at her feet in a submissive position. That, she thought, would be much more interesting.

Once again these thoughts surprised her. She had never felt inclined to dominate a man before, and certainly believed that she could not have respected a man who would allow her to do so. But she remembered how she felt when Sinclair took command of their sexual adventures, allowing her to simply relax and wait expectantly for whatever new excitement was coming next. Perhaps a man would also sometimes enjoy feeling the same way?

The idea would have seemed ridiculous to her a few months ago. But, she thought, that was just another example of how she had changed. How Sinclair had changed her, whether he had intended to do so or not. One more example of her hidden sexual personality that he had helped bring to the surface.

She looked down at the kneeling man. The expression on his face clearly reflected the erotic pleasure he was getting from the scent of the leather, the shape of her foot, the height of her heels. Suddenly he shuddered, his eyes shut, his mouth half-open, as orgasmic tremors shook him. He clung to her legs for a moment and then, with sigh, sat back on his heels and stood up.

'Beautiful,' he said. 'Thank you. May I buy you both a drink?'

'Yes,' Sinclair said, before Genevieve could say anything.

The man ordered drinks and paid, and after a few more casual words wandered away and disappeared.

'Surprised?' Sinclair sounded amused.

'That's putting it mildly,' Genevieve said.

'You must have known some people are turned on by shoes and boots, particularly high heels?'

'I suppose I knew it,' Genevieve admitted. 'I just didn't expect to be involved in it.' She had a sudden thought. 'Isn't he afraid I might meet him again somewhere, and remember him?'

'Probably not,' Sinclair said. 'One of the unwritten rules of this club is that people are discreet. That's why it's so popular. People feel safe to be themselves.'

'Is that why you come?' she asked. She felt like adding: have you brought Jade Chalfont here too? Does this kind of scene turn her on as well?

'I'm a member,' he said. 'But I don't come that often. I find it a little too well mannered. And I prefer my fantasies to seem spontaneous.' He grinned suddenly. 'Even if they often take weeks of planning.'

Genevieve looked round. She saw a large woman drinking and chatting to a group of female friends. Her booted feet were resting on a man crouched on the floor in front of her. Another man controlled his female companion by a leash attached to a dog collar round her neck. But for all the odd costumes and odd behaviour, she realised what Sinclair meant about the club being well mannered.

There was a strange feeling of decorum about the whole scene. She felt a sense of unreality about this fantasy world that she had never felt when participating in Sinclair's erotic games. She tried to decide why and realised that it was because the club lacked danger. With Sinclair there was always a sense of the unexpected. A fear of discovery. Here everything was safe. You asked politely for what you wanted. You did nothing that was not requested. There were no surprises. It was all terribly civilised.

The crowd on the dance floor suddenly parted and Genevieve noticed a small raised stage against the wall. Black curtains were pulled back to reveal a square-shaped frame. It glittered as lights played over it and she saw that there were steel manacles attached to each corner.

There was a murmur of conversation that stopped when two people stepped out of the crowd and walked toward the stage. One was a small woman in typical bondage leathers: a tight-laced corset, spike-heeled thigh boots, straps and chains wrapped round her body. Following her was a tall man, with the well-muscled torso of a body builder. His tanned skin gleamed with oil. He wore a silky posing pouch that emphasised his sexual endowments rather than hiding them, and a black hood that made him look like an Elizabethan executioner.

He carried a flexible riding crop ornamented with silver bands.

Genevieve glanced at Sinclair. 'Your professional CP couple?' she asked.

'Professional in attitude,' Sinclair said. 'No one here gets paid anything.' There was a trace of a smile on his lips. 'Unlike you, Miss Loften, they all do it for love.'

'It takes two to make an agreement,' she reminded him crisply. 'It was your idea, remember? And your terms.'

Sinclair did not reply and Genevieve turned her attention back to the stage. She waited for the leather-clad woman to be chained to the frame, but to her astonishment the man turned, knelt and offered the woman his whip, bowing his head in a gesture of obedience.

As the woman strutted round the stage, slapping the whip against her boots, two volunteers from the audience spread-eagled the man against the frame, fixing the manacles round his wrists and ankles. The woman turned and said something to her partner that Genevieve could not hear. He replied, and she laughed. She stepped back, curved the whip between her hands and then cracked it against her boot again.

The man, obviously expecting the blow to land on him, jerked in anticipation. The audience took a collective inward breath. The woman paused, then stroked the whip across the man's buttocks, gently. Again his body quivered expectantly. The crowd was as silent as if they were watching a theatre performance which, Genevieve thought, in a way they were.

The third time the whip landed in earnest. It drew a bright-red line on the man's neat, muscular behind. His whole body trembled, shaking the frame. Three more lashes followed in quick succession, each one raising a long, straight mark.

Then the frame began to revolve, slowly. The woman

followed it as it displayed her victim to the audience. Each time the whip landed, the man's hips jerked strongly, as if he was in the throes of sexual passion. The woman, obviously not holding back, delivered the punishment with enthusiasm, but Genevieve had no doubt that her victim was enjoying his predicament. His erection bulged against his brief posing pouch and when he began to plead with the woman to stop, his voice did not carry much conviction.

Sinclair finished his drink. It was difficult for Genevieve to decide whether or not he was actually enjoying the fantasy being played out for them. Personally, she had mixed feelings about it. Could she have whipped Sinclair like that? She would definitely have felt uncomfortable about humiliating him in public, and she was certain he would not have wanted it. But in private? She was not sure. It seemed to be taking domination a bit too far. To her it seemed like a drastic – and almost unnatural – role reversal, although she realised that many men found it stimulating.

But when she thought of Sinclair with Jade Chalfont in Japan, maybe giving her one of those slow and sensual visual assessments that she found so arousing, she felt much more sympathetic towards the idea of such punishment. Suddenly the thought of his body, stripped down to erotic near nakedness and spread-eagled on that frame, seemed extremely attractive. She tried to imagine him in a brief posing pouch and once again realised that she had never seen him completely nude. She had felt the movement of his muscles under her hands as she pulled him closer to her, holding him during the rhythms of love, but she had never been able to explore him fully with her eyes. Would she ever have that pleasure? She doubted it. He seemed unwilling to strip for her.

The couple on the stage had completed their ritual. The

woman released the manacles and held out the whip. The man knelt and kissed it. Then he stood up and kissed the woman on the lips. She laughed and patted him on the rear. He flinched, and she laughed again. Together they came down from the dais and were immediately surrounded by the crowd, who had already started to gyrate as the music rose in volume.

Genevieve realised that, despite her misgivings, the scene had made her feel sexy. Sinclair was lounging against a bar stool, and on impulse she reached out for him. He was semierect, but not hard. Obviously the stage display had only a limited effect on him.

'The rules here are that you always ask before touching,' he said.

But he did not move away. She massaged him gently but firmly, and felt his cock swell under her hand. As she continued to work on him, she could not believe that she was actually behaving like this in public. And enjoying it. His dark eyes watched her.

'Turned you on, didn't it?' he asked softly.

'Mildly,' she said. 'What about you?'

He glanced down at her moving hand. 'What do you think?'

'This is turning you on more,' she said.

He pulled away from her. 'Too much,' he said. 'And too early.'

She reached for him again and although he tried to avoid her he did not have much room to manoeuvre and she caught him, rather more roughly than she intended. He gave a subdued grunt of protest. That's for going to Japan with Jade Chalfont, she thought, pleased.

'All this is party stuff, really,' he said. 'Some people would find it pretty mild. There's more specialised entertainment if you want it.' He stood up. 'I'll show you.'

He led her across the dance floor and out into the foyer again. The cheerful receptionist was still there.

'We want privacy,' he said.

She reached for a key rack, found a key and handed it to him. 'The dungeon is free at the moment. But I can only allow you an hour. It's been booked for the rest of the night.'

'An hour is fine,' he said.

He took the key and led Genevieve down a narrow passageway until their path was barred by a heavy door with huge iron hinges. Sinclair unlocked it and, as it swung open, lights sputtered into mock flames on the walls. Genevieve walked forward and the door banged shut.

The room had stone walls and no windows. The air felt cool. There were so many pieces of equipment standing about that she did not know which one to look at first. There was a medieval rack, sitting and standing stocks, a whipping bench, a strange-looking padded vaulting horse with chains and shackles attached. There were several large metal frames obviously intended to secure victims in a variety of uncomfortable positions. There was even a complicated chair that seemed to be wired up to an electric socket.

There were hooks on the ceiling, and in the walls, and racks containing an assortment of whips. Genevieve walked round the room, looking and touching, and trying to decide how anyone could find any of this sexually arousing.

'Like it?'

Sinclair's voice startled her. She had almost forgotten he was there. She had a sudden horrible feeling that he wanted to use some of this equipment. 'No,' she said. 'Not really.'

'A lot of people find this a turn-on.'

'Do you?' she challenged.

'No,' he said. 'I don't need props like these.'

He took a whip from the wall rack and showed it to her. She

was amazed to see that the leather thongs had small pieces of bone and metal twisted into the end. He swung the whip suddenly. It made a vicious, swishing sound.

'These,' he said, 'are intended to hurt.'

'All this stuff is intended to hurt,' she said.

'It depends on how seriously you use it.' He put the whip back. 'But basically you're right.' He turned to the door. 'Come on. Let's go back upstairs.'

She was glad to leave the dungeon. It had depressed her. It reminded her too much of Ricky Croft's pictures, and of sexual pathways that she did not really understand. She was very glad that Sinclair did not seem to be interested in the dungeon's dubious attractions either.

Sinclair waited while Genevieve slipped into her fur coat, then followed her up the stairs and into the street again. He took her arm.

'The car's just round the corner.' Her heels clicked on the pavement as she walked beside him, taking two or three steps to his one. He opened the car door for her. She climbed into the front passenger seat, and by the time he was sitting beside her she had removed her mask and shaken out her hair.

'You looked relieved when we left the dungeon,' he said. There was a touch of humour in his voice now. 'Did you think I was planning a session in there?'

'I thought you might be,' she admitted.

'And you'd have gone along with it?'

'We have an agreement,' she said. 'Remember?'

'How could I forget?' he said, abruptly. He turned. His face was inches from hers. 'So let's see you perform.'

She reached for him, but he pushed her hands aside and twisted his fingers in her hair, forcing her downwards.

'This way,' he instructed, hoarsely.

'It's illegal in a car,' she said demurely.

'Only if you're caught,' he said. 'Get on with it.'

She reached forward, unzipped his trousers and took him in her mouth, moving her lips over the length of his shaft. She felt him growing hard. Her position was far from comfortable and he held her head down strongly, almost roughly, pushing his hips upwards and making sure she did not lose contact.

'That's right,' he said in a voice so low she could hardly hear it. 'That's good. It's almost as good as when I'm inside you. As good as fucking you.'

She ran the edge of her teeth lightly against his sensitive skin, then flicked the ridged end of his cock with her tongue, and he groaned.

'Make it last,' he entreated. 'Do that again. With your tongue. Do it.'

For the first time she felt that he was not in control. He needed her. Or maybe, she thought, he just needs the sex. Was it stupid of her to believe that it was only her mouth, her hands, or her body that could turn him on? It could have been anyone. Black-haired, sword-swinging Jade Chalfont. A geisha girl. Any of the dozens of other women he had probably made love to in his life.

As usual the thought of him with anyone else made her angry. Instead of caressing him slowly, prolonging his pleasure, she worked faster. And suddenly she felt his hands pulling her away.

'I said slow down,' he said harshly. 'Haven't you learned yet to obey orders?'

He shifted back in the seat and zipped himself up. She glanced sideways at him, seeing his profile against the street lights. His face was shadowed. For all their previous intimacy, he was still a stranger. She still did not understand him. He switched on the ignition and she heard the powerful engine purring into life.

She knew he was trying to keep his temper under control but instead of taking her home he drove to his house. Once again she had to clamber awkwardly up the steps in her high heels. He let her into the hall and pointed to the first door.

'In there,' he said abruptly. 'And strip. But keep the boots and gloves on.'

The room smelled just as she remembered it, of polish and leather, a sexy masculine scent. A small table stood by one of the armchairs. There was a padded, box-shaped stool near to it, on small stubby legs. She took off the leather dress slowly. In her thigh-high boots and gloves that came up over her elbows she realised that she must have looked like a hooker. She walked carefully round the room, her heels tapping on the wooden floor. She sat in the large armchair, leaned back and closed her eyes, and remembered the feel of him in her mouth. Thought about how his mouth would feel, moving over her body, lingering wherever he sensed a reaction.

'Get up.' Sinclair's voice startled her out of her dream. He had shed his coat and looked slightly sinister in the black polo neck and black trousers. He pointed to the padded stool. 'Over there, Miss Loften.' She went to sit on the stool but he shook his head. A smile touched his mouth, briefly. 'Bend over it,' he ordered. 'And part your legs a little.'

She obeyed, feeling rather undignified. She could not see him but she heard him. A drawer opened and shut. Then he was next to her again, kneeling. Quickly he fastened her wrists to each of the stool's legs with a heavy silk cord.

'Obedience,' he said. 'That's just to remind you not to move.'

It wasn't really uncomfortable. Her knees were on one of the thick rugs. It was simply humiliating. She could hear him moving about, but could not see him. She heard the clink of a glass. She tried to twist her head, but she was tipping too far forward and the stool's enclosed sides obstructed her vision. She was certain he was looking at her, and the thought made it difficult for her to keep still.

Then she heard him walk across the room. Heard the door open and click shut. She was alone. She pulled at her bound wrists. Probably if she had really tried she could have freed herself. She waited. Nothing happened for such a long time that she began to seriously consider working her wrists free.

When he finally returned she heard the clink of cutlery and glass. Although she could see nothing, she knew that he had put a tray down on the table next to the armchair. She waited for him to untie her. Instead she heard the faint creak of the chair as he sat down. The gurgle of something she assumed to be wine being poured into a glass. The sound of a knife cutting.

'Stop wriggling,' he said, as she tried to twist round.

'You're eating,' she accused.

'How perceptive of you, Miss Loften.'

'Did it occur to you that I might be hungry too?'

She heard him stand up. The sound of his footsteps coming towards her. She saw his feet, in their elegant, handmade, black leather shoes, inches from her head. A piece of chicken dropped on the floor near her head. If she had stretched forward she could have picked it up between her teeth.

'So eat,' he said.

She stifled an impolite retort. The chicken stayed where it was.

'You're not *that* hungry,' he observed.

He picked the chicken up and went back to his chair

'It's very tasty,' he said, after a few minutes. 'You don't know what you're missing.'

By now the leather boots were beginning to feel uncomfortably tight around her knees. She tried to stretch.

'Keep still,' he said.

'How long *for*?' she asked.

'Until I'm ready for you,' he said. 'And keep your legs apart. I want to see more of what I'm getting later on.'

How much later, she thought. Now she was beginning to get cramp in her legs, and pins and needles in her arms. She heard the clink of the wine bottle again. Despite his orders to keep still, she wriggled angrily.

'Thirsty?' he asked, politely. Again she heard him coming towards her. There was a clink of china against glass and then he put a saucer filled with wine on the floor close to her head. 'Drink,' he said.

'Does it constitute a breach of our agreement if I don't?' she asked tightly.

'Certainly not,' he said, lightly. 'I'm just being a good host.'

She was tempted to lap up the wine, but her pride forbade her to do so. After a moment he picked up the saucer.

'How long would you really hold out, Miss Loften?'

'You mean you're not going to try and find out?' she challenged.

He laughed softly. 'I've got a feeling you're tougher, and more stubborn, than you look. Now if I was a lord of the manor in the old days, and you were a rebellious servant, just think how interesting that could be? I could keep you prisoner for days. Weeks, even. Until finally you'd do anything I asked. You'd beg for food and lap water from a saucer like a cat.'

He was very close to her now. His fingers smoothed over her bottom, first softly then with increasing intensity and pressure. Under the magic of his hands she forgot all about her previous discomfort. Kneeling behind her, he slid his hands up under her body and massaged her breasts with his long fingers. She could feel the silky, smooth cloth of his polo neck shirt and the hardness of his muscled chest against her back.

She could feel the bulge of his cock pressing between her buttocks.

His hands moved down to stroke between her legs, his finger finding, and sliding over, the moist little bud of her clit, leaving it to find her breasts again, pinching her nipples into erection. He kissed the back of her neck, first lightly, then nipping her skin with his teeth.

'Want it now, do you?' His breath was soft against her skin. 'Well, you'll have to wait. Wait until I'm ready. And I like to hear you ask for it, lady. Remember that.'

Being bound no longer felt uncomfortable. Now the delicious feeling of being helpless excited her. His hands moved downwards and he found her clit again, erect and swollen now. Positioning his finger accurately on its sensitive tip, he pushed back against her pubic bone, driving her to a frenzy with strong circular movements. She made inarticulate moaning noises, deep in her throat.

'Ask me,' he murmured. 'Ask me. You want me to fuck you? Ask for it nicely.'

'Fuck me,' she moaned, writhing under him.

'Louder.'

She repeated it louder. And again. Repeated it in a frenzy of frustration until he was satisfied. Swiftly he unzipped and entered her just as the waves of pleasure were beginning their unstoppable rush and her body began to shake. His thrusts suddenly became less controlled. Her orgasm overtook her and she lost herself in waves of intense sensation. When her body had stopped trembling and she relaxed, she realised that he was still close to her, holding her, although he was no longer inside her.

'Good, was it?' His voice was low and intimate.

She murmured something, afraid that forming words would break the spell.

'And for me,' he said.

She realised suddenly that this was the closest they had been. This warm afterglow, with his body covering hers, was deliciously intimate. She wanted it to last but he broke the spell by standing up. In a moment her wrists were untied. His hand on her arm helped her to stand. She felt a stab of regret.

'Have a glass of wine,' he said. 'And I'll take you home.'

When she settled into the car again she still felt comfortably at ease. She felt as if their relationship had changed. But Sinclair did not seem to feel the same way.

'Not long to go now, Miss Loften.' He sounded both cynical and amused. 'Think you'll last the distance?'

'I've lasted this far.'

'A lot can happen in a short time.'

What was that supposed to mean, she wondered, as she let herself into her flat. It almost sounded like a warning.

A note in her diary reminded Genevieve of her conversation with Georgie. She was hesitant about ringing. Did she really want a night out in a lesbian club? Would she really enjoy it? Then she remembered that apart from her activities with Sinclair she had not had a social evening out for months. Maybe it would do her good to relax, chat, drink some wine, and not have to think about the approaching end of the ninety-day agreement. She phoned Georgie, who sounded delighted, and they made arrangements to meet.

'We'll go to Goldie's,' Georgie said. 'Parking's useless, I'm afraid. Can you take a cab?'

Armed with detailed instructions, Genevieve found Goldie's without any trouble. Georgie arrived on time in another cab. The club entrance was down a steep flight of stone steps, with a discreet sign outside. A large female bouncer nodded to them, stone-faced.

'Goldie owns the place,' Georgie said. 'You'll see how she got the name when you meet her.'

Georgie was a walking advertisement for her own talents. Her leather trousers were skin tight and she wore a snug white T-shirt. Genevieve herself wore a pale sleeveless dress, fashionable but understated.

The club was lit by subdued wall lights with multicoloured shades. Smoochy music murmured from the speakers, and several women were dancing. Tables stood round the side of the small dance floor, wooden partitions giving the occupants a measure of privacy. A bar ran along one wall. A good-looking young barman smiled at them, but it was only when 'he' spoke that Genevieve realised the elegant 'young man' was a woman.

'Hi, Jan,' Georgie said. 'This is a friend of mine. She's never been to a queers' club before.'

Jan nodded cheerfully, and did not seem offended by Georgie's description of the club, but Genevieve felt distinctly awkward and was glad when she was able to hide herself in the shadows of one of the tables by the wall.

'I thought "queer" was an insult?' she said.

'Depends on who's using it,' Georgie said. 'And I wanted to let Jan know, in the nicest possible way, that you were straight. Otherwise she'd have been over here as soon as she came off duty, chatting you up.'

'How do you know I'm her type?' Genevieve asked.

'Any beautiful woman is her type,' Georgie said. She glanced up. 'Look, there's Goldie.'

An enormous woman had appeared behind the bar and was now talking to Jan. Apart from her size, the other extraordinary thing about her was the amount of gold jewellery she was wearing. Earrings dangled to her shoulders, her fingers were hidden under glittering rings. Chains covered her chest, and bracelets heavy with charms were pushed halfway up her arms to make room for the wide slave bangles on her wrists. Genevieve calculated that if the gold was genuine Goldie should have been kept in a padlocked safe.

'It's genuine,' Georgie confirmed when Genevieve questioned her.

'Isn't she afraid of being robbed?' Genevieve asked.

Georgie shrugged. 'If you asked Goldie she'd probably say "easy come, easy go". She loves wearing the stuff, but I don't think she's hung up over it. Mind you, she very rarely goes out. This place is fully alarmed, and Billie's here most of the time, too.'

'Billie?' Genevieve questioned.

'You saw her on the door,' Georgie said. 'No one gets in here unless Billie approves. You wouldn't have got in without me.'

Genevieve remembered the hefty 'doorman'. 'Are they – er – lovers?' she asked.

Georgie grinned. 'No. Just friends. And business partners. Lesbians can be *friends* with each other, you know?'

'Oh, stop being so touchy,' Genevieve said, good-humoured.

The music changed to a brighter beat. A couple of women began to dance with each other.

'Things get more lively later on,' Georgie said. 'That's why I brought you early. I didn't want you getting embarrassed.'

'The orgies start later?' Genevieve enquired, smiling.

'That's right,' Georgie agreed. 'Billie won't let you in unless you've got a ten-inch dildo in your handbag.'

Genevieve sat back and enjoyed her drink. Two more women walked onto the dance floor. They were dressed plainly in T-shirts and skirts, but they were as poised as ballet students. Interpreting the music's beat in a series of rhythmic and sinuous movements, they moved slowly round each other without touching. It was graceful and theatrical. Genevieve was so engrossed in watching them that she did not notice the two new customers at the bar until a loud laugh from Goldie caught her attention. She leaned forward, and looked round the wooden cubicle partition.

A man and a woman stood together. The woman looked like a fashion model, in a figure-revealing, knee-length dress. She had the kind of stunning red hair no one could ever get out of a bottle. It cascaded to her shoulders in glossy waves. The man looked relaxed and elegant in a dark tailored suit. He was talking to Goldie, but he had one hand possessively on the redheaded woman's bottom. As Genevieve watched, she saw his long fingers massaging his companion's curving buttocks. Not only did Genevieve know that this was definitely a man, she knew his name. It was James Sinclair. She drew back so quickly that Georgie looked at her in surprise.

'What's the matter?'

'I didn't think you allowed men in here.'

'We do,' Georgie said. 'Mostly gay men, but unless Billie knows them really well they have to come in with a genuine club member. We don't get many straight men. Most of them only want to gawk at the freaky women who don't like cock, and this isn't really a voyeur's club. Why? Who's just come in?' She peered round the cubicle. 'Oh, that's Marsha. She's an actress, or a model, or whatever takes her fancy. I don't know who the man is.' She glanced at Genevieve. 'Do you?'

'Er – yes.' Genevieve felt she had to admit that much. 'But not all that well,' she added hastily. 'I know him from work. And I don't want him to recognise me.'

'Relax,' Georgie said. 'Sit back. No one will see you.'

Genevieve could accept that Georgie did not know Sinclair. He had probably conducted all his dealings with her over the telephone. But what was he doing in this kind of club?

And with a ravishingly good-looking woman like that? It was quite obvious from the way he was fondling her, and the way she was reacting, that they were more than just good friends.

'Marsha certainly isn't gay,' she observed, tartly.

'She is sometimes.' Georgie glanced at Genevieve and grinned. 'Marsha swings both way. Fancy her, do you? Want me to arrange an introduction?'

'Certainly not,' Genevieve said, primly.

She toyed with her drink and then peeped quickly round the side of the cubicle again. Goldie had moved further down the bar to talk to another customer. Jan was pouring a drink. Sinclair leaned towards Marsha and whispered something, and Marsha laughed. Sinclair lifted the heavy fall of her shining red hair and it was obvious from the way his head was moving, and from the way Marsha squirmed with delight, that he was using his tongue in and around her ear, probing and caressing, kissing her lightly, while his hand flattened against her bottom and pulled her closer to him.

'Hey, you two,' Goldie called from the other end of the bar. 'Why don't you just hire a bedroom?'

Genevieve heard Sinclair laugh. 'Good idea,' he said. 'Come on, sweetheart. Let's go.'

They left the club together and as she watched them Genevieve realised that she was furious. And jealous. First Jade Chalfont, and now this redheaded bisexual. Or maybe Jade Chalfont *and* Marsha whatever-her-name-was. And who else? She sat there silently fuming. Then she remembered the torture implements at the bondage club and suddenly the idea of Sinclair chained to a rack or a flogging post seemed positively attractive.

'Hey?' Georgie touched her arm. 'Loosen up. So you like him. So he hasn't noticed you yet. Maybe he will. But even if he doesn't, it's not the end of the world. You've already got a fella, haven't you?'

Have I? Genevieve thought. It looks as if I'm just one on a long list of Mr James Sinclair's available playmates. What was he going to do with redheaded Marsha that evening? What was he doing at that precise moment? Was he driving, telling her what he had arranged for her later? Or was he sitting in a taxi with his fingers smoothing the soft inner skin of her thigh, finding the warmth higher up, tempting her legs apart while the driver, oblivious to what was happening on the back seat of his cab, headed for whatever destination Sinclair had planned.

Would he take her home? Would Marsha strip for him? Or would he strip her? Would she end up naked, bound to the door, with Sinclair looking her over with that possessive, slightly cynical and infuriatingly attractive smile, as he decided which part of her body to stimulate first? The thought of him was making her wet. She hated him! She hated Marsha! She swallowed the remainder of her drink and slammed the glass back on the table.

'Really fancy him, don't you?' Georgie said quietly.

'No, I don't,' Genevieve snapped back. 'I hardly know him.'

'If I was into men,' Georgie said, reflectively, 'I think he'd be the type I'd go for.' She glanced at Genevieve. 'But I wouldn't get ulcers over him. Or over a woman either, come to that.'

'Well, I am into men,' Genevieve said. 'And he's definitely *not* the type I go for.'

'How do you know?' Georgie asked innocently. 'You just said you didn't know him all that well.'

'You can see what he's like. A conceited womaniser! A male chauvinist pig!'

It had spoiled her evening. She tried to put it out of her mind but it was impossible. Although Georgie attempted to entertain her with amusing anecdotes, Genevieve cut the evening short. Leaving Georgie with her friends, she took a taxi back to her apartment.

She tried to forget what she had seen. She tried relaxing in a warm bath (which somehow did nothing to relax her), and then watching a video. Unfortunately she picked one with a leading man who looked vaguely like Sinclair. She switched the film off.

She was angry with Sinclair for being able to affect her like this, and angry with herself for being affected. She knew that she had no claim on him. He had never said that their agreement, even while it lasted, was exclusive. She had simply assumed that he was not seeing any other women while he was seeing her. He had not forbidden her to see other men. As long as she was available when he wanted her, she thought, he probably did not care what she did in her spare time.

Even that angered her. She realised that she *wanted* him to care. Damn him! What was he doing in a lesbian club with that redheaded bitch in tow? What was he doing right now? She felt her body shiver as she imagined his mouth moving over Marsha's body, his hands exploring, expertly, finding different ways to turn her on.

She wished he was here with her. She wished he had come in while she was in the bath and dipped his hands under the froth of bubbles and found her warm skin, slippery from the oil that scented the water. She imagined the sensation of his hands searching her body, lingering down her spine, fondling her nipples just roughly enough to excite them, sliding between her legs.

Maybe he would strip, and join her. She would feel his skin next to hers, his hard erection pressing against her. But he would save himself. They would shower the soap from their bodies. She imagined the shine of his tanned skin under the cascade of water. The sight of his cock, straining upwards. She would tease him, gently cupping his balls and maybe even taking him in her mouth, arousing him still further. He would lift her into his arms and carry her over to the bed.

You romantic idiot, she told herself. That's never going to happen. That's the way lovers behave, and James Sinclair is not your lover. He's a business proposition. And to him you're an amusement. He's selling, and you're buying. You're using each other. That's what the ninety-day agreement is all about.

And my usefulness is coming to an end, she thought suddenly. James Sinclair is already looking round for a replacement.

She began to wonder if she was going to get the usual feedback from Sinclair. If there was even going to be another meeting. Then the courier brought a small parcel and a large white envelope. The parcel contained a length of heavy silk cord and in the envelope was a large white invitation card: YOU ARE CORDIALLY INVITED TO A CELEBRATION. COSTUME AND MASK TO BE WORN BY ALL GUESTS. The address was Hilton Hall, Essex. The date, the thirtieth of the month. It was the day her agreement with Sinclair ended.

8

Genevieve put the invitation card on the shelf of the small Welsh dresser in her kitchen. She read it each morning, and each time it depressed her. It sounded terribly final. Was this really going to be her last private meeting with Sinclair? She believed it was. He had not shown any sign of wanting to continue their relationship. Was he already enjoying Jade Chalfont's company more than hers? With Marsha adding a little spice to the mixture? Perhaps Marsha and Jade were willing to perform a twosome for him, with variations that she and Bridget had not had the time – nor, in her case, the inclination – to try?

She did not want to imagine them together, but the pictures kept forming: Jade Chalfont, slim and tall as a super-model, but with hidden muscles from her martial arts training, and Marsha, with her more rounded curves and stunning red hair. What would they do? Would they use whips and chains? A cock-shaped vibrator? A strapped-on dildo? Surely Sinclair would not find that sort of thing a turn-on?

Or maybe he would. Maybe she did not know him at all. He had certainly shown no particular interest in the more extreme pleasures on offer in the dungeon, but was that just because he guessed she was not interested? Although part of his pleasure clearly came from making his partner aware of sexual needs she had not previously been aware of – or had deliberately refused to acknowledge – he did not seem to want to force a woman into any sexual games she did not enjoy.

But she was certain he would be equally good at discovering what those games might be. Was he already planning to get her to back down on the last day of their unusual contract? Would that amuse him? She remembered his words: if anyone breaks our agreement, it'll be you. He had quite obviously enjoyed the feeling of being in control. This would be the ultimate proof of it.

Would he do it? She was still not sure.

'How are things progressing?'

Genevieve had hardly had time to check her appointments for the day, before George Fullerton arrived at her office, making a rather obvious attempt to look as if he had been casually passing by, had seen her and just dropped in.

'How am I getting on with Mr Sinclair, you mean?' Genevieve countered.

'That too,' Fullerton agreed. 'I understand the Japanese trip was successful, but the rumour is that Barringtons haven't a hope in hell of getting Sinclair's account.'

'That rumour's been going round a long time,' she said.

'And nothing much has happened here to disprove it,' Fullerton commented, quietly.

'I told you, George,' Genevieve said, with a touch of irritation fuelled by the knowledge that she was not sure if she was telling the truth, 'Sinclair has been buying time. Now that the Japanese deal is finalised he'll start to reorganise his marketing campaigns. With us.'

'I wish I shared your confidence,' Fullerton said honestly. 'But I'd feel a lot happier about Mr Sinclair's sincerity if gossip didn't also claim that he's been seeing rather a lot of Jade Chalfont. Maybe it's just for sex – knowing Sinclair's reputation

235

that wouldn't surprise me – but you can't tell me they never discuss business. Chalfont's one of Lucci's account managers, after all.'

'They call them reps,' Genevieve said.

'I don't care what they call them,' Fullerton said sharply. 'That Chalfont woman set her sites on Sinclair almost as soon as she joined Lucci's. She probably got him into bed after their first meeting.'

'That doesn't mean she's also going to get him to sign on the dotted line,' Genevieve said.

'Obviously not,' Fullerton agreed. 'But if they're having a fling, I'm sure it hasn't harmed Miss Chalfont's chances. Of course, I don't expect you to use the same tactics, but you did give me the impression that things were moving nicely before that Chalfont woman appeared on the scene. Very nicely, if I remember rightly. After that,' he smiled slightly to show that this was only a friendly criticism, 'negotiations seemed to have come to a standstill.'

'I told you, George,' she said patiently. 'Sinclair wanted time.'

'He's had time,' Fullerton said. 'How much longer do you think he wants?'

'Oh, good heavens, George.' Genevieve felt her temper slipping. 'I can't push a prospective client too hard.'

'Make an informed guess,' Fullerton requested.

'I'd guess at next week,' she said. 'One way or the other.'

And which way would it be? she wondered, later that day, as she made her way home from work. The more she thought about it, the less certain she was that Sinclair would choose Barringtons' services. She had believed him to start with. But was that because she had been attracted to him and had wanted to believe him?

Would he really risk the ideas offered by a young and admittedly relatively inexperienced creative team, rather than trust an international track record, like that of the equally up-and-coming Lucci's? Would he stay with Randle-Mayne in the end? She had only his word that he was having creative differences with them.

How would her career stand if her predictions proved wrong? She knew nothing drastic would happen, at least not immediately, but she would certainly lose credibility, especially as she had insisted so strenuously that Sinclair was going to bring his account to Barringtons. Damn you, Sinclair, she thought suddenly, angrily. You've messed up my life in more ways than one.

That evening she did an internet search on Hilton Hall and found that it was a private house owned by a city financier whose name was familiar to her from the newspapers. A respectable figure who had never been linked with any kind of scandal. But, she remembered, the Knights of the Banner had been a genuine organisation meeting at a legitimate venue. She suspected that the celebration at Hilton Hall was not as conventional as it sounded.

The week passed slowly. On Thursday a small white envelope landed on her mat. Inside was an appointment card. Variety Costumes, she read. The telephone number and address were printed, but a time and date had been added by hand with a request for confirmation. The date was the evening before the one on Sinclair's invitation card. He was obviously assuming that whatever costume she wanted would be available from this supplier. She telephoned, and a girl with a Sloaney voice seemed very anxious that she was happy with her appointment time and asked her if she had 'any ideas'. Totally confused, Genevieve said that she hadn't. What would the girl suggest?

'Does the party have a theme?'

'I don't know,' Genevieve said. 'I don't think so. My invitation just says it's a celebration.'

'Well, aren't you lucky,' the cheerful voice informed her. 'You can go as absolutely anything.'

Somehow this made Genevieve feel depressed again. Usually Sinclair dictated what she would wear. Now it seemed as if he was no longer interested enough to care.

Variety Costumes gave the impression of being as chaotic as a jumble sale, but it was soon clear that the assistants knew exactly where everything was. Dresses, coats, hats, shoes and accessories were labelled and coded. One assistant worked a computer. When a customer asked for a particular costume, the computer found its number, and an assistant fetched it for approval and fitting.

Faced with so much choice Genevieve found it impossible to make up her mind. She could be an exotic Eastern dancer or a maid in a short black dress with a fresh white apron and cap. She could swathe herself in furs and jewellery or go semi-naked as a belly dancer. She could be a clown (in fact she was rather tempted) or a wasp-waisted lady in a high-necked, lace-fronted blouse and a wide-brimmed hat heavy with flowers and colourful feathers.

Then she saw a top hat. On impulse she tried it on. The assistant turned her towards a mirror.

'That really suits you. How about going as Marlene Dietrich? The *Blue Angel* look, you know? You could wear a man's tailcoat and high heels. Your hair's the right colour and with the correct period make-up you'd look super.'

Although she had been thinking of a glamorous historical outfit, Genevieve found this idea appealing. She knew she had good legs, and they'd look fine in black silk stockings and high heels. Combined with a man's coat and the top hat, the effect should be sexy and unusual. Even if Sinclair did not appreciate it, she would feel happy knowing that she looked good.

When she tried the complete outfit, she knew she had made the right choice. The band of white flesh visible between the tops of her stockings and edge of her black silk briefs added to the erotic image. The black tailcoat, cropped at the front, and the white shirt beneath, disguised her feminine shape but somehow made her look and feel more sexy than if she had worn a low-cut gown. This outfit promised and tempted rather than revealed. She put on the top hat and tilted it rakishly sideways. The assistant smiled in enthusiastic approval.

'Absolutely great. Your husband's going to love you in that.'

'I'm not married,' Genevieve said.

'Well, your boyfriend, then.'

'I haven't got a boyfriend either,' Genevieve said, and before the assistant could comment she added quickly: 'I'll need a mask.'

The assistant smiled. 'I know just the right one. I'll get it for you.'

Left on her own Genevieve posed unselfconsciously in front of the mirror. Maybe Sinclair would be attracted by this costume. It was strange how the right combination of masculine clothes and feminine accessories emphasised femininity. This *Blue Angel* look promised something not quite conventional, a hint of the forbidden, the unusual. The assistant returned with a mask that looked as if it had been sprayed with Christmas-card glitter.

'Here you are,' she said. 'This will go with your costume. A contrast to all that black.'

Genevieve had to admit that she was right. And the sparkling mask under the brim of the top hat disguised her completely. She left the shop well-satisfied with her visit.

The taxi that came to collect her had no other passengers. Genevieve wore her fur coat over her costume. The taxi driver was cheerful and talkative, making the journey through London and out into the Essex countryside pass quickly.

It was getting dark by the time they branched off the motorway and turned into roads that quickly grew narrower and devoid of traffic. The driver seemed to know his way, rarely hesitating to consult sign posts at junctions or crossroads. He finally slowed at an imposing pair of wrought-iron gates, and turned into a driveway. Coloured lights glittered in the trees. At the end of the drive, Hilton Hall stood illuminated with spotlights. Music spilled from the open doors.

The welcoming atmosphere was slightly spoiled by the two burly bouncers in smart suits who checked Genevieve's invitation card with an electronic scanning device. But, once she was through the doors, smiling staff took her coat, offered her a selection of drinks, and explained that there was a permanent buffet in the blue room, the cinema was showing a continuous programme, there was dancing in the ballroom, the indoor pool was heated and the viewing area was open. If she wanted a private room, the first floor was available. Theme rooms were provided. If she did not know her way around the Hall, any member of staff – dressed in royal-blue, page-boy uniforms – would direct her.

Not all of this made immediate sense to Genevieve. She loitered in the foyer, wondering if Sinclair was looking for her. A masked couple wandered past, the man dressed conventionally as a vicar and the woman as a bare-breasted ancient Egyptian. Another couple, who had probably started off in Edwardian clothes but were now down to their period-style underwear, went up the wide main staircase together. Obviously heading for the private rooms, Genevieve thought.

She was beginning to feel awkward. Guests arrived in pairs or groups, in various stages of dress and undress, smiled at her and then wandered off together laughing and talking. Where was Sinclair? Would she recognise him? He would certainly recognise her, even with her mask on. She felt certain he had contacted Variety Costumes for details of the outfit she had chosen. Surely he was going to attend this party? And if he wasn't, what was the point of sending her all the way out here?

She decided she might look less like a wallflower if she started to walk about. Passing a door marked CINEMA, she slipped inside, more to confirm her suspicions about what kind of films they would be showing than from any particular desire to watch.

She realised immediately that she had guessed correctly. On the huge screen bodies writhed together. The camera zoomed in to a close-up: a man's mouth caressing a woman's breast, the tip of his tongue tracing a line under its curving weight, to end up on a nipple. His tongue circled. The woman's gasp of pleasure as his lips sucked her were amplified on the sound track. Memories of Sinclair's mouth performing the same erotic tricks on her made Genevieve feel tense with frustration. The camera moved to another couple, another mouth, a pair of hands stroking an erect cock.

It was a well-made film, with soft colour and excellent picture quality. As Genevieve watched, the camera picked out another couple, their legs entwined around each other, their bodies rocking. Once again the hidden speakers magnified the sound of their delight.

'Looks like fun.' The unexpected voice startled her. She turned quickly. The man next to her was tall and powerfully built, and dressed as an American policeman. He had a soft American accent that she thought was genuine and not just assumed because of his costume. 'But the real thing's better still.'

There was a suggestive invitation in his voice that Genevieve did not like. 'That depends on who you're doing it with,' she said coolly.

She saw his teeth gleam in the flickering light from the screen. 'You wouldn't be here if you were bothered who you did it with,' he said.

'I was invited by a friend,' she answered shortly.

'Yeah? Where is he – or she?'

'*He* is waiting for me by the pool,' Genevieve improvised. 'So if you'll excuse me?'

She pushed past her unwelcome companion, and for a moment it seemed as if he was going to try and stop her. She felt the hard bulk of his body. She smelled the faint sharpness of an expensive aftershave. 'Excuse me, please,' she said abruptly.

He laughed then, and stepped back, allowing her to escape into the light. She decided that she would go to the pool anyway. Maybe she could borrow a costume and have a swim. She asked directions from one of the staff and hurried down a long corridor. A harlequin in a brightly patterned bodysuit passed her, followed by a woman wearing a brief and revealing school girl's gymslip and a boater hat.

She tried to imagine the kind of costume Sinclair would wear. She had only ever seen him in a suit, combats, and his motor-cycle leathers. Her mind clothed him in various uniforms, her favourite being a hussar: tight white trousers and glossy boots, his cropped jacket ornamented with masses of gold braid. It would suit his tall, athletic figure. She kept the image in her mind, trying to blank out the memory of the American.

She reached the pool and found it crowded with swimmers, laughing and shrieking. None of them, she was surprised to note, wore any kind of mask. When a few of them pulled themselves out of the water she realised that they were not wearing costumes either. One of the pool staff came up beside her.

'If you want to see better, go down to the viewing-room.'

He pointed to a door. Genevieve went down some steps and found herself in a room below pool level. Music filtered from hidden speakers. Men and women stood in groups watching the action through a thick glass wall. Their bodies were dappled with watery reflections, making them look strangely surreal. As Genevieve stood watching, the swimmers began to move away from the viewing panel. Before she could work out why she heard a voice behind her.

'Recognise anyone?'

She smelled the familiar sharp aftershave and turned round. The American policeman was grinning at her. She could see the dark stubble on his chin beneath the black mask.

'Please stop following me,' she said coldly.

'I'm not following you,' he said. 'I've come to watch the fun.'

He gestured at the glass wall. Genevieve realised that there were only two swimmers in the pool now. The naked bodies of a man and a woman trod water and then reached for each other. As she watched they began to stroke and caress each other, in time to the music. Their supple bodies floated in the water in a series of weightless and erotic gymnastics. They looked like aliens from outer space, their skin patterned with rippling shadows. Even when they joined together in their sexual finale their hip-thrusting was in slow motion, and seemed oddly innocent. Genevieve felt that she was watching a ritual dance rather than a sex show.

'I still say nothing beats the real thing,' the policeman said.

He put his hand on Genevieve's bottom and patted her. 'How about it, baby? You and me? I do a good strip search.'

She moved away from him and walked towards the door. 'I've told you, I'm waiting for a friend.'

He followed her. 'So what? Leave him a message. If he turns up, he can join in.'

'I don't think he'd be very happy about that,' she said, walking faster.

'Listen,' the policeman said. 'I'm used to getting what I want. And right now I want you.'

'That's a pity,' she said, 'because I'm already booked for the evening.'

He grinned. 'Make me a promise? Introduce me to this boyfriend of yours. We'll do a deal. I'll trade him two very acrobatic brunettes for you.'

'Why don't you make use of the brunettes?' Genevieve said, sweetly. 'And leave me alone.'

'Because they don't surprise me any more,' he said. 'And I think you will. I fancy a bit of class, and you've got it.'

'What I've got, I'm keeping,' she said. 'So please go away.'

He laughed. 'I just hate it when women give in too easily. But the night is young, as they say. I'm going to have you, and you'll probably love it.' He touched his cap in a mocking gesture. 'See you around, sweetheart.'

Despite his easy manner she sensed a ruthlessness about him. She believed his claim that he usually got his own way. Once again she wished Sinclair would appear. Where *was* he? A rush of anger swept over her. What was he playing at? Leaving her on her own at a party like this made her an obvious target for unattached men. Was that what he wanted? Did he hope a stranger would pick her up and take her to one of the first-floor private rooms so that he could follow her discreetly, and watch?

She did not want to believe this of him. She knew he had called her an exhibitionist, and she accepted that it was partly true. But she realised now that if she was going to have an audience, she only wanted to perform with him, not for him with another man. She remembered Bridget but, for Genevieve, somehow it seemed different with a woman. Almost like making love to yourself. Pleasant, but without any emotional commitment.

If he was planning to pair her with someone else, would she refuse? She prided herself on being a modern woman. Surely a quick bout of sex with a man she did not like was not an impossible final price to pay for a career success? Or was it? She did not want to have to make the decision. She could no longer give a confident affirmative answer. Sinclair had changed all her values.

She made her way to the buffet but the food, delicious as it was, tasted like sawdust in her mouth. She inspected the costumed revellers for anyone who looked remotely like Sinclair in size and height. She tried to avoid gazing too intently at any particular guest in case they took it as an invitation. Even without any advances on her part she was approached by several men, and some women. Happily they took her refusal in good part and wandered off to find more obliging playmates.

As she was trying to decide whether to hide herself in the cinema or go out into the floodlit grounds Genevieve felt a tap on her arm. Turning she found a man in royal-blue staff uniform. He held out a plain white envelope with FROM JS on the front.

'I believe this is for you, ma'am. Do the initials mean anything to you?'

'Yes, they do,' she confirmed.

'I was told to look for a Marlene Dietrich lookalike, ma'am,' he said. 'Although in my opinion you're more beautiful than the original.'

Genevieve smiled her thanks at the compliment. She opened the envelope and recognised Sinclair's writing. The message was simple: TAKE PART IN THE AUCTION.

The staff man had begun to walk away. Genevieve moved forward to catch up with him.

'What is this auction? Where do I go?'

'The charity auction?' He stopped and turned towards her. 'You want to volunteer?'

'I think so,' she said. 'But I haven't got anything to sell.'

The man laughed. His eyes moved over her body in a quick assessment. It was friendly rather than lecherous and Genevieve felt that she had been complimented again.

'I think you have, ma'am.'

'All right,' Genevieve said, returning his smile. 'Explain.'

'The auction is a feature of parties at Hilton Hall, ma'am. Volunteers go on stage, and bidders pay for the removal of a chosen item of clothing. You can stop whenever you like, but if you do, you have to pay a forfeit. If the volunteer agrees, the purchaser can also buy some of their time at the end of the auction, to be spent in one of the private rooms. That's a personal choice, of course. There's no forfeit if you refuse.' He smiled at her. 'To be honest, I'm sure the volunteers know who's buying them anyway. The arrangements are made in advance.'

Genevieve thought that sounded exactly like something Sinclair would enjoy, and if he was in the audience watching, she would enjoy it too. She began to feel a lot happier. She had no doubt that he would bid for her time at the end.

'Who gets the money?' she asked.

'The charity of your choice, ma'am. You tell the auctioneer before the bidding starts.'

Fine, she thought. I know a good charity that promotes medical research without the use of animals. Mr James Sinclair can add substantially to their funds.

She was in the buffet, enjoying the food this time, when the auction was announced. She followed the moving crowd to a large room adjoining the ballroom, registered her charity and was given a number to carry. The volunteers laughed and joked together. Most of them were masked, but despite this they seemed to know each other.

A woman in a medieval gown was teasing a man dressed as a samurai.

'Can't wait to show your pecs, can you, Miles? You're such an exhibitionist.'

The samurai grinned. 'I aim to show more than pecs if Amanda's bidding for me. Providing I can remember how to get these odd clothes off.'

'You should have chosen something simple,' the medieval lady said. 'With a body like yours, you could have been a lifeguard or something.'

'You can't see my body,' he objected. 'Not in this skirt.'

'I've got a photographic memory, darling. I remember all my men.'

'Don't tell Amanda,' the samurai laughed. 'You might shock her.'

'You think she doesn't know? We've already swopped performance details.'

'Women!' the samurai complained. 'You've no scruples at all.'

Genevieve could see the darkened ballroom through a door. The band began to play a fanfare and the first volunteer, a girl dressed as a cat, walked down an aisle formed by the bidders and onto the stage. A spotlight picked her out and stayed with her. She stood on a small dais and held her number above her head. The dais began to revolve slowly. The band began to play. A voice over the loudspeaker suggested an opening bid and someone from the audience responded enthusiastically.

The girl stripped off her catsuit quite sexily, but since it was a one piece outfit and she was only wearing a bra and pants underneath she was not on the dais for very long. Her figure was lithe and slim, with small breasts. She posed while the audience cheered, and the voice from the speakers announced the sum of money she had raised. I can strip better than that, Genevieve thought smugly. If Sinclair wants a show, I'll give him one.

When she finally stepped into the ballroom the glare of the spotlight followed her. Dazzled, she could not make out any of the faces in the audience. She stood on the revolving dais and felt her body begin to move in response to the beat of the music. This was going to be easy. She was going to enjoy it. She felt certain Sinclair was watching her but when the first bid came out of the darkness she did not recognise the voice. It sounded slurred.

'Twenty-five for the hat.'

'I am bid twenty-five pounds for the lady to take off her hat,' the auctioneer announced over the speaker.

Genevieve almost smiled. If that was the way the bidding was going she stood to make a healthy profit for her charity. She took off the top hat with a flourish.

'And loosen her hair,' the bidder added.

'An extra fiver for the hair,' the auctioneer demanded.

'A fiver? I can't afford it!'

There was laughter, boos and catcalls.

'Has he paid his fiver?' the auctioneer persisted. 'The hair stays up until he's paid.'

Genevieve could not see any money changing hands. She

was dependent on the hidden auctioneer for instructions. While she waited for the good-natured argument to end she moved sinuously on the dais as it turned.

'A hundred pounds for the coat!'

She removed it, taking her time, sliding it back off her shoulders, wriggling it down her arms. finally she bent over and caught the dangling tails, whipping the coat between her legs, as she stood up again, and flinging it away.

'A hundred for the shirt.'

'More for the shirt,' the auctioneer demanded.

'A hundred and fifty.'

Genevieve lifted the edges of the shirt provocatively. High enough for the lower curve of her breasts to be visible. High enough for the audience to see that she was not wearing a bra. She stayed there, waiting.

'More for the shirt,' the hidden auctioneer repeated.

'Two hundred.'

'Two hundred for the shirt.' The auctioneer accepted the bid.

Genevieve took her time. Toying with the buttons. Lifting the edge of the shirt just high enough to tease, then dropping it again. Finally easing the garment off her shoulders, bunched in front of her, still covering her breasts, always moving with the music. She was aware that the audience were quieter now. She had captured them. When she tossed the shirt aside there was a cheer and several wolf whistles.

The bids went on for the rest of her clothes. None of the voices sounded like Sinclair. A hundred pounds for her suspender belt. A hundred for each stocking. Three hundred for the black silky pants. Now she wore only a brief G-string, her glittering mask and her shoes. How much for the G-string, she wondered?

'Five hundred pounds.'

The voice from the audience answered her question. Her hands went to the narrow silk thongs that held the brief garment in place.

'A thousand pounds for an hour of the lady's time.'

This was a different voice. There was a gasp from the audience, then clapping. Then the first voice again.

'A thousand pounds for the G-string.'

More clapping and cheering.

'Two thousand.' The second voice interrupted the applause. 'For two hours of time.'

It certainly sounded like Sinclair, although the noisy reaction from the audience made it difficult to be sure. But who else would pay so much money for my time, she thought. The note she had received had definitely been in Sinclair's handwriting, and he would have been the only one who knew the costume she was wearing.

'The lady has the choice,' the auctioneer was explaining. 'Either way her charity will benefit, but will it be by one thousand pounds or two?'

Genevieve was so convinced that Sinclair had bid for her she did not hesitate. 'I'll sell two hours of my time,' she said.

More cheering, clapping, whistling. She revolved once more on the dais, acknowledging – and enjoying – the applause. As she left the dais someone handed her back her clothes. She put on the tailcoat, feeling the lining silky and cool against her flesh. 'Room 32,' a staff member told her. 'It's a beautiful room.'

Genevieve went out into the brightly lit foyer. The wide stairs were softly carpeted in deep red. She walked up them. Sinclair would be waiting for her in Room 32. She was sure of it. She paused outside the door, almost afraid to go in. This could be their last meeting. She would have to accept that he was not the type who wanted a permanent relationship. Or if he did, he certainly didn't want one with her. When she saw him again, it would be in her professional capacity, and they would probably treat each other as if they were polite business acquaintances. She put the thought of it out of her mind. It depressed her.

When she pushed open the door the first thing she noticed were the mirrors. Ornately framed in gilt they reflected each other, and made the room seem much larger than it really was. The second thing that caught her attention was the bed. It was a huge four poster, with fluted gold posts. Gilt cherubs held white draperies so light they moved and billowed in the draught from the open door.

Then she smelled the sharp tang of aftershave.

'Two hours,' a voice said. 'And I'm going to enjoy every minute of it.'

She spun round. A tall, muscular man dressed in an American policeman's uniform appeared in the open door that led to an adjoining bathroom. He was no longer wearing a mask.

'Surprised?' he said. 'Expecting someone else? Well, I'm real sorry to disappoint you, but you've ended up with me, just like I promised.'

For a shocked moment Genevieve thought she had come into the wrong room.

'Don't be shy,' he drawled. 'Take your coat off. Make yourself at home.'

For an answer she drew the edges of her coat closer together. She saw his eyes stray downwards to the black silk triangle that only just covered her pubic hair and linger there.

'I'm told you're a natural blonde,' he said. 'Like to prove it?'

She stood like a statue, not believing what she was seeing and hearing. Had she really mistaken his voice for Sinclair's during the bidding? She could not believe it. It was deeper, and his accent was too distinctively American to disguise.

'I can't imagine who told you that,' she said, with icy disdain.

'The same guy who put in my bids for me,' he said.

She stared at him, not wanting to believe him. He walked over to a small table, opened a box, took out a cigar and lit it. 'One of my vices,' he explained. 'I've got quite a few.' He grinned. 'You might like some of them.' A cloud of fragrant smoke wreathed his face. 'Doesn't bother you, does it? I know you don't smoke.' He shifted the cigar in his mouth. 'I know quite a lot about you, Genevieve.'

She did not bother to ask him how he knew her name. Despite the warmth of the room her body felt cold. Her mind still refused to accept that Sinclair had bid for her, knowing that she would come in here and find this – stranger.

'I'm Bradford Franklin.' The American sat down on the bed. 'My friends call me Brad. That can include you, if you like. Or not, it doesn't bother me. But something else does.' He patted the bed. 'At a grand an hour you're costing me about sixteen English pounds a minute. That's serious money. Come and lie down.'

Genevieve stayed where she was, her back to the door. She could see herself reflected in the carefully placed mirrors. A long-legged figure, her blonde hair loose, a man's black tailcoat clutched round her.

'There's been a mistake,' she said.

Brad shook his head. 'No mistake. You agreed to the auction.'

'But I thought . . .'

'You thought someone else was doing the bidding?' He laughed. 'Well, you were right. My friend James owes me a favour. Quite a few favours, as it happens. I suggested a way of paying some of them off. He agreed. Neat idea, huh?'

'It was mean,' she said, angry now. 'Mean and under-handed.'

But was it really, she thought bleakly. She had agreed to

Sinclair's terms at the start of their agreement, and if forcing her to go with someone else was part of his idea of erotic entertainment she supposed he had a right to arrange it.

Bradford Franklin seemed to think so too.

'Oh, come on.' He lounged back on the bed. 'Stop trying to convince me that you're little Miss Prim and Proper. I know all about your arrangement with James. You're a smart lady. You want to get on. I like that.' He patted the bed again. 'C'mon, baby. It's not that bad. You and James had a good time together and you'll do well out of it.' He shifted the cigar in his mouth, watching her. 'But how much higher can you get in a firm like Barringtons? I've got connections. America, Canada, Europe, you name it. I can get you into the kind of positions you've never even dreamed about, and I'm not just talking sex. You've proved you're open to suggestions. Here's one for you. Another ninety days – with me. We play some good games together and I'll push your career like you won't believe.' He took the cigar out of his mouth and blew a perfect smoke ring. 'How about it, baby? Sound good to you?'

'I'm not interested,' she said.

'Don't you even want to think about it?'

No, she thought. Before I met James Sinclair, maybe I'd have considered it. Just maybe. But not any longer. Not as a career move. Not on any terms. Sinclair had woken her up to the kind of sexual fantasies she enjoyed, but she knew that she enjoyed them because she was acting them out with him. It had been easy for her to forget that they were not really lovers. Would she have enjoyed them with anyone else? She doubted it now.

'There's nothing to think about,' she said.

'And I thought you were a hard-headed businesswoman.' He shook his head in mock reproach.

So did I, she thought. And I was, until I met James Sinclair.

'Well, I'll just have to make do with my two hours.' He stubbed out his cigar. 'Come over here and show me how well you can perform with that pretty mouth of yours.'

'Sorry,' she said. 'That deal's off, too.'

He stared at her for a long moment, then grinned lazily.

'Are you sure you mean that? You want to lose everything you've gained? James wants me to fuck you, baby. And I want it, too. I've even agreed to pay two grand to a charity for the privilege.'

'Sorry,' she said. 'I'll pay the charity. But I'm not for sale.'

Brad stood up and hooked his thumbs in his belt.

'Sorry's not good enough. So what the hell's wrong with me? Maybe I don't look like one of those pretty-boy movie stars, but you could do a lot worse.'

'There's nothing wrong with you,' she said. Now that she had made her decision she felt as if a weight had been lifted off her mind. She could almost feel sympathetic towards Brad Franklin. 'I think there's something wrong with me.'

He gave her a slow once-over that reminded her of the way Sinclair had looked at her. 'You look OK to me. What's bothering you?'

'I think it's called being in love,' she said.

He stared at her for a moment, then gave an explosive snort of laughter. 'Who the hell with? Sinclair?' When she did not answer, he persisted: 'You can't be serious? This is real life, darlin'. You're in it for profit. Your career.'

'I was,' she admitted. 'But not any more. Maybe I'm in love. Maybe I'm falling in love. But either way, the deal's off. I can't go along with it any more.'

'Well, for God's sake,' a voice drawled from behind her, 'it's taken you long enough to admit it.'

She spun round. James Sinclair was leaning against the

bathroom door, elegant in evening dress. The first emotion Genevieve experienced was relief, followed immediately by a rush of anger.

'Where the *hell* have you been?' she demanded.

'Around,' Sinclair said, with an infuriating smile. 'Watching. Waiting. Listening.'

'And what exactly is that supposed to mean?'

'It means he set you up, honey.' Brad grinned. 'With my help. He set you up, then stood around and watched the show. Sounds a bit unkind, but it was all for a good cause.'

'Set me up?' She stared at the two men. 'I don't believe this. I trusted you, Sinclair!'

'Don't be too hard on him, sweetheart,' Brad said. 'He wanted to hear you say those three little words: I love you. Touching, isn't it?' He put his hand on his heart. 'Gets you – right here.' Genevieve stared at him, still not really believing him. 'It gets me, anyway,' Brad added. 'But then I'm just a big softy, really.' He walked over to the door. 'Helping you two lovebirds come together has really made my day, but now I'm beginning to feel like the unwanted guest.' He blew Genevieve a kiss. 'Been nice meeting you, sweetheart, and don't worry. Discretion's my middle name.'

The door shut behind him. Genevieve twisted round to face Sinclair. 'Lovebird isn't the word I'd use to describe you right now,' she said furiously.

'Or ever, I hope,' he said. 'I'll accept handsome. Irresistible. Sexy, even. But lovebird? Never.'

'You've made me look a complete idiot.'

He laughed softly. 'All I've done is get you to admit a lot of things about yourself that you were repressing. Including your feelings for me.'

'Well, if that isn't just about the most conceited thing I've ever heard!' She was still furious, as much with relief as anger.

'You're fooling yourself, Mr Sinclair. Right now, the only feeling I have for you is a strong desire to punch you.'

'You'll get over it,' he said, grinning. 'You know I don't deserve it.'

'You deserve it. You blackmailed me.'

'I've never blackmailed anyone in my life.'

'Ninety days as a sex slave, or no signature?' she stated. 'If that isn't blackmail, what is?'

He stared at her for a long moment, and then began to laugh. 'You didn't take that seriously, did you?'

'Damn right, I did!' She had been calming down, but now his laughter infuriated her again. 'Are you trying to tell me you were joking?'

'I'm a businessman,' he said. 'How far do you think I'd get if I really made deals like that?'

'You never intended to transfer your account to us?'

'I always intended to,' he said. 'Randle-Mayne haven't been coming up with enough fresh ideas. I wanted new blood. I like some of the work your creative team have been producing. And I might be interested in buying into an advertising agency quite soon. A small one, with some fresh young talent is just what I'm looking for. Barringtons would be my first choice.' He paused and walked towards her. Standing in front of her he put his hands on her shoulders. 'Come on now, Genevieve. You wanted me. From the moment I made you strip for me in your office you were hooked. You couldn't wait to find out what else I could make you do. The ninety-day agreement was just an excuse, for both of us. Don't try and tell me you didn't know that.'

'I didn't,' she said. 'Why me? I'm not even your type. With your money you could get any woman you fancied.'

'Thanks for the backhanded compliment,' he said drily. 'And why are you so sure you're not my type?'

'I've heard about the kind of women you like,' she said.

'You've heard about the kind of women other people think I like,' he said. 'It's true I've escorted a variety in my time, but if a woman's too blatantly sexy it actually turns me off. And if she's just some bimbo who wants me as a status symbol, I might try her out in bed but that's as far as I want to go.' He smiled. 'I like independent women, and I don't feel threatened by women with brains. I'm intrigued by the combination of ice and flames.' He paused. 'That's why I liked you. You were a mixture of intelligence and sexual heat. An iceberg with internal fire. It was an irresistible turn-on. Does that make sense to you?'

'No,' she said. 'I wasn't even trying to turn you on.'

Or was I, she thought. You attracted me. Did it show in my eyes? My body language?

Sinclair put his hands on her shoulders, and she felt their warmth.

'You tried to act the remote businesswoman when we first met,' he said softly. 'But I'm afraid you weren't very convincing. Apparent indifference is quite a turn-on for me, as long as I'm sure it's only a bluff.' His fingers tightened on her shoulders. 'And I knew yours was. You looked like a cool, pure maiden, very prim and proper in your elegant suits. I knew you were nicely built, but I had a great time imagining exactly what you'd look like when I stripped you.'

'You told me to strip,' Genevieve reminded him. 'And you felt me up as if I was in a slave market.'

'And you loved it,' he agreed. 'The problem was, you wouldn't admit it, even to yourself. All you did was insist that everything we did was strictly business, that it wasn't me you were interested in, it was our final agreement.'

She put her hands lightly on his. 'I thought that was what you wanted,' she said. 'I went along with it. I suppose I tried to switch off my feelings most of the time. I didn't want to get hurt. I thought you were using me. You have a reputation for it.'

'I suppose I deserved that,' he said. 'To be honest, I've encouraged people to believe it. In many ways it's helped me. People who don't know the truth about me, never know what to expect.'

'You don't use people?' she asked, faintly sarcastic.

'Of course I do,' he said 'If they let me. Everyone does. Including you. But it's often a two-way process.' He grinned. 'I used Jade Chalfont.' He saw her expression change and his grin broadened. 'A classic case,' he said. 'She wanted me as her first success at Lucci's. I knew she'd be useful to me in Japan. She obligingly decided to arrange her holiday at the same time that I'd arranged my business trip. She even managed to book out on the same flight as me.'

'But I thought . . .' Genevieve began.

'You thought I'd invited her as a little bit of convenient entertainment?' He laughed. 'So did a lot of other people. Like I said, it didn't do my reputation any harm. Here, or in Japan. The Japanese really admired her – the English sensei. When it comes to beating people up with a sword she certainly knows her stuff.'

'And what about in bed?'

He laughed.

'You don't give up easily, do you? I wouldn't know. Actually I don't fancy Miss Chalfont at all. Her attitude's too masculine. And I'm sure she doesn't fancy me either, for the same reasons, although I don't think she'd have refused me, if she thought she'd profit by it.'

'You think she's a lesbian?' Genevieve asked, curiously.

'I think she's bisexual,' Sinclair said. 'But I'd guess she prefers women.'

'Well, at least you've got that in common,' Genevieve said drily.

'We both played a manipulative game,' he said. 'And we both knew it.' He smiled lazily. 'But I won. I got my Japanese contract. She won't get her client. That's the way it goes.'

'Didn't you even wonder what she was like in bed?' Genevieve insisted.

'No,' he said, innocently. 'I was too busy remembering what you were like.'

'In bed?' She almost smiled. 'As far as I can remember, we've hardly ever made love in a bed.'

'That can soon change,' he said softly.

He moved closer to her and she felt her body begin to respond to his physical presence. He pulled her towards him and kissed her. The kiss was long and deep and when they parted she felt deliciously out of breath.

'Why didn't you do that before?' she murmured.

'I just needed a hint of encouragement.' His breath was warm against her cheek. 'I didn't think I was ever going to get it. The last time we were together, in the car, I had the feeling you just wanted to get things over with. You wanted to get away from me. And let's face it, every time I tried to get a positive response out of you, tried to get you to admit your feelings, you turned it back on me. You always said it was business. You always brought up that damned agreement. There were times when I really regretted using the ninety-day idea.'

'I was worried,' she said. 'I thought you were planning to get me to do something really unpleasant.'

'You really have a low opinion of me, haven't you?' he murmured.

This time she relaxed completely when he kissed her. His mouth brushed hers lightly at first, and the tip of his tongue gently probed between her lips, pushing them apart. His fingers massaged the nape of her neck, bending her head back so that he could kiss the curve of her throat and round to her ear. His lips traced a light path that made her skin tingle.

'Blackmailer?' He kissed her neck. 'Womaniser?' He kissed her again. 'It's a wonder you're letting me do this.'

'And thug,' she added.

He pulled away from her, surprised. 'That's a new one. I've never been called that before.'

'What about Ricky Croft?'

He lifted an eyebrow. '*What* about him?"

'The rumour says you beat him up.'

'The rumour's true, for once,' he agreed.

'Why did you do it?'

'You don't want to know.'

'But I do,' she insisted. 'Was it something to do with those porno drawings he does?'

'As I told you,' Sinclair said. 'I'm not interested in that sort of thing. I prefer the genuine article.'

'Ricky told me Jade Chalfont had bought some of his pictures and given them to you.'

'Wishful thinking,' Sinclair said. 'Jade Chalfont wouldn't buy anything off him. She'd be more likely to punch him in the mouth.'

'And you did,' Genevieve said. 'I want to know why. I can't believe it was because you were shocked.'

'I saw another set of pictures,' Sinclair said. He paused. 'Without going into details, the ones I saw featured you. Mr Croft obviously thought I'd be amused to see you in some – er – rather strange positions.'

Genevieve had a brief memory of some of Ricky's drawings. Knowing how he felt about her she could imagine the kind of sexual indignities he had probably depicted her indulging in.

She didn't want to think about it, but her imagination forced her to do so anyway.

'I'll kill him,' she said, furiously.

'That's how I felt,' Sinclair said. 'But he isn't worth the jail sentence. So I tore the pictures up, damaged him a little and I told him that if he ever did it again, or talked about what had happened, it'd be the last time he drew anything for a very long time, because I'd come back and break his fingers. One by one. Slowly.'

'I think he believed you,' Genevieve said. Looking at Sinclair's grim face she believed him too. 'Why would Ricky do something like that to me?'

'Revenge.' Sinclair shrugged. 'He wasn't any friend of yours. He blamed you because no one would employ him. He'd already been starting a few rumours of his own, linking us together, and bad-mouthing you. Unfortunately, there are people around who believe anything they hear, regardless of the source. He even hinted to me that you might like it if I beat you up for real.'

Genevieve stared at him, horrified. 'Why would he say that?'

'Perhaps he hoped I might try it on you. It misfired, because I tried it on him instead. Anyway, I always thought he was a liar. I didn't think you were into the heavy CP, and when I took you to the dungeon I knew it. Forget him. I don't think he'll bother you again.'

'He could have made plenty of money,' Genevieve said. 'He was just so damned unreliable. I could never recommend him to anyone.' She smiled suddenly. 'It must have been a novelty for you, playing a knight in shining armour.'

'It came naturally,' Sinclair said modestly. 'I hate the sexual exploitation of women.' He paused, and smiled slowly. 'Mind you, Mr Croft certainly has a fertile imagination. Some of the positions he put you into were – er – interesting, to say the least.' His hands strayed down her back and cupped her buttocks. 'There were a couple I wouldn't mind trying.'

'I thought you hated sexual exploitation?' she said.

'That would come under sexual experimentation,' he explained. He massaged her soft flesh. 'Legitimate research.'

She felt her body responding to him, but pushed him back. 'Don't let's waste the bed,' she murmured.

'I don't intend to,' he said. 'This is costing me two thousand pounds, remember.' He stepped back and looked her over slowly. 'And I'm going to get my money's worth.' He began to take off his jacket. 'Starting now.'

But she stopped him again. 'No. I want to do it. You've stripped me. Now it's my turn.'

He grinned. 'Sounds good to me. But take that coat off first. It makes you look like a boy.'

She opened the front of her tailcoat and let it slide down her arms to the floor. She stood in front of him wearing only the brief black G-string and her high-heeled shoes.

'Have you ever seen a boy who looked like this?'

'Yes,' he said. 'In Thailand. Out there they'll pay a fortune to a surgeon to get a figure even half as good as yours.'

He reached for her breasts but she eluded him.

'On the bed,' she ordered.

She sat on the edge of the bed herself, and swung her legs towards the opposite side, twisting round and then kneeling. He stretched out next to her. She crouched beside him and began to unbutton his shirt. His hands reached for her again, the tips of his fingers brushing her nipples.

'Behave yourself,' she said.

'You really have got the best-shaped ass I've ever seen,' he murmured.

She saw that he was looking above her. Turning her head

she realised that there was a mirror inside the four poster canopy reflecting the entire bed. Her rounded bottom was beautifully displayed as she knelt.

'Puts a new angle on things, doesn't it?' He reached out and pressed a hidden button. Curtains parted revealing another mirror behind the bed's high-piled pillows. 'And how about this? Be your own blue-film star.'

She watched herself opening the front of his shirt, revealing the hard muscles of his chest and nipples that were as erect as her own. She leaned over him, closing her mouth over the nearest one and felt his body shudder as she sucked and nipped him with her teeth. Her fingers caressed the other nipple, rubbing and stroking just has he had so often done to her. He groaned and reached for his zip. She pushed his hand away.

'Don't be in such a hurry.'

'I don't have your self control,' he said.

She sat astride him, pressing against his imprisoned erection, both hands holding his wrists above his head, while she tormented him with her mouth, kissing him, running her tongue round his ear, and teasing his nipples into even harder peaks. She could see him watching the overhead mirror, and knew that seeing her on top of him, as well as feeling the things she was doing to him, doubled his erotic entertainment.

She encouraged him into a sitting position and slipped the shirt down his arms, twisting it suddenly behind him, round his wrists, and then pushing him onto his back again. When he struggled to free himself she swiftly unzipped his trousers and reached between his legs.

'You're my prisoner,' she said. 'Enjoy it.'

She massaged him gently and watched with pleasure as his body reacted, his hips thrusting forward as she stroked and kneaded. She felt his prick swell beneath her hands, until it was straining and massive under her fingers. Only then did she slowly pull his trousers down fully, and stretch the tight briefs he was wearing over the captive organ so that it sprang free and he groaned with relief. Quickly she removed his shoes and socks and then the trousers and pants.

She sat back on her heels and looked at him. It was the first time she had seen him totally naked. She admired the full heaviness of his balls and the length of his cock, rising from the thick black pubic hair. The same colour hair matted his chest. His body was lean and tanned, with long thighs and narrow hips. She could see the ridges of his abdominal muscles. She reached out a finger and circled one erect nipple, then the other. Each time she heard him draw his breath in sharply.

'Does this feel the same for you as it does for me?' she murmured.

'If it does,' he said huskily, 'no wonder you like it.'

'Turn over,' she instructed.

'Why?' he asked, his eyes half-closed. 'I feel fine this way.'

'You've seen my ass. I want to see yours.'

He grinned lazily and shifted position with slow elegance. She admired the way his muscles moved when he turned. She admired the tight curve of his buttocks. She looked at him on the bed and then in the overhead mirror, his body darkly golden against the white bed cover. Lying on his stomach, with his legs slightly apart and his wrists still entangled with the shirt he gave the impression of being helpless. She knew it was a fantasy, but it was a pleasant one. She could do what she liked with him.

She ran her tongue down to the end of his spine, where she drew little circles on his skin and delighted in the way his body reacted. She drew patterns on his taut buttocks with the tips of her fingers. When she touched certain spots he jumped and shuddered in a most satisfactory way. Moving slowly upwards again, she finally kissed the nape of his neck lightly, below the slightly jagged line of his glossy black hair. She felt his body quiver. She stroked the inside of his thighs, her finger brushing the sensitive skin of his balls.

'You've explored nearly all of me.' His mouth was muffled by the pillow. 'Do I meet with your approval?'

Suddenly she moved her hand forward slightly and tightened her hold on his balls.

'Did Marsha meet with *your* approval?' she whispered silkily in his ear.

His head jerked up from the pillow and he half turned. She kept hold of him.

'Be careful,' he gasped. 'That's hurting.'

'Marsha?' she insisted. 'The lovely bisexual redhead. Surely you haven't forgotten her already?'

'I don't know anyone called Marsha,' he said.

He tried to get on his knees and escape, but she pushed him back on the bed, still keeping his sexual equipment firmly captive.

'You were stroking her bottom in Goldie's club,' she reminded him. 'Then you went off together looking as if you were planning to be a lot more than just good friends.' She squeezed her fingers, not too roughly, but enough to make him yelp with surprise. 'Just tell me all about Marsha. And don't you dare say you don't know her.'

She massaged him with her fingers, enjoying the reaction it caused.

'Oh,' he gasped. '*That* Marsha!'

'Oh?' she repeated, mimicking him. She handled him more gently this time. 'Yes. *That* Marsha.'

She felt his body shaking and realised that he was laughing.

'Jealous, weren't you?'

There was only one way he could have known that. 'You set that up, too?' she accused. 'With Georgie?'

'Of course,' he said. 'If you hadn't reacted so strongly I might not have asked Brad to help me out this evening.' He glanced up at her. 'I would have been worried you might have accepted his offer. I wouldn't have liked that.'

She sat back on her heels. 'You're the one who reckoned you knew exactly how I felt,' she said. 'You should have known I'd never do that.'

He stared at her, not smiling now. 'There was always an element of doubt. I admit that. I sometimes wondered if I was indulging in a bit of wishful thinking. You were always so cool and self-possessed. And always insisting that everything we did was business. I didn't want to make a fool of myself.'

Cool and self-possessed, she thought. If only you knew!

'Now kindly let go of me,' he requested. 'Or I won't be in any fit state to give you what you want.'

'And what do I want?' she asked, still holding him.

'Fucking, I hope,' he said. 'It seems a shame to waste this room and this bed. The mirrors should appeal to you, too. You can watch yourself from all angles in here.'

He had freed his hands without her noticing, and he sat up suddenly, grasped her wrists, and rocked her until she sprawled flat on her back. In one swift move he was astride her, gripping her with his knees. He kissed the side of her neck and moved to her mouth, his tongue entering gently, then insistently. His hands found her breasts and captured them, thumbs moving over her nipples.

She moved her head until she could glance upward over his shoulder. In the canopy mirror she saw a woman with her blonde hair spread wildly and a lithe, tanned man holding her in delicious captivity. As she watched the man raised himself up. As if in a dream she saw the woman shift position, and the man move with her.

'Which way?' Sinclair murmured, close to her ear. He licked her with tantalising slow movements. 'From the front, or behind? It's your choice.'

'I thought you were the one who gave the orders,' she said.

'Not tonight,' he said. 'Maybe I'll get back into character later.'

'From the front,' she said.

She wanted to feel overpowered by him. She wanted to see his face above hers and watch his expression when he came. She wanted to look over his shoulder and enjoy the reflection of his thrusting movements in the mirror.

When he entered her she was already wet with need, and as his cock drove into her she closed round it and pulled him deeper. His hands tightened on her breasts. She put her legs round him and clasped him strongly. She felt that she could not get close enough to him. She wanted to share his heartbeat, his breath, his life. She lost track of time and abandoned herself to pure sensation. She moved her hand down between her legs and rubbed gently.

Sinclair gave a deep groan of pleasure and his body shook in orgasmic release. Her own orgasm came only moments later. It was not as intense as some of those he had already given her, during his carefully arranged fantasies, but she knew that she would treasure this particular memory because, for the first time, she felt that they had been entwined in a true lover's knot. He relaxed against her for a moment, and she felt the warmth of his body against hers. Then, gently, he withdrew and lay next to her.

'That was good,' he said simply. He turned to her. 'And for you, too?'

'It's always good with you,' she said. 'Even when I'm strapped into a bondage corset. Even when I'm tied to your door, or to a motor-bike.'

'I knew you'd like playing games,' he said. 'I'm a great judge of character.'

'So you won't be surprised if I start discussing business?' she teased. 'You know what a hard-headed woman I am.' She pointed to the small clock on the white and gilt dressing table. 'It's midnight. Our agreement is over. You owe me a signature.'

'You'll get it,' he said. 'It wasn't ever in doubt. And later, when we discuss my possible financial investment into Barringtons, you might get a lot more than that.' He caught her wrist and pulled her back towards him. 'And now let's mix business with pleasure again. I've paid two thousand pounds for the pleasure of your company. Two hours, wasn't it? How many orgasms do you think I can give you in two hours?'

'I don't know.' She relaxed on the bed and glanced sideways at him, admiring the lean strength of his body. Even looking at him turned her on. 'But I've got a feeling I'm about to find out.'

London, Genevieve decided, had never looked better. She suddenly knew why people came from all over the world and took photographs of the buses, the pigeons, the Thames. Never mind that the buses were frequently late, snarled up in traffic, the pigeons unintentionally ruined buildings, the Thames was sluggish. London was beautiful. She loved it. She had decided to walk to work from the Underground partly because it was sunny and partly because she felt more like dancing than sitting behind a desk.

She crossed the road and saw a familiar figure walking ahead of her, his arm round a girl, his mouth close to the girl's ear. His hand rested, flat but possessive, on the girl's behind.

Genevieve ran forward. 'Philip!'

Her brother's head turned quickly. 'Gen?' He looked positively guilty. 'What're you doing here?'

'Going to work,' she said. 'You know? It's what you do when you leave university.'

'I didn't know you walked.'

Genevieve looked from her brother to his companion, and back again. 'And I didn't know you . . .' she began.

'This is Ingrid,' Philip interrupted her firmly. 'My girlfriend.' The girl smiled at Genevieve. 'She's doing economics. Ingrid, this is my sister Genevieve. She's a lot older than me.'

'She doesn't look it,' Ingrid said.

'And she's in a hurry to get to work,' Philip added. 'How's work going, by the way?'

'Fine,' she said. 'I've just netted a really big client. He's even interested in investing in the agency. It's made me very popular.'

'That's great,' Philip said. 'All you need now is a nice boyfriend, and your life will be complete.'

'I think I'll take a vow of celibacy,' Genevieve said sweetly. 'That should do the trick.'

Ingrid stared at her in surprise. 'What an odd idea,' she said. 'How would that help?'

Genevieve smiled at them both. 'Ask Philip,' she said.

In the middle of the week a messenger arrived at Genevieve's apartment with a small parcel.

'From Mr Sinclair,' he said cheerfully. 'Sign please.'

When she opened the box a solitaire diamond ring winked in the light. She looked at the small card with it. It said, simply: MARRY ME?

About the author:

Lucinda Carrington lives in Essex.